KT-525-443

Behind Her Back

JANE LYTHELL worked as a television producer and commissioning editor for fifteen years. She has been Deputy Director of the BFI and Chief Executive of BAFTA. She is the author of four novels, including *Woman of the Hour*, the first title in the StoryWorld series, which was published by Head of Zeus in 2016.

ALSO BY JANE LYTHELL

The Lie of You

After the Storm

StoryWorld
Woman of the Hour

Behind Her Back

JANE LYTHELL

HEAD
of ZEUS

First published in the UK in 2017 by Head of Zeus, Ltd.

Copyright © Jane Lythell 2017

The moral right of Jane Lythell to be identified as the author
of this work has been asserted in accordance with the
Copyright, Designs and Patents Act of 1988.

All rights reserved. No part of this publication may be
reproduced, stored in a retrieval system, or transmitted in any form
or by any means, electronic, mechanical, photocopying, recording,
or otherwise, without the prior permission of both the copyright
owner and the above publisher of this book.

This is a work of fiction. All characters, organizations,
and events portrayed in this novel are either products of
the author's imagination or are used fictitiously.

9 7 5 3 1 2 4 6 8

A catalogue record for this book is available from
the British Library.

ISBN (HB): 9781786690760
ISBN (XTPB): 9781786690777
ISBN (E): 9781786690753

Typeset by Adrian McLaughlin

Printed and bound in Great Britain by
CPI Group (UK) Ltd, Croydon CRO 4YY

Head of Zeus Ltd
First Floor East
5–8 Hardwick Street
London EC1R 4RG

WWW.HEADOFZEUS.COM

To Barry, with love

Behind Her Back

CHAPTER ONE

EARLY AUGUST
Chalk Farm flat, Sunday, 2 p.m.

As soon as we got in, Flo looked for Mr Crooks our cat and started to panic when he wasn't in the flat or our garden. She was straight on her mobile to Janis who reassured her that he'd been fine when she'd been in to feed him this morning. He had probably gone for a wander.

I stuffed dirty clothes into the washing machine, two weeks' worth, some of which were still powdered with sand from the beach at Bordighera. For the first time in years, having Simon as my deputy had allowed me to have a complete break from StoryWorld and I had returned with a good tan and a hole in my finances.

I was heading back to work on Monday and needed a briefing from Simon. I made a mug of tea, black because I'd forgotten to buy milk, and called him.

'Welcome back. Was your flight OK? Heard there were delays at Heathrow,' he said.

'We didn't fly. We were on the overnight train from Ventimiglia and it was brilliant, though I didn't sleep much.'

'Good holiday?'

'Fantastic. Pasta and ice cream to die for and we swam in the sea most days. How have things been?'

'Fine, really, no mishaps to report, and Ledley is going from strength to strength.'

'Glad to hear it. Fizzy is back next month, you know.'

1

'So I heard. He's taken to it so well. Maybe he'll find it hard going back to a weekly slot,' Simon said.

Ledley, the StoryWorld chef, has been sitting in for our star presenter Fizzy Wentworth. She's been on maternity leave and he's been a hit with our viewers. Fizzy had her baby in late May and is only taking three and a half months off. She's determined to be back on the sofa at the beginning of September. She's worried that if she stays away longer Ledley will get too entrenched in the anchor role.

'And Lori Kerwell arrived last week,' Simon said, and there was something in his voice, the verbal equivalent of rolling his eyes.

'What's she like?'

'She's scary; really scary. All pent-up energy and dead eyes.'

'Oh dear!'

'She insisted on coming to the morning meetings and by the second day was commenting on the output.'

'I hope that's a short-term thing. It's an editorial meeting,' I said.

'Yeah, but she said it will help her understand where she can develop business tie-ins.'

'And is Julius OK with that?'

'Not sure. He put her in her place on Friday.'

The gossip at the station was that Julius Jones, our director of programmes, was not overjoyed at the appointment of Lori Kerwell to develop sales and marketing. She had been appointed by the MD, Saul Relph. He is the money man at StoryWorld. Julius, who is the ideas man, was not involved in her selection and employment. There is often conflict between the editorial and the business sides in television.

'Can you talk me through the running order for tomorrow?'
I said.

'Loula is our celebrity interview of the day.'

Loula was the latest winner in ITV's blockbuster talent
show.

'That's a good signing.'

'Harry got her for us. And Molly's story is on FGM.'

Female genital mutilation was a challenging topic for my
researcher Molly to have chosen.

'How did she cover that?'

'She found this young Somalian woman, Beydaan, very
brave. She shopped her parents to social services because she
doesn't want her younger sister to go through what they did
to her. Liz, she was seven years old when she was cut.'

'Bloody hell!'

'I know. Molly had to shoot the interview so you can't see
her face. And we've changed her name, of course.'

This was making me uneasy. Ours is a morning show and
we have to be careful about the content we put out.

'And who will Ledley talk to about it?'

'We've booked the officer from the Foreign Office who
runs the FGM Unit.'

'That's a good call. Are you sure Ledley is OK with this?'

'Molly briefed him at length on Friday.'

'Well, huge thanks, Simon, for all you've done. Let's both
sit in the gallery tomorrow and we can go to the morning
meeting together.'

'It's good to have you back.'

I unlocked the French doors and stepped into our garden.
Dead blooms and leaves had accumulated and it needed a
good sweep. I have a tiny shed in the corner and I rummaged

out the garden broom. My beloved hollyhocks needed water too. I filled the watering can and gave them a good soaking. Their large pale pink and yellow blooms rested against the warmth of the back wall. There is something satisfying about watering plants. The hollyhocks are too big really for our small patch but I love them so much and looking at them lifts my spirits. The washing cycle had finished so I pulled the clothes out and hung them over the drying frame which is a job I hate doing as the frame is not large enough. I wondered if I should call Ledley and talk through the FGM story with him. It is not the easiest subject for a male presenter to deal with. But I had left Simon in charge and I trusted him. The cat flap clattered and Mr Crooks emerged, blinking, into the sitting room. When he saw me he let out an outraged yowl.

'Flo, Mr Crooks is back and he's got the hump,' I called out.

Flo came out of her room. She had stripped down to her panties and a white T-shirt and I admired her long tanned legs as she walked across the kitchen and picked up Mr Crooks. My rosebud was turning into a rose.

CHAPTER TWO

StoryWorld TV station, London Bridge

I was in the green room with Loula, our celebrity guest of the day, and her father, who introduced himself to me as her manager. He was wearing a navy blazer with brass buttons and a cravat, of all things. He looked more Golf Club Man than Stage Dad. Loula was in high demand so we had done well to get her on the show but she was a right little madam. I took her into make-up and then returned to the green room. Loula's father was being difficult with Ziggy, my runner, who served the refreshments and booked taxis for the guests. He was complaining about not being allowed to accompany his daughter into make-up. I explained that it was a small salon and we liked guests to have a moment to compose themselves before they went on air and would he like another coffee. I was being polite and gritting my teeth. I recognised the type; a doting father who had sent his daughter to stage school and had entered her into the TV talent competition which she had won. His daughter's moment of fame had come and he was grabbing it with both hands.

I returned to make-up. Loula was giving Ellen, our make-up woman, a hard time.

'I hate all that foundation. God, I look like a Barbie doll now.'

'I can tone it down,' Ellen said calmly.

I watched as Ellen reached for a sponge and started to wipe

Loula's face. Loula snatched the sponge from Ellen and I felt like slapping her. It is always so revealing how a celebrity behaves with the back-room staff. Her rise to celebrity had been meteoric. She was twenty years old and there was a greediness and a gracelessness about her, like her father. She had a good singing voice but I hoped that her fame would be short-lived.

When the programme was over Simon and I waited for Ledley at the studio door. As he emerged he gave me a hug.

'Hey, you're back.'

'That was a terrific interview with Loula,' I said.

'Thanks.'

Predictably, Loula had changed her manner once seated on the sofa next to Ledley with the cameras running. She had giggled and flirted and had been charm itself. Ledley and I walked up the stairs together and I was struck again how he looks so much smarter these days. When he became the main anchor in May, the deal was that he had to spruce up. Ellen had overhauled his wardrobe and gone was his street-style look: the faded black jeans tucked into big boots. This morning I had noticed how he's getting more polished in his interview techniques too. When he started there was a spontaneous, rough-around-the-edges quality which I liked and was sorry to see go.

We entered the meeting room and I spotted Lori Kerwell straight away. She was sitting at one end of the table with a lever arch folder open in front of her and what looked like tables of figures. Julius was behind me.

'Welcome back, Liz. You haven't met Lori yet?'

I walked over and shook hands with her. She looked like she was in her late forties and she was wearing a turquoise suit with a statement necklace. She had fluffy blonde hair, that I think of as poodle hair, which was pinned up with a frizzy fringe shading her forehead.

'Liz oversees all our feature content,' Julius said.

She had dark opaque eyes. I recalled Simon's memorable description of them as dead eyes. Certainly, she gave nothing away as she said: 'Pleased to meet you.'

I sat down and Julius opened by saying how much he had enjoyed Ledley's interview with Loula. He always watches the show on the TV in his office and he makes detailed notes every day. He never misses it when an item goes wrong and criticism rather than praise is the norm from him, so this was welcome.

'It was smart to get her talking about food, Ledley. That gave us a fresh insight,' I said.

'You learn a lot about people from what they like to eat and boy, did she have faddy tastes,' Ledley said.

'Rice cakes, pot noodles and Bounty bars and not a fruit or veg in sight; bizarre, but interesting to hear,' I said.

'Why did we run the FGM story?' Lori asked.

The expression on her face was like someone who had eaten something that was off.

'Because it's a compelling story,' I said.

'But hardly one that would speak to our demographic?'

She pointed to the tables in her folder which I saw now were the detailed breakdowns on our viewers' class and geographical spread.

'Over five thousand cases were reported in the UK last year,' Simon said.

'It's a topical story which also has a universal element to it; an older sister trying to protect her little sister from the pain she'd been subjected to. Our viewers can relate to that,' I said.

'I'm not convinced,' Lori said.

I gave her a long look.

'It's *our* job to find important and moving stories that our viewers will respond to. We found a brave young woman willing to share her story and I'm proud that we carried it.'

I had emphasised the word 'our'. It was her second week here and already she was demanding that we convince *her* about our output. She was well out of order and I was simmering. Julius said nothing throughout this exchange but he had noted it. Bob, the news editor, looked like he wanted to support Lori, to keep the pressure on me, of course. He hates me because of something I know. But even Bob could see that for the news editor to go against this kind of story would not ring true. Last month, a rival station had run a hard-hitting story on FGM and Bob had praised it. Julius closed the meeting and asked me to join him in his office.

'Good to have you back. You look well,' he said.

'Thanks. It's amazing what rest and sun will do.'

As I said this I wondered how long it would take for StoryWorld to turn me grey and tired again.

'I wanted you to know that the tone of voice of the features has been slightly off the last two weeks,' he said.

'What do you mean by off?'

'It's been a bit earnest, a bit feminist, a bit preachy.'

'Is this about the FGM story?'

'No, I thought that worked OK, though it's edgy for a Monday morning. We're the home of cheerful stories.'

'Yes, the pastel station,' I said.

He narrowed his eyes at that. Last year, Julius had decreed that all our presenters had to wear light, bright colours on camera to cheer up our viewers. Black had been banished as the colour of misery – one of our presenters had defied Julius and been sacked.

'It's the summer season. Make sure we get the balance right, OK?'

He has snarled at me so many times in the past but this morning his voice was neutral and he was being reasonable.

'Fair point, will do.'

'I went to see Fizzy yesterday,' he said.

'How is she?'

'She's exhausted and also aggrieved.'

'She's got a two-month-old baby so exhausted is to be expected. Why aggrieved?'

'Says she feels cut off from StoryWorld and that none of us are keeping her in the loop.'

'Before I went on holiday I offered to carry a weekly slot on her and the baby, post up pictures and get viewers to coo over them. She bit my head off; said she wasn't one of those dreadful celebrities who parade their children for profit,' I said.

I had got close to Fizzy in the early months of her pregnancy because she had confided to me how conflicted she was. She had booked in to have a termination and I had gone with her to a private clinic in the country, but she couldn't go through with it. As her pregnancy advanced she had become irrational and paranoid. She had got it into her head that I was out to get her permanently replaced by Ledley who she felt I favoured over the other presenters. This was nonsense but I hadn't been able to shift her suspicions.

I was also the only person who knew the identity of the father of her baby.

'Go and see her. Give her some support,' Julius said.

'You know I would love to see Zachary.'

Fizzy had given her baby son a suitably showbiz name.

'Ring her. And I'm on holiday from Wednesday, for a week. Will you chair the morning meeting for me?'

'Happy to do that. You going anywhere nice?'

He hesitated. Julius is the kind of man who doesn't even like to share his holiday destination.

'Cornwall,' he said.

I called a team meeting and Simon, Molly and Harriet joined me in my office. Ziggy sat outside to field calls for us. I had bought a box of almond biscotti for the team so I offered these to Ziggy and she took one. She is such a thin little thing.

'Take a few more, *please*,' I said.

She scooped up two more and placed them on her desk.

'Did Loula's father behave himself after I'd left?'

'He was a pain, to be honest, but nothing I couldn't handle.'

'A nasty little man, but there are a lot of pushy dads like him out there.'

She smiled shyly at me. 'It's nice to have you back.'

The team sat in their usual places and I passed the box of biscotti round and told them briefly about my holiday.

'And so to work: well done, all of you, it was a good show today. The FGM story was powerful, Molly, but I was glad we had Loula on the sofa to counteract it with something lighter.'

'I pulled strings to get her,' Harriet said with a small smile.

Harriet's father is the editor of a national newspaper and I wondered if that was what she meant. She had had a troubled start at StoryWorld but now she was making celebrity interviews her thing and getting us good guests, as well as overseeing the fashion items.

'Excellent, a real coup.'

Harriet was pink with pleasure and she glanced over at Simon who gave her an encouraging grin.

'And what's the response been like to the FGM story, Moll?'

Molly had a printout with her. 'Not a huge number of comments but those we've had are overwhelmingly sympathetic. Simon told me what Lori Kerwell said.'

I wished that Simon had kept his counsel on that. I always made a point of filtering what was said in the morning meetings. 'I need you to collate the comments into a single document, please. I plan to send them to Julius and to Lori Kerwell.'

'Will do. I'd like to do a follow-up story with Beydaan. She's had to leave home, you know, and she's getting support from social services and an activist group. We don't know for sure that her sister will be spared.'

'Maybe in September, Moll. We need a light touch to the features in August: holiday fashion, summer food, good books for the beach, that kind of thing.'

We spent the next forty minutes going through ideas for feature items. As they left my room, Harriet hovered by the door.

'That Lori Kerwell came to see me,' she said.

'When was this?'

'Middle of last week. She said fashion is a great area for marketing tie-ins and she wants me to introduce her to Guy. Should I set that up?'

Guy Browne is our fashion expert and he's been doing a weekly slot for us for the last six months.

'We have to keep a clear line between editorial and advertising,' I said.

'I remembered you said that.'

'If she wants to do tie-ins we need to keep control of it.'

Harriet had found Guy for us and was protective of him and proud of the slot.

'You know the fashion houses are beginning to trust us.' She said it almost sadly. Harriet has hooded eyelids and I find it hard to read her face.

'What's worrying you about this?'

'She's pushy. She's mentioned it twice already and I'm worried she'll put pressure on Guy.'

'OK.'

'And want to go downmarket. I didn't know what to say to her.'

'Set up a meeting with the three of us. We need to agree some ground rules on how any fashion tie-ins will work. Don't let her speak to Guy until we've got clarity on that,' I said.

I stood at my window and looked at the scene below. Londoners had ventured into shorts and summer dresses and sandals but somehow they lacked the style of the people Flo and I had seen at Bordighera. Most evenings we had sat on the terrace of our small hotel and indulged in people-watching and then we would stroll down to the family gelateria to buy ice cream. I loved the fact that young Italians would have an ice cream cone rather than a pint of lager as their evening treat. But I was back in London now and needed to get my head back into work mode.

I thought about Guy Browne and how we might use him. When he did his screen test for us last year he had been wickedly witty about fashion disasters at the Oscars. He had made us laugh, but at heart Guy was a serious man, certainly serious about fashion. Harriet told me he had wanted to be a designer but for now his work was as a writer and a critic.

There was something of the ascetic about Guy. He would arrive at StoryWorld on his racing bike and change before he went on air. He favoured asymmetric cuts and neutral palettes. One week, when he had done a fashion makeover with a member of the public, I thought his choice of outfit for her was verging on the extreme. It was very stark and hadn't really worked. You would need to be a true believer in the High Art of Fashion to carry it off. But Fizzy has adored Guy from the beginning. She said he was so New York and cutting edge and that she was delighted at last to have someone in the StoryWorld line-up who pushed at the boundaries.

Molly came in. She had collated the comments on her FGM story and I read these through with satisfaction. I attached them to an email addressed to Julius and copied to Lori Kerwell and wrote:

> Please see attached all the comments we received
> on the FGM story. A positive response. I do think
> we underestimate our viewers at our peril. Liz

I deleted the third sentence. It sounded pompous. Lori Kerwell had been appointed by Saul Relph, and there was no point in getting into a fight with her.

I put in a call to Fizzy's home and Loida, her housekeeper, answered. She told me that Fizzy was having a nap. I heard a baby start to grizzle close by.

'Hush, angel.' She was picking up the baby. 'Call in two hours,' she said.

In my lunch hour I went food shopping at a street market near London Bridge station. It's a cheerful noisy place and over the years the stalls have become more international and foodie and you can get every kind of ingredient there now. I bought a slab of parmesan cheese, fresh pasta, onions, two fat white garlic bulbs and a bag of courgettes. I was going to try to recreate a fantastic courgette sauce that Flo and I had eaten one night in Bordighera. There's a greasy spoon café tucked behind the fruit and veg stalls and I was surprised to see Lori Kerwell sitting at one of the tables. I stopped and peered through the window which was misted with condensation. She had a plate of egg and chips and was reading a tabloid newspaper spread out on the table in front of her. She didn't see me.

I got through to Fizzy at three o'clock and suggested I visit her. I kept my voice warm but still half expected her to rebuff me.

'Are you up for a visit? It would be so lovely to see you and Zachary.'

'God, I've been in purdah for weeks. I need to talk about something other than feed times and sleep cycles and the colour of his poo.'

'Happy to oblige. I'm just back from holiday in Italy.'

'Lucky you. Come for tea on Wednesday and meet Zac,' she said.

As I was leaving for the day, Harriet stopped me.

'Lori Kerwell says can we meet tomorrow?'

'That's so soon.'

'I told you she was pushy.'

'OK, put it on the calendar for noon.'

It was clear that Lori Kerwell was a woman in a hurry.

Chalk Farm flat, 7.30 p.m.

I've made a new arrangement with Janis, a local woman and

now a friend, who has been looking after Flo since she was seven years old. I've always hated the idea of Flo coming home from school to an empty flat. And during the school holidays I can't leave her on her own for the whole day. But now that Flo is fifteen we needed a new deal. We've agreed that Janis will come round at five-thirty, make Flo her supper and stay till seven-thirty. If I'm honest, this is more to reassure me than anything else.

Flo was in her room Skypeing with her dad, Ben, my ex. Most evenings I cook something for myself as a way to relax. I had a go at making the courgette sauce and Flo joined me in the kitchen as I was draining the spaghetti.

'Do you fancy some of this?'

'No, thanks.'

She sat at the table with me.

'We need to fix a week for you to stay in Portsmouth,' I said.

Ben's parents live in Portsmouth and are active grandparents. I depend on them a lot and they have offered to have Flo stay with them for a week. She still had nearly four weeks of holiday left so this was very welcome. My mum lives in Glasgow and sees far less of Flo and me, which I regret.

'Granddad said this time we can go out in a rowing boat,' she said.

'That will be fun.'

She watched me piling pasta onto my plate and adding the sauce.

'Maybe I'll try a bit.'

Flo spooned three heaped teaspoons of parmesan on to her portion and we ate the spaghetti. I love to see her eat. It was tasty but my sauce did not reach the heights of the one we'd had in Italy. I will make it again and get better at it.

I went into my bedroom and booted up my laptop. I couldn't stop myself looking up Todd's new girlfriend on Facebook. Todd and I had been lovers for about two years but he'd had to return to Sydney last autumn when his father was diagnosed with cancer. His father died in February and Todd said he would have to stay in Sydney for a few months to support his mum. His emails had become less frequent and less communicative and in May he wrote to say that he had taken up with a woman he first dated when he was in high school. He told me her name. She is always posting up photos of her and Todd doing fun coupley things with annoying captions like *Happy with my new man*. I live in terror that one day I might accidentally 'Like' one of her posts and reveal myself as a stalker. I sat up and thought about what I was doing and was ashamed of myself. I shut down my laptop and made a resolution; I was not going to look at her account any more. Todd and I were over, had been for months. I was a single woman again.

CHAPTER THREE

StoryWorld TV station, London Bridge

Lori Kerwell arrived at my office at noon on the dot and I asked if she'd like anything from the Hub.

'I've got a drink with me.'

'Harriet?'

'I'm fine, thank you.'

I asked Ziggy to get me a coffee. Lori took out a can of Red Bull from her bag although she was already fizzing with energy. She pulled out her laptop, which was in a neon pink metallic case, and booted it up.

'I've prepared a PowerPoint, done an analysis of the brands our viewers favour. Shall I start?' she said.

'Some background first,' I said. 'This is a fairly new slot and Harriet has been working hard to get fashion houses on board. We're at the reputation-building phase and need to agree some ground rules around any marketing tie-ins.'

'Guy's slot is good. I've watched the last three months' worth, but it's not what our viewers are wearing, as I will show you,' Lori said.

'Perhaps not, but the point of Guy's slot is to be aspirational. He brings glamour into the show. Viewers love to see what celebrities wear, to see gowns that cost the price of a car,' I said.

'But he does high street sometimes. I can recall at least three slots,' she said.

'It's nearly always to show how you can create designer looks from high street shops,' Harriet interjected.

'And we're keen to keep an exclusive feel,' I said.

Lori was looking at me, knowing we were engaged in a negotiation; I was struck again by her dark eyes which gave nothing away.

'That's the area I will focus on, those high street brands with aspiration. Let me show you what I've learned from our viewers.'

'You need to know that Guy can't be closely identified with any one brand. He has to be free to be critical to maintain his credibility. We agreed this when we took him on, but please go ahead.'

Her PowerPoint lasted ten minutes. She had done a survey with a small number of viewers on which fashion brands they bought or liked. Harriet's face is not expressive but I thought she looked glum as Lori clicked through. The last slide was a pie chart which summarised her findings and she talked us through this with great confidence.

'I'll use this to target our advertising and tie-ins,' she said.

'Thank you for that. It's always useful to be given an insight into our viewers' tastes. Your sample, however, was small,' I said.

'This one was quick and dirty. I plan to do more in-depth surveys in the autumn.'

'How do you want to use Guy Browne?'

'I'd like him to front any fashion tie-ins I secure.'

'What would that entail?'

'It could be a range of things from in-store promotions, an internet Q and A with fashion tips, maybe even a roadshow doing makeovers with the public, you know the kind of thing.'

'Guy is incredibly busy,' Harriet said. 'You know he's fashion director at *The Gloss*? He's always travelling to shows in Paris and New York.'

I could tell that Harriet was appalled at the ideas Lori had rattled out, which also had a tired, old-fashioned feel to them.

'We do have a limited amount of time with Guy, but I think the key issue is his requirement to stay unconnected to any one brand,' I said.

'We wouldn't ask him to do any of this for free. The companies would pay him well, probably very well,' Lori said.

She had ignored my point about his need to be free to criticise designs and focused solely on the money aspect of any deal. I knew at that moment that Lori Kerwell and I would have difficulty reaching agreement. Appeals to her about editorial integrity would fall on deaf ears. She would, however, understand contractual obligations.

'Our first ground rule has to be that Guy is not required to do these promotions. Contractually, he has the right of refusal,' I said.

She sits in an upright posture but she straightened her spine even more at my words.

'That will make my job harder.' There was a distinct edge to her voice.

'I'm sorry about that, but the brands you've identified can take advantage of our slot and put their ads around it.'

'Yes of course, that's a given. But this is about taking it to the next level. Those brands want some of his stardust.'

'It only stays as stardust if he retains his status as high-end and objective,' I said crisply.

'I write a weekly report for Saul on marketing initiatives

and he was the one who identified food and fashion as two key areas for me to work on,' she said.

She held me in her look, her dark eyes unblinking. I knew she had lobbed in Saul's name as a tactic to get her own way. I took a sip of my coffee, which was cold, to give myself time to think.

'I can see one way we could involve Guy. Say you ran a competition with a design college for a young designer of the year. I'm sure Guy would be willing to be a judge and it would make nice television.'

'That would be very labour intensive,' Lori said.

'Yes, it would, but worthwhile, and we could run a series of items on it. It's exactly the sort of thing a sponsor might like. Think about it. We'd work with you on it.'

She clicked her laptop shut and put it into its case. She stood up and put on her jacket and handed me three copies of her PowerPoint presentation.

'I'd like Guy Browne to see my presentation.'

'Of course, I'll get his feedback,' I said.

I watched her walk away and Harriet picked up the printed sheets.

'Ugh, these brands are all either downmarket or mumsy,' she said.

'Yes. My goodness she works hard. She's been here, what, two weeks and she's already watched back episodes of Guy and done a survey!'

'I'm glad you said what you did. In-store promotions! I don't think so.'

'But we do need to try and work with her, somehow,' I said.

'Do I have to show Guy her presentation?'

'I'll have a word with him when he's next in.'

After Harriet had gone I brooded on how Lori had invoked Saul's name in our discussion. She was his appointment and she reported directly to him, not to Julius. They were both people who thought the bottom line was all that mattered. I recalled seeing her in that market café reading a tabloid. And out of nowhere I had a memory of a conversation I'd had with Julius shortly after I'd started work as a junior researcher. He'd said: 'You can't get all your stories from the *Guardian*. You need to read the *Sun* and the *Express* and the *Mirror* too. We're broadcasters, not academics!' This was a dig at me because shortly before I joined StoryWorld I'd given up my Masters in History. His comment rankled but Julius has a genuine talent for popular TV. He knows what issues and personalities our audience like and I've learned a lot from him.

Around two, Martine called and said could I pop down to see Julius. She is his PA and his gatekeeper. He's the only executive who still has a dedicated PA. I have a mirror by the door and I combed my hair quickly before I went down to his office. We all envy Julius his room. It's the corner one with double-aspect windows and the best views of the river. It always looks pristine, too, because it's painted every year while the rest of us have to wait longer to get our offices decorated. My office was looking distinctly tired at the moment. His furniture is all high-tech and contemporary except for his chair. This is an ancient leather Baedekar, a glimpse of the private Julius, and I've come to associate the chair with him. Julius likes the good things in life. He spends a lot of money on his clothes too. The pale blue shirt he was wearing was simple and perfectly cut. He has the kind of face that can change from pleasant to menacing in an instant and I've spent years watching his expression; more so since our great confrontation last November. Today, his expression was pleasant.

'You doing anything on Friday night?' he said.

'Vegging out at home with Flo.'

'Only I've got a ticket to the People's TV Awards. It's yours if you want it.'

He handed me the thick cream card with its embossed gold lettering. The ceremony was being held at the Grosvenor House Hotel and Julius, as director of programmes at StoryWorld, would be on one of the best tables. I felt a flicker of excitement as I held the invitation in my hand.

'That would be fun. Thanks, Julius.'

'I'm off now. I want to miss the traffic. Back next Wednesday.'

'Are you going to the Lizard?'

'Why do you ask?'

'Flo and I were there two years ago, at Lamorna Cove, stunningly beautiful but no mobile reception at all; something to do with the geology.'

He knew I was digging to find out more about his plans.

'I'm taking Steven to the Eden Project. And no calls is fine with me. I've told Martine you're in charge,' he said.

'I hope you both have a brilliant time and thanks for the invitation.'

I left his office. Steven is his younger brother and he lives with Julius. Steven has Down syndrome and Julius's love for his brother is the nicest thing about him. I wondered if Amber, the woman Julius has an on/off relationship with, was going with them. Somehow I doubted it. Amber is a stylist and a city woman through and through. I couldn't picture her trekking round the biospheres of the Eden Project. This was the friendliest phase Julius and I had gone through for months.

Last year we had a falling-out that was almost terminal. But he is a man who does not forget a grudge and I knew that this period of sunniness between us was unlikely to last.

When I got back Ziggy told me that Simon and Betty, our agony aunt, had gone down to the Hub to go through viewers' letters.

'Betty asked would you join them when you got back,' Ziggy said.

I didn't want to do this. Simon was perfectly capable of helping Betty choose which letters she would discuss on air tomorrow. There was something more pressing I needed to do.

'Thanks, I'll go down in a while.'

I went into my office and closed the door. The pressing matter related to Ziggy. She joined us last August on the intern scheme I had set up with the child protection team at Southwark Council. Every year we offered a one-year paid internship to a young person who had been in care. Ziggy's time was nearly up but I didn't want her to go. Two months ago I had asked the council if we could delay choosing the next new recruit until January. I was sure that by then I could get Ziggy placed in a permanent role at the station. The council had been sniffy about it for weeks and had left a message for me that morning. I called Fiona, my contact person at the council.

'The point of the scheme was to help as many young people as possible and we would prefer to stick to a summer or at least an autumn handover,' she said.

'Yes, but the point was also to help our interns build a career path in television. You told me that Ziggy had a record of running away from things.'

'Running away from her foster homes,' Fiona said.

'Yes, I remember. As you know, Ziggy is training to be a digital technician and she's showing enormous promise and staying power. I have an agreement with the director of programmes that the next junior post that becomes vacant goes to her. Now that would be a tremendous result for the scheme. And we'd be happy to welcome a new intern next year.'

'And what if a post doesn't come vacant by then?'

'I'm ready to commit to a new intern in January. You have my guarantee on that,' I said, feeling my irritation rise.

'We feel that Ziggy is getting special treatment,' she said.

I nearly snapped at Fiona because I did have a special feeling for Ziggy. Somehow, I kept my voice level.

'If so, it will be the first time in her life that has happened. Please reschedule the scheme for January.'

'As you wish,' Fiona said.

We said goodbye to each other coldly. I looked out of my office and could see Ziggy at her desk tapping away on her keyboard. Both her parents were dead, from heroin. She was bright and hard-working and I was determined to keep her at StoryWorld.

By the time I got down to the Hub, our staff café, Betty and Simon had selected the letters.

'Sorry I couldn't join you earlier. What have you gone with?'

'We had two good letters on cosmetic surgery; one that's gone horribly wrong and one from a woman who wouldn't get married unless her fiancé paid for her to have a facelift before the wedding,' Betty said.

'How romantic!' I said.

'She's sent us some before and after pics and honestly she looked better before the surgery,' Simon said.

'She's in her forties and this is her second marriage. Clearly she wanted to look younger but she does look very *Stepford Wives* now,' Betty said.

They showed me the two photos and Simon was right. The woman had looked more interesting and attractive before her face had been stretched and her nose made smaller. Cosmetic surgery often gives faces that wind tunnel look and nothing makes a person look older than striving to stay looking young. We wouldn't use the photos, though, as we always change the names and locations of the letters we use.

'You know, ten per cent of brides now have surgery or botox injections before their weddings. So I'll discuss the pressure to look perfect and, at the more serious end, body dysmorphic disorder,' Betty said.

'Good topic,' I said.

I accompanied Betty to the exit. She gets irritated if I don't show her these small attentions.

'Your ratings for last month were excellent,' I said.

'That's good to hear. You know, I thought Ledley might find the more intimate letters difficult to discuss but he's a delight to work with,' she said.

Chalk Farm flat, 7.30 p.m.

I tapped on Flo's door. She was lying on her stomach with her earphones in. She took these out.

'All good, sweets?'

She rolled into a sitting position and crossed her legs, beaming at me.

'Dad's sent me some money. I told him I was broke last night and he's put money into my account.'

Ben was back in funds and was being generous again. I was curious to know how much he had transferred to her account but didn't ask. It was Ben who had set it up, saying it would be good for her to have independent access to funds. It would teach her how to use money. Certainly it made her feel grown-up.

'And it's forty degrees Celsius there.'

'God that's hot!'

'He swims in the pool in his block and it's Olympic size,' she said proudly.

In December Ben had started a new job and a new life in Dubai as an aerial photographer on a land development project. He had bags of money but the life there sounded awful, living in an air-conditioned compound for the privileged. Flo, however, was enthusiastic about Dubai and had visited him in the Easter holidays. I sat down on her bed.

'I was wondering if you could organise to do a sleepover on Friday, maybe at Rosie's?'

'Why?'

'I've got a ticket to the People's TV Awards and I'd like to go.'

Now she looked interested.

'What are you going to wear?'

'I was thinking my little black dress?'

'No way, Mum! You have to really dress up for that. Haven't you watched it? It's ball gowns.'

'I'm not going to wear a ball gown.'

'You need to buy yourself a new dress.'

'Not for one night, darling. Maybe I could hire a dress.'

'Can I come and help you choose?'

'Yes, I'd like that. I'll check out some places.'

An hour later, fortified by a glass of wine, I called Ron Osborne. He's a crook of a builder. I need a new pair of French doors because the ones that open onto our garden are warped and difficult to open in the winter. I had asked around and the guy who lives in the flat upstairs said this Osborne had put in his new kitchen and was a proficient carpenter. I met with Ron Osborne in February. I remember he was deeply tanned which I found off-putting.

'Been in Gran Canaria for a month. Always take my holidays in the winter as jobs get stacked up once the weather improves,' he said.

He measured the doors and sent me a detailed estimate that a pair of new doors made from hard wood would cost one thousand seven hundred pounds. Friends said that was the kind of figure I'd have to pay. We scheduled the work for March and he asked for a deposit of a thousand pounds at the end of February. I thought this was a large deposit but I paid it. In March he had a minor accident to his left leg and said he needed to put the job back to April. In April he said he needed surgery on his leg. In May he said he was unable to drive after the operation so wouldn't be able to get over to Chalk Farm. In June he said he had a major job he had committed to which would take two months and he would slot my doors in during August. With each postponement my anxiety had grown. I took a deep breath and called him.

'We really need to get the date in August nailed down, Ron.'

'I'll do the job as soon as I can, Liz, but I can't commit to a date at the moment.'

'Why not? You said August.'

'Yes, but there's been some slippage, you see?'

'I don't understand.'

'I'm going to have to fit it in around some other jobs that are pressing.'

'My job is pressing. It's been postponed since March.'

'You know the reasons for that,' he said in a wounded voice, a voice I was growing to hate.

I found that I was holding the phone tightly and could feel sweat in my palm.

'I've been very patient but I can't wait any longer. I need the new doors before the summer is out. I think it best that we cancel the job and you return my deposit,' I said.

'Can't do that.'

'Why not?'

'I've bought the materials, see. I said I'd slot the job in and I will. I just can't give you an exact date.'

I know what is going on here. Ron Osborne has had my thousand pounds since March. He has spent it and there is little incentive to put himself out for the remaining seven hundred pounds. He thinks I'm a lone woman and a pushover. But I'm not going to let him get away with it. I poured myself another glass of wine and took out the papers that related to the job. I'm going to take legal action against him even though I know it will be a chore. His company is called Ron Osborne Maintenance UK Ltd but what I hadn't noticed before was that he had only put his email and mobile on the estimate. There was no postal address. I'll need his address if I'm going to serve papers on him.

I wished I could call my best friend Fenton and talk about it. She is so grounded and is brilliant with conflicts like these. She would never allow a builder to get the better of her. She's been like a sister to me since we met at university and I rely on her for emotional support more than anyone else.

She's away for a week, in Barcelona with Bill, her sexy detective. I googled Ron Osborne. Surely there would be something online about him: a club membership or a trade directory, that ChekaTrade thing? I could find nothing. I emailed my neighbour upstairs asking if he had Ron Osborne's postal address. Only two days back from Italy and my holiday afterglow was fading fast.

CHAPTER FOUR

StoryWorld TV station, London Bridge

Mid-morning, Gerry Melrose, our astrologer, dropped by my office to show me his script. Every week, as well as his forecasts, Gerry chooses a hot news story and does an astrological take on it.

'You look fabulous, Liz,' he said as he sank onto my sofa.

'Thanks. I switched off completely.'

'Simon did a good job in your absence.'

'He's wonderful. Anything happen here I should know about?'

'Well, there's been even more speculation about who Zachary's father is. Poor Fizzy, it's been intense. I don't think the press will let it go.'

'How very tiresome of them.'

'But inevitable. When you're in the public eye people will probe, and she did say it was a married man. Her vowing never to reveal his identity was like throwing down the gauntlet. Anyway, apparently a journo from one of the tabloids knows one of the news reporters here and he got hold of Geoff's name.'

Gerry raised his eyebrows and gave me a meaningful look. The widespread assumption at the station was that Fizzy had got pregnant by Geoff. He was a married consultant who Fizzy had had an affair with for several years. But I knew that he was not the father.

'Did they run with it?'

'Not yet. Maybe they'll wait till she's back on the sofa,' Gerry said.

It was common knowledge that after Zachary was born Fizzy had pulled up the drawbridge and no visits were allowed. But Julius had seen her on Sunday and I wondered if the recent thaw had extended to Gerry.

'Have you seen the baby yet?'

'I have; this weekend. Zachary is a gorgeous little Gemini, like you and your Flo. I cast his chart and went through the reading with Fizzy. That little boy has some interesting transits.'

One of the ways that Gerry shows his affection for you is by preparing a personal astrological chart, and his readings can run to several pages; he did one for me last year. People pay a lot for this service. He believes absolutely in the truth of astrology and that it should guide your decisions in life.

'I'm going to see her later. How did she seem with him?'

'Thrilled to have a son but overwhelmed by it all. Quite honestly, she couldn't cope without Loida. Loida was making the bottles and doing the nappies.'

'I hope she's not trying to come back too soon,' I said.

I had his script and read it through. His topic was a celebrity's right to privacy. There had been a row running for weeks about an injunction which a celebrity couple had taken out to prevent disclosure of the infidelity of one of them. Their whole public persona relied on the idea that they were a happy and wholesome couple and a number of their sponsorship deals hinged on this image. But according to the tabloids, one of them had indulged in three-in-a-bed romps. Everyone in the media knew who the couple were, of course, but their names could not be published. In his script Gerry had analysed how different star signs need different levels of privacy. Apparently Sagittarians let it all hang out whereas Scorpio was the most secretive of signs. Gerry had taken some celebrities as examples of these traits, not the two in the news, and it was well-written enjoyable nonsense.

'Excellent script. We're trying to keep the mood light-hearted this month,' I said.

Gerry was looking thoughtful now.

'I've just this minute had a thought. This issue of privacy relates to Fizzy too, doesn't it? Is that going to be a bear trap?' he said.

I often spoke to my team and the presenters about the need to avoid bear traps and banana skins. A bear trap was when a story came back and bit us and a banana skin was a foolish mistake that sometimes got through. I read his script again more carefully.

'This will be OK. Everyone will be thinking about the injunction couple in this context, not Fizzy,' I said.

He stood up. 'Good. I've got to dash but shall we do lunch or dinner soon?'

'Definitely; I'll check the calendar.'

After he had gone I looked up Ron Osborne Maintenance UK Ltd. It is not registered with Companies House which came as no surprise. I googled how to make a small claim and it is quite straightforward but I will need his address.

In my lunch break I headed for an upmarket gift shop by the river walk as I wanted to buy something for Zachary. There was a mountain of soft toys on display in the window. Since the end of May sackfuls of baby toys have arrived at the station, sent in by our viewers. It is Ziggy's job to write thank-you letters to every one of them on behalf of Fizzy and we've donated the gifts to a community hospital in Bermondsey. The toys in the shop were enchanting, though, and I made myself resist the softest blue bunny for Zachary. Instead, I bought a Peter Rabbit bowl with a matching mug which came in nice boxes.

Fizzy lives in Pimlico in an exclusive cobbled mews. Her home comprises two mews houses which have been knocked together with a central entrance between two garages which occupy the ground floor. They are not greasy-rag garages though, far from it; both offer services for high-end cars. It's exactly the kind of pretty and tucked-away house you would expect a TV star to live in. Loida opened the door and I followed her up the steep stairs to the sitting room which runs the length of the two houses. A child-proof gate had already been installed at the top of the stairs, though Zachary can't be crawling yet. Fizzy looked pretty in a loose pink dress. She is slightly plumper and less perfectly coiffed and made-up than when she's on air. I liked that she looked softer. She got up off the sofa and we exchanged kisses. Zachary was fast asleep in a Moses basket next to her.

'Thanks for coming over. I look a fright,' she said.

'I was thinking how pretty you looked.' I handed her the Peter Rabbit boxes.

I peeked in the Moses basket. Zachary was lying on his back with a cream blanket with a thick satin hem tucked loosely around him.

'He looks blissfully asleep and extremely kissable,' I said.

I joined her on the sofa as she undid the boxes and took out the mug and the bowl.

'Thank you for these. I like old-fashioned things.'

'How are you doing?'

'The breastfeeding was ghastly. I stuck it out for a month to give Zac's immune system a boost but I couldn't go on with it.'

Loida brought in a tray with tea things and a plate of those little French biscuits, cat's tongues they're called.

'Has he been asleep long?' I asked.

Fizzy looked over at Loida.

'About forty minutes. He'll wake soon. I'll be in my room if you need me,' Loida said.

Fizzy poured tea from the pot and handed me a bone china cup and saucer.

'Is Loida staying here now?'

'Yes, thank God. She's fantastic with Zac.'

She passed me the milk jug and offered the plate of biscuits and I took one.

'I've got a month to lose half a stone,' she said.

'Don't put pressure on yourself. You look lovely.'

'I have to. The cameras add a stone, you know.'

'You've had a baby. The viewers will love it if that shows a bit.'

'Mmm, I'm not sure about that. Julius and Gerry have both been over but I've not had a peep out of Ledley.' She sounded resentful.

'I think most of us got the impression you wanted a period of complete rest and privacy. I'm sure he'd love to see you.'

She pulled a face and I thought I shouldn't have defended Ledley.

'Well, please don't say anything to him. I'm sure he's far too busy being the anchor,' she said.

Ledley was a sore point between us and I decided to confront it directly.

'Fizz, you need to know that I have never championed Ledley to replace you. I suggested him as the temporary stand-in rather than bringing in another woman presenter. I'm so looking forward to you coming back and to Ledley returning to being our chef.'

She had stiffened at my comment.

'Why do you say that?'

'I don't know. He's become too polished recently, almost slick. I preferred the scruffier Ledley who made mistakes and made us laugh.'

She put her cup down on the tray.

'Maybe I was overreacting, Liz, but I've seen it too often; presenters demoted or replaced after a break. Remember what happened to Yvette?'

Yvette had been a high-profile presenter on a rival channel who had taken six months off to front a charity project to combat malaria in the Ivory Coast. On her return to London the younger woman who had stood in for her kept the job. Yvette had spoken to the press about ageism and won the moral argument but she had lost her TV slot.

'She never has come back full-time, has she?' I said.

'That's exactly my point. She gets the odd gig, but mainly as a replacement presenter.'

Fizzy wrinkled her pretty nose in disgust at the thought.

'But she was never as big as you, Fizz.'

'Granted, but her presenting career is pretty well over now.'

'You're in a different league.' I said it again to bolster her.

She must have been thinking about this and worrying about it. This was what was driving her to come back in September.

'Julius knows how important you are to the success of the show. I've always thought one of our unique selling points is that StoryWorld bucks the trend and has you as our sole anchor,' I said.

'We work in a ruthless industry. I have no illusions about loyalty from the station, none.'

She filled my cup again and I added milk and leaned back against the sofa. I was glad I had broached the subject of Ledley. It was a pretty room, a reflection of Fizzy's taste, feminine with vases of flowers and lamps on small tables and a lot of framed photographs of Fizzy at various stages of her career. There was a shot of a younger Fizzy standing in front of a weather map looking pert and pretty. Her first on-screen role at StoryWorld had been to do the weather and she had been an almost instant hit with the viewers. There was little evidence of a baby in the house apart from the Moses basket on the floor. When I had Flo our small house had overflowed with baby things and it used to irritate Ben. I guessed that Zachary had his own dedicated nursery and the toys and changing mats and other baby paraphernalia would be there with Loida keeping everything in perfect order. Fizzy poured herself more tea and gave me a guarded look.

'So, strictly between you and me, Bob rang me a week ago. It's the first time I've heard from him since the birth,' she said.

Mentioning Bob meant she was willing to treat me as her confidante again.

'He said he wants to see Zac. What should I do?'

I wasn't going to give her any advice this time. Getting too involved before had made Bob my arch enemy. He had been very aggressive and told me to butt out of her pregnancy. My knowing he was the father made him fear me because

I could spill the beans to his wife Pat and wreck his marriage. Not that I would do such a thing in a million years! I leaned towards her.

'What do you want to do?'

'I don't know. He said he was sorry he hadn't been in touch, that he'd been thinking about me all the time but didn't know how to be around me any more.'

'Well, I'm sure that's true,' I said.

She tossed her head in a dismissive way.

'Easy enough to say he's thinking about me. I judge people on what they actually do.'

'He must feel so conflicted. It's a big secret.'

'He's scared; terrified Pat will find out and kick him out. But he's also dead chuffed to have a son. I could tell that was the real draw, not me.'

She took a biscuit and nibbled on it.

'I love these biscuits. I know I shouldn't but…'

'They're tiny,' I said, and took another two to encourage her.

'He's got daughters, you know. He's always wanted a boy. Anyway, I told him he couldn't possibly come here. Most days there's some paparazzi posted outside watching who's coming in and who's going out.'

'Creeps, they should leave you alone,' I said.

'I know,' she sighed. 'It means I can't go out without the full slap on.'

Zachary started to stir and opened his eyes and slowly he came awake. Fizzy knelt down by his basket, lifted him up and cradled him in the crook of her arm. He was a pretty little baby, with her pointed chin.

'He's *gorgeous*, Fizz.'

She smiled proudly. 'He sailed through his six week check-up,' she said.

Loida came in with a bottle for the baby.

'I'll feed him this time,' Fizzy said.

I left soon after. Feeding her baby was a moment for her to savour without company.

CHAPTER FIVE

StoryWorld TV station, London Bridge

I was sitting in the gallery with the director watching Guy Browne do his fashion slot which was on 'Dressing for the British Summer'. Guy had initially written 'English' summer in his script but thankfully I had spotted it in time and changed it to 'British'. We get a furious response if we refer to our stories as being English rather than British and I've learned to look out for this.

'Every year we have high hopes of soaring temperatures but the reality of the great British summer often disappoints. So I have a few simple rules,' Guy said. 'Invest in a lightweight trench coat. It's by far the most elegant way to combat our unpredictable weather. I'm not talking of a dreary, detective trench. There are some playful versions out this summer.'

Ledley was doing his best to look interested but he rarely comments, whereas if Fizzy was back she would have engaged far more. She loves talking fashion. Guy had told me he had to rush off after his slot so I didn't mention the Lori Kerwell survey to him. Straight after was our interview of the day and this was with Jasmin, an actor turned activist who cared passionately about the fate of the bee. She wanted to ban the insecticide that was killing bees, had got a social media campaign going and had started a petition which had taken off. She was delivering this personally to Number Ten that morning. She and Ledley had a lively discussion and at the end she presented him with a jar of honey.

'Bees are the good guys of our planet. Please help me save them,' she said.

With Julius away I was chairing the morning meeting and Bob hated this. He had hardly sat down before he launched into Jasmin.

'I mean, Jasmin and her bloody bees! She's rent-a-gob and it's well known she'll go to the opening of an envelope,' he said.

Ledley protested. 'That's harsh. She really cares about bees and I thought she was great on that.'

'She was,' I said. 'And she'll be on the lunchtime bulletins delivering her petition to Number Ten and we had her on the sofa first. We might even be able to syndicate one of her quotes. Well done, Ledley.'

Bob was so transparent in his hostility. It was strange how when Julius was away the importance of these discussions drained away. Lori was present but she didn't say anything.

Ledley walked back to my office and sat on my sofa. He had closed the door with a firm click, his expression puzzled and slightly pained.

'Why is Bob being so aggressive towards you?'

'Oh, he's furious that Julius asked me to chair the morning meetings,' I said.

'That's stupid. Downright petty. I thought there might be something else going on?'

Ledley's intuition was sound and Bob's animosity went far deeper but I couldn't explain any of that.

'No, just the usual news versus features nonsense,' I said.

'Anyway, I wanted you to know that tomorrow I'm having lunch with Lori Kerwell and my food producers. She's hoping she can do business with them,' he said.

Ledley has a deal with a food manufacturer who use his name on a marinade for meat and fish which is called Go Luscious with Ledley. He fronts their advertising campaign and we've been carrying the ads since January, which has been a good earner for the station.

'Thanks for letting me know. Lori certainly has hit the ground running.'

'Telling me. She gets in very early. I've seen her coming in when I'm heading for make-up.'

'And she's still at her desk when I leave,' I said.

Lori Kerwell had an office which was the mirror image of mine but was on the other side of Julius's corner room. I'd been past it a couple of times and peered in. All our offices are glass boxes. She had a pink sofa and a shelf with colour-coded lever arch files running the length of one wall. When most of us left for the night you could see her desk light still burning. There was something alarming about the intensity with which she worked. It was more than working hard; she was a workaholic.

'I heard you went to see Fizzy,' he said.

'I did. Yesterday. Zachary is gorgeous.'

'Is she up for visits now?'

'I think so, yes.'

'Only she was cold when I rang her about two weeks ago. Gave me the distinct impression that my call wasn't welcome.'

This was odd. Fizzy had complained to me that she had heard nothing from Ledley. And she had asked me not to say anything about it either.

'She's under a lot of stress. There are paparazzi outside her house most days, which must be awful,' I said.

'They won't leave until they know who the father is. They're like a dog with a bone. I think I'll send her a bunch of flowers and wait for an invitation,' he said.

'Good plan. And let me know how the meeting with Lori goes.'

After Ledley had gone I felt low and I realised it was because I hadn't been able to be straight with him, either about Bob's aggression or about Fizzy. So often at work I can't say what I think and have to be guarded in my choice of words. I once thought Ledley was someone I could have got close to but this gap between my real take on things and my diplomatic StoryWorld version can be a bar to true friendship. I sometimes worry that I've got into the habit of concealing my thoughts and feelings. My mum is a person who sets great store on telling the truth and she brought me up to think that was fundamental to a good life. But a lot of the time in television you can't be honest. We all engage in a mixture of flattery, superlatives and half-truths and I still get these little stabs of self-reproach when I do it.

I had stood Janis our childminder down for the day and Flo came into the station at four. She sat outside with Harriet and the team while I finished my emails. Flo has a thing about Harriet and thinks she is super cool. Harriet helped her last year on a disastrous night I still don't like to think about and to her credit Harriet talks to Flo like she's an equal. I know they keep in touch on WhatsApp.

We took the Tube to Sloane Square and headed up the King's Road to a dress-hire place I had researched. The walk took a while because Flo kept stopping at the shops on the way.

The money Ben had transferred into her account was burning a hole in her pocket and she said she couldn't decide what to spend it on. Finally, we reached the dress-hire shop which had a dark red interior and was heady with the fragrance of expensive candles. Jewel-coloured Tiffany lamps glowed on small tables. There were long rails holding every type of evening dress from elegant sheaths to Disney princess to Christina Aguilera vamp. Flo was impressed that as well as dresses you could hire jewellery, shoes, evening bags and even beaded hats and fascinators. The sales assistant said she'd be with us in a while and we should browse. She was dealing with a thin demanding woman with a loud voice and an expensive handbag on her bony arm.

Flo was gleeful as she worked her way down the rails, picking several dresses for me to try on. I was drawn to the less ornate dresses and found a couple I liked. We carried our haul to the changing rooms. I tried each dress on and came out to the larger mirror to twirl for Flo. There was one I liked a lot, a simple cream satin sheath that was cut on the bias.

'It's too simple, Mum.'

'I like simple,' I said.

The sales assistant had seen off her demanding client and joined us. She was a stylish middle-aged woman.

'That looks good on you but with your dark bob I'm thinking you could go for a Louise Brooks look,' she said.

'Oh, I adore Louise Brooks,' I said.

'Who is she?' Flo asked.

'She was a star of the silent screen, darling.'

The saleswoman returned with a beaded shift dress on a satin padded hanger.

'This is one of our few vintage nineteen twenties dresses.'

The dress was knee-length and the neckline a deep V. Silver, black and midnight blue glass beads had been sewn into a series of concentric circles and glittered dully under the changing room lights. She handed me the hanger and I was surprised at how heavy the dress was. She helped it over my head and as I looked in the mirror I shivered with pleasure. It was beautiful, exotic, and it made me feel glamorous.

'Mum, you look gorgeous!' Flo said.

When you moved the dress moved with you and set up a gentle rustling of the tiny beads.

'Oh yes, you have the face and the body for that dress. You'd think it was made for you,' the saleswoman said.

'Thanks so much for the suggestion. I would never have thought to try it on.'

She slid the dress into a protector bag and zipped it up.

'With a vintage dress you need to accessorise carefully.'

She talked me into hiring a pair of 1920s-style black bar shoes with a small heel, and a metal mesh bag. I was on a high, had thrown my usual caution about spending to the winds and treated us to a taxi home with the precious cargo laid out on the back seat while Flo and I sat on the pull-down seats.

'I'm going to have to take all this into work tomorrow. I won't have time to come home and change.'

Flo had been busy googling pictures of Louise Brooks.

'Oh, Mum! I wanted to help you get ready.'

'I guess you and Rosie could come to the station at teatime, if you think she'd like that. You can help me get ready there.'

Chalk Farm flat, 7.15 p.m.

Flo got on the phone to Rosie while I made us a salad niçoise.

I hadn't felt as excited about an event for ages. We aren't up for any awards this year so I'll be able to relax and drink the champagne and watch my industry at play. I was in such a good mood I decided we should eat outside so I gave our garden table a quick scrub and carried out two chairs. I opened a bottle of white wine and tossed the salad. Flo helped me carry out the plates and we sat across from each other.

'Thanks for coming with me, sweets. I'm really excited about that dress.'

She was picking out the black olives from her salad and putting them on my plate.

'You looked different in it; different in a good way,' she said.

Later, I went to my room and checked my home email. My neighbour upstairs had replied.

> No I'm sorry I don't have Ron's postal address. We
> did all our business by email. Is there a problem?
> Jason

I was careful when I wrote back to him. He might still be in touch with Ron Osborne and I didn't want that crook getting wind of my intentions.

> Thanks for getting back to me. There's been a
> delay on my job but it can be resolved. All best, Liz

I hope it can be resolved. I can't afford to lose a thousand pounds. My finances are usually on a knife edge. When I separated from Ben I took on a larger mortgage than I can comfortably afford so that I could buy this two-bedroom flat. A great chunk of my salary goes on it every month. But my flat is my haven and I'm determined to hang onto it.

CHAPTER SIX

StoryWorld TV station, London Bridge

I watched from the gallery as Gerry did his rundown on how different star signs view the issue of privacy.

'The way I see it is that just as on Facebook you can choose the privacy settings you want, so with the star signs you will find a wide range of preferences on this. Sagittarians are happy for everyone to have access to news about their life. But those secretive Scorpios cringe at this openness and choose the highest privacy settings possible.'

Gerry ran through the celebrities he had picked to illustrate his point and we flashed up their images as he spoke.

'I get that, Gerry, but don't you think that if you are a celebrity you can't expect to put up these walls? I mean, you get all the advantages of fame and it's your fans who put you there. Don't you have to accept there'll be interest in your private life?' Ledley said.

'Granted, but there needs to be limits, don't there? No one can live their life under the spotlight all the time.'

'When I hear celebrities complaining about this it seems a bit rich to me,' Ledley persisted.

'But if your zodiac character is to be private you will find press attention more difficult to take. It has been known to make people ill,' Gerry said.

Ledley looked into camera. 'We'd like to know what you think about this, and, tweeters, please include the hashtag StoryWorld.'

God, we have an unforgiving audience sometimes. All the comments sided with Ledley and said why should overpaid celebrities have their cake and eat it. They got all the benefits of fame and should get over themselves.

Later, I had a coffee with Gerry in the Hub.

'That was a lively discussion this morning,' I said.

Gerry stirred a heaped teaspoon of sugar into his cappuccino and sprinkled more on top.

'I was actually surprised at Ledley's vehemence. It was almost like he was on his soapbox, wasn't it?'

'I haven't seen that side of him before. He's usually more laid-back. Our viewers were with him on the privacy issue though,' I said.

I could tell Gerry had something else he wanted to say but he didn't want to be overheard. He scanned the café and took a sip of his drink. He moved closer to me.

'I think Ledley is going to have problems returning to a weekly slot after all this airtime. You can see how he's loving the limelight,' he said in a low voice.

Simon had said the same thing and I felt a stirring of unease. Ledley came to us as a chef with a weekly cooking slot. I had talent-spotted him and up till now had found him the most accommodating presenter to work with.

'Maybe, but that's the way it has to be,' I said.

Around four, Flo and Rosie arrived at the station. Rosie hadn't been there before and she was impressed by our large, light-filled atrium and by the Hub. She liked the lime-green and orange tables and chairs. She and Flo circled the food and drink bar which caters for all tastes and all types of allergies, but in the end they both settled for a pizza and a Coke. I treated them and went off to find Ellen in make-up to do my hair. The girls joined me there later while Ellen was starting on my face. Flo watched intently as she shaded my cheekbones and lined my eyes. We moved to one of the dressing rooms and the girls helped me into my dress and secured my shoes. I did a twirl for them and I felt excited, heady and giggly. As we left the room we encountered Henry, the floor manager.

'Wowza! Pretty lady! I'd like to whistle but I know that's not allowed any more,' he said, grinning at me.

I tipped my head to one side and tried to look vampy.

'Oh, I don't object to the odd whistle,' I said.

'Mum, you were flirting with him. Gross!' Flo muttered as we went up the stairs. Flo hates me to show any interest in men. I'm Mum and I'm supposed to be asexual. We approached my office where Molly, Simon and Ziggy were at their desks.

'You look amazing,' Simon said.

'Like you stepped straight out of the nineteen twenties,' Molly said.

'Mum's based her look on Louise Brooks,' Flo chipped in.

'Who's Louise Brooks?' Ziggy asked.

'She was a star of the silent screen.'

Flo got up some pics on her phone and was showing these to Ziggy. There was no sign of Harriet.

'Thank you, all. I'm glad you approve. We're off in ten minutes so I hope you all have a lovely weekend,' I said.

'Harry and I are going to a do tonight too,' Simon said.

'Where are you off to?'

'Lori Kerwell gave these invites to Harry; a cocktail bar that's opening in Covent Garden tonight.'

He showed me a black card with the word *Hayworth* written in flowing gold letters across the front.

'It's in homage to Rita Hayworth and they've invented a cocktail called the Gilda.'

'That sounds fun.'

'She offered us four invites. Told Harry she doesn't drink so she wasn't planning on going,' Simon said.

So Lori didn't drink. It was Friday, let your hair down day, and I wondered if she ever allowed herself to unwind.

'That was kind of her. You don't fancy it?' I looked over at Molly and then Ziggy.

'Not my thing,' Molly said.

'I think you have to dress up for those places, don't you?' Ziggy said. She was wearing her usual uniform of boyfriend jeans and a grey T-shirt.

Harriet had arrived back.

'You can still come, Zig. This is an opening and they won't turn us away,' she said.

Ziggy looked alarmed at the notion of being turned away.

'No, ta, I'm all right.'

'What a stunning dress,' Harriet said. 'Are the beads made of glass?'

'Yes, and it weighs a ton.'

I did a little wiggle and the dress moved sinuously around my hips. Ziggy reached out and touched the beads.

'So beautiful.'

Harriet was looking at my feet. 'Those shoes are perfect with it.'

'We *must* have a photo,' Simon declared.

Ziggy is the best photographer in the team so Harriet gave her phone to her. The whole team insisted I walk back to the stairs. There are two staircases in our building, on either side of the atrium. One leads to features on the left and the other to news on the right and they are rather showbiz in the way they sweep up. Harriet positioned me halfway down.

'Now chin up, right leg slightly in front and left hand on your hip,' she ordered.

I did as she asked but felt foolish as Ziggy took the shots, especially when I saw Bob approach and walk down the right-hand staircase. He was dressed in black tie and the thought flashed into my head: could he be going to the People's TV Awards? He shot me a baleful look.

Finally, we were in a taxi heading for the Grosvenor House Hotel. I asked the driver to take the girls on to Rosie's house and gave Flo some cash. I was spending too much money but had decided that this was going to be a treat evening and I'd be careful for the rest of the month. I waved goodbye and as I started to walk up the red carpet it began to spit rain. A burly steward in evening dress stepped forward, held a large umbrella over my head and accompanied me all the way to the entrance. A couple of photographers took shots of me which was rather thrilling.

The champagne reception was hosted in the legendary Red Bar. It was a crush in there and guests were spilling out into the foyer. I took a glass and hung back by the wall watching the throng of loud and beautiful and needy people who circulated and air-kissed and looked over their shoulders to scan the bar for A-listers. I recognised a few faces and pondered how certain beautiful women from a past era, Louise Brooks and Rita Hayworth, were still being celebrated today. I doubted that our film and TV industry produced actors with the same enduring appeal. I had the feeling that someone was watching me and as I turned I saw Bob leaned up at the bar staring at me. As soon as my eyes met his he looked away, took a glass of champagne from a tray and went out into the foyer. It gave me a jolt seeing him like that because we are colleagues and he hadn't even acknowledged me. I prayed he wasn't on the same table as me. That would spoil the evening.

After thirty minutes, when the crush in the bar had started to get uncomfortable, we were asked to move into the ballroom. This was a long stately room that had been themed in silver and white with every table graced by silver candles, already lit, and posies of tiny white rosebuds in glass bowls. It looked pretty and elegant and more understated than I expected. Last year's People's TV Awards had been written up as too neon and flashy and this year the organisers had gone to the other extreme.

I was on an excellent table near the stage and my table companions were all well-known folk. Thankfully, Bob was not amongst them. We shook hands and introduced our-selves before we sat down. To my left was a Queen of the Theatre who had recently won accolades for her portrayal of Saint Joan. Next to her was ITV's political editor with his trademark floppy fringe, and next to him the celebrity editor of *Glamour* magazine. The seat on my right was empty. I peered at the place name which said 'Douglas Pitlochry'. He's the newscaster for a rival TV company, News Nine. They are bigger than us and often in competition for stories. Douglas Pitlochry is described by the tabloids as the housewife's choice and the newscaster most women would like to sleep with. I was disappointed that he was a no-show. The next chair along was occupied by a former newspaper editor who now fronted an interview show called *Celebrity*

Tribe. He was known for being an attention-seeker and for making provocative comments on Twitter to his four million followers. To his right sat a distinguished-looking woman in her sixties. When she introduced herself as Claudia Buck I realised who she was. She used to head up a secret government department. On her retirement she had written a thriller which one grumpy Conservative MP had objected to, saying it sailed close to breaching the Official Secrets Act. Now, her book had been made into a three-parter for television and she was the only person on our table who was up for an award.

The lights were dimmed and the bright pink and gold logo of the People's TV Awards was flashed up on the huge screen behind the stage. The logo faded into a slick two minute promo which listed the awards that would be unveiled after the dinner. The lights came up and a phalanx of waiters entered the ballroom carrying the starters on silver trays. And Douglas Pitlochry sat down next to me. There were drops of rain on his fair hair and on the shoulders of his dinner suit. We shook hands briefly and I saw him glance at my place name.

'Traffic was awful. I got out of the taxi and walked the last three blocks,' he said to me. He reached for the wine bottle in the ice bucket. 'Want a refresh?'

'Yes, please.'

He filled my glass before pouring some for himself. I've seen him on screen but this was the first time I had met him. I was struck by how well his suit hung on his broad shoulders, but the most memorable thing about him was his voice. It's a rich broadcaster's voice with a trace of his Scottish roots discernible in certain words. I could tell at once that Douglas Pitlochry did not like Mr Celebrity Tribe to his right. He sat so that his body was angled towards me and addressed all his remarks my way.

Our starters were fried green tomatoes sitting on goat's curd with basil sorbet on the side.

'Unusual and delicious,' Douglas Pitlochry said to me.

'Mmm, yes, this basil sorbet is amazing.'

Our starter plates were whipped away and we were presented with wild bass or sirloin steak or Lancashire cheese and prune filo according to our preferences. Douglas Pitlochry and I had both chosen the fish. Mr Celebrity Tribe had gone for the sirloin and he started to complain to the table: 'This is too well done. A good sirloin should ooze pink and there's no ooze, no ooze at all.'

I glanced at his plate and thought that his steak looked pretty rare to me.

'I think the food is nicely done considering they are catering for hundreds,' the Queen of the Theatre said as she took one tiny mouthful of the filo.

Douglas asked me about Fizzy.

'Is she coming back soon?'

'Yes, at the beginning of September.'

I hoped he wouldn't probe me about the paternity issue. I was enjoying talking to him and didn't want to close it down.

'She's good but I like your Ledley too,' he said.

I was surprised that he watched our show.

'Have you ever tried to make any of his recipes?' I asked in a teasing tone.

'No, but maybe I should. I'm trying to teach myself to cook these days,' he said.

After two glasses of wine, on top of the champagne I'd had

earlier, I started to tell Douglas about my difficulties with Ron Osborne.

'I feel such a fool. I should have spotted there was no address and my neighbour hasn't got it either. I can't take legal action against him without an address.'

'There are tracing agents, you know. They could get his address for you,' he said.

'Tracing agents?'

'Yes, private investigators. You've got his phone number and email?'

'Yes, his mobile and email.'

'They should be able to track down his address from that.'

To my surprise the thought of hiring a private detective appealed to me. I had worked up a lot of resentment against Ron Osborne.

'How do you find them?'

'The usual way: an internet search.'

'Sounds expensive and maybe it's shady?' I said.

He smiled at me and I decided that he had a rather lovely mouth.

'Not shady and not too expensive either. He's the one who's being shady. I can check it out for you. What's your email?'

'Really?'

'It will be my pleasure.'

I wrote my work email on the back of the menu card.

'Give me your number too,' he said.

Our pudding arrived and it was café gourmand: a cup of espresso accompanied by tiny portions of crème brûlée, île flottante, chocolate soufflé and fresh strawberries all arranged artistically on the plate. The pudding divided the table along gender lines. All the women loved it and we cooed over the tiny diamond-shaped dish that the île flottante was resting in. The men looked bewildered at the diminutive portions and asked why not have a decent-sized serving of one thing instead?

The lighting in the room changed and the award ceremony began with a well-known comedian doing the compèring. Claudia Buck did not win for the dramatisation of her novel. Douglas and I commiserated with her and she was robust in her protestations that it wasn't a problem at all. I was thinking about inviting her on to our show and decided I'd call her on Monday from the office.

There was a brief interlude before the technical awards were due to start and the compère referred to this as a comfort break. I've always found that phrase ridiculously euphemistic. As I headed for the Ladies I saw Bob. His table was much further back in the room and it was all men. I guessed it was a gathering of news editors. Bob's face was flushed and he had loosened his bow tie. There were a lot of empty wine bottles on their table. I joined the queue at the Ladies and had the inevitable conversation with the woman in front of me that even at the Grosvenor House Hotel there was not enough provision for women. I was moving back through the tables when Bob walked into my path – he had deliberately sought me out. He is a man who always gives the impression of barely containing the anger within him and I could see that he was on the edge of drunk.

'So you're sitting on the boss's table with all the luvvies,' he sneered.

'And good evening to you too, Bob,' I said.

'You seem to be his blue-eyed girl at the moment. What have you got on him then?'

I don't know why I even tried to answer him. To placate him, I suppose. I felt hot and embarrassed seeing him like this, hardly an ambassador for StoryWorld.

'Julius gave me his ticket because he's on holiday.'

'But that's how you work, isn't it? Digging up secrets; you like to get things on people, don't you? Gives you a sense of power.'

His look was openly hostile and I quailed inside. He has been aggressive towards me before and though I didn't think he would strike me I wanted to get away from him.

'You've drunk too much,' I said, trying to move past him.

He leaned in closer to me and his expression was venomous.

'If you say anything, anything at all about me and Fizzy, I'll make you pay, I really will.'

'Bob, hello!'

It was Douglas and he was standing by my side. He had made his greeting loudly and I felt so grateful to have him there. Bob took a small unsteady step back from me.

'Douglas.' He nodded his head at him and walked away.

'Are you OK? He looked really angry.'

I was trembling and Douglas noticed it. He put his hand gently on my lower back and steered me to our table. By the time I sat down I had thought how to explain away what Douglas had just witnessed.

'That was so stupid. He's drunk far too much and you see there's a lot of rivalry between news and features at StoryWorld. Bob is very put out that I got to sit in Julius's place tonight,' I said.

'Was that all it was? He seemed positively threatening.'

Douglas gave me a searching look as if he was assessing the truth of what I had said. He couldn't have missed how aggressive Bob was and I needed to deflect him from probing any further.

'How do you know him?' I asked.

'He freelanced with us a few years back. He's a solid news man but he has a short fuse.'

'He certainly does,' I said with feeling as the lights dimmed and the technical awards started.

Ten minutes later Douglas leaned over and whispered in my ear: 'My boy's been away and he's back tonight so I'm bailing out. I'll be in touch.'

He picked up the menu card on which I'd written my details and left. I thought about the way he'd looked at me when I gave my lame reason for Bob's blatant aggression. It was the look of a journalist not believing a story he was being told. But what could I do? He works for a rival TV station and there was no way I could have told him the truth. The question was whether he had overheard what Bob said to me and caught that mention of Fizzy. With his leaving it felt to me like the evening was over.

CHAPTER SEVEN

Chalk Farm flat, Saturday, 4 p.m.

The beaded dress, the dress of transformation, had to be back at the hire shop by ten a.m. on Monday or I would incur an additional charge. I had taken the Tube to Sloane Square and handed it over to the saleswoman with a pang of regret. It had cost a lot to hire but I had loved how it made me feel and meeting Douglas Pitlochry had been exciting. The only thing that had spoiled the evening was Bob's aggression. He was clearly under a lot of pressure and had drunk too much but what a stupid place to confront me. I had no intention of sharing his secret but hadn't been able to tell him that. And anyway, would he believe me? He was determined to think the worst of me.

As I let myself into the flat I could hear Flo crying in her bedroom. I hurried in and she was lying on her bed sobbing as if her world had come to an end. The shutters were closed and the room was in near darkness.

'What's happened, sweetheart?'

She sat up and I saw that her beautiful brown hair was now a nasty brassy blonde! I rushed over to her and put my arm around her and the story came out between great hiccoughy sobs. She had decided to use the money Ben had put into her account to get her hair bleached. She thought that going blonde would be edgy so she and Rosie had set off after breakfast to look for a salon she could afford. The high street ones had been too expensive so they found some cheap backstreet hairdresser who must have applied a gallon of peroxide to Flo's tender scalp. Honestly, I think the bloody woman had used toilet bleach! When she saw the result Flo knew it had been a terrible mistake. Rosie had tried to comfort her but she was inconsolable and had run all the way home. I was shocked when I touched her hair, not just at the colour but that her normally healthy hair felt dry and brittle.

'My scalp is burning,' she said.

That worried me.

'Will I go bald?' she wailed.

'Of course not,' I said firmly, while thinking that it was not impossible. 'I'm going to look up some advice now,' I added, as calmly as I could manage.

I went into the kitchen and furiously googled how to deal with a bad job of bleached hair. I found a terrifying article which said you should inspect the burn area. Redness and irritation could be treated at home but if there were open wounds, blistering or tissue damage you had to go to hospital. Vomiting and feeling faint was also a symptom of chemical burn. Flo had joined me in the kitchen and I shut down the article quickly.

'I need to look at your scalp, darling.'

She let me inspect her head. Her scalp was red but there was no sign of blisters.

'You're not feeling sick or anything like that?'

'No, not sick; all hot and itchy.'

'OK. We need to get hold of some aloe vera lotion. That

should soothe your scalp. I'm going to the pharmacy now. Do you want to come with me?'

'No! I can't leave the house.'

'OK, well I think you should run some cold water on your head to cool your scalp down.'

I guided her into the bathroom and got her to kneel down and run cold water from the handheld shower onto her head.

'Keep running the water as long as you can and I'll be back in fifteen minutes.'

Chalk Farm flat, Sunday

By this morning Flo's scalp had calmed down a bit. She told me it wasn't hot any more but was still dry and itchy. It was a beautiful sunny day and I suggested we go to Regent's Park and eat out, or maybe go on the boating lake which is one of our places. Her response had been emphatic.

'No way am I going out looking like this!'

She was determined to stay holed up in the flat all day. I got out our two deckchairs from my tiny shed and sat in the sun reading, reconciled to a day at home. Finally Flo emerged and stood on the threshold watching me. The deckchairs were new ones we bought recently as our last pair had fallen apart. Flo had chosen them and she always insisted on sitting on the one with the yellow and white stripes and left the green and white one to me. She sank down sorrowfully with a deep sigh and started a long phone conversation with Rosie in which she made her promise several times not to say a word about her hair to anyone.

I went inside and made a jug of sparkling water with lime cordial, adding lots of ice cubes, brought the jug out and poured us both a beaker. I deadheaded the flowers and watered the plants in their pots and finally Flo said goodbye to Rosie.

'Darling, were you given a skin test at that salon?'

'A skin test?'

'Yes, sweets, they're supposed to test the bleach on your skin before they do anything. They're supposed to do it twenty-four hours before.'

'Nothing like that...'

'What's the name of the salon?'

'Are you going to complain?'

'Damn right I am. The woman is a menace and I'll try to get your money back.'

'It had a stupid name, Scissor Sisters,' she said reluctantly.

She hates me to make a fuss about anything relating to her. She started in on me then. Her position was that normal life could not resume until I paid a good salon to dye her hair brown again and why was I being so mean as to say no to that.

'Because I've read up on it. Every article said you *have* to wait and let the scalp and hair recover before attempting any more colour changes.'

'I can't wait.'

'You'll have to. It's not the end of the world.'

'I look like a freak.' Her voice was rising which usually meant that tears were on their way.

'Of course you don't,' I said, privately thinking, Whose fault is that?

We argued on and off for the next hour.

'I was thinking maybe you'd like me to move your trip to Portsmouth forward?'

She nodded.

'At least no one knows me down there,' she said tragically.

I went inside and called Grace, Ben's mum, and we agreed Flo would travel down on Tuesday. Pete would meet her at the station and she could stay ten days if she wanted to. I briefed Grace on the great hair drama and she promised me she would be diplomatic about Flo's appearance and would stop her doing anything else to her hair. I returned to the garden and told Flo about the new arrangements.

'It means I'll miss Sophie's party,' she grumbled.

'But you said you didn't want to go out.'

'I don't, but if you'd pay to get my hair done...'

'Once you're back from Portsmouth I'll book you into my salon.'

'Why do I have to wait?'

I'd had enough of her endless whining.

'I've told you. That's enough, Flo!'

'You're *so* mean.'

'And you brought this on yourself. No one told you to go to that stupid salon.'

She stormed off to her room in a fury and I heard her bedroom door slam. I sat down and picked up my book, wanting to escape into it, but I couldn't settle to read. I went inside and tidied the sitting room and emptied the bins. I flattened our empty water bottles for the recycling box with more force than usual. I was fed up. The weekends are when I recharge my batteries in preparation for the week ahead. I resented Flo's histrionics which had dominated most of the last two days.

CHAPTER EIGHT

StoryWorld TV station, London Bridge

Bob, Lori, the director, Ledley and I had assembled for the morning meeting to discuss the show. I was not looking forward to being in a room with Bob. Lori sat next to him, as I've noticed that she does every day. He avoided eye contact and said virtually nothing. I wondered if he felt ashamed about his behaviour at the awards ceremony. Ledley was looking smart in a cream linen suit with a pink shirt underneath. He kept pulling at his cuffs and I guessed the suit was new. When Julius had made the wearing of pastel colours a requirement for all presenters last year, I had told him there was no way I could get Ledley into a pink shirt. Times had changed indeed.

As we rose to leave I heard Lori say to Bob that she'd like to buy him a coffee and they headed off together.

'Have you got a minute, Liz? I wanted to brief you on my lunch with Lori,' Ledley said.

'Oh yes, how did it go?'

'It was good, thanks. Fast and furious and she's come up with loads of ideas and they all entail me fronting them.'

'Do you like the ideas?'

'Yes, I do. I'd go into more detail but I'm needed at a photoshoot in Bond Street. Can I get my agent to send them through to you? I know you have to clear that kind of stuff.'

'Good plan.'

'Angela Hodge has taken me on,' he said.

'I've heard of her.'

Angela Hodge had a reputation for being hard as nails. She would fight for the last penny for her clients and squeeze TV companies until the pips squeaked.

'She's great, a smart cookie. I'll get her to call you.'

This is the first time Ledley has wanted to get an agent involved. Our exchange was typical of our altered relationship. He would know of Angela Hodge's reputation and in the past we might even have joked about it. Now he was calling her a smart cookie and not letting me into his thinking. We were talking in the coded language we so often use in television. I guess it was inevitable that with his higher profile he would see the need for an agent to fight his corner. We parted at the staircase and I joined my team.

'Did you have a good time at the awards?' Simon asked.

'I had the best time; the company, the food, it was great. And how was the cocktail bar?'

'Good,' Simon said as Harriet said, 'Tacky.'

They looked at each other and grinned.

'I didn't see you holding back on the tacky cocktails,' he said.

'The cocktails were good but you've got to agree the decor *was* dead tacky,' she said.

'Ideas meeting at twelve noon in my office,' I said, and left them to it.

Guy Browne had sent through the script for his fashion slot. I always check it because although Harriet is learning fast she still sometimes misses things. His main item was the new focus on geometric prints. But he opened his script with a rundown on the fashion winners and losers from Friday night's People's TV Awards and he had included a photo of me among the winners! I was startled to see my picture attached to his script. Harriet must have sent him Ziggy's photo of me on the Story World staircase. It was a good photo but I felt hot and awkward and got on the phone to him at once.

'Thank you so much for your kind words but I can't agree to you showing that pic of me.'

'Why ever not?'

'It would look like blatant self-promotion.'

'I don't think so. I chose it because you looked so good. That dress was the perfect choice for you.'

'Thank you again, but I really am a behind-the-camera person. In fact, the very thought of you showing that pic makes me cringe.'

'OK, I'll drop it. Shame though, I loved that dress. They knew how to design beautiful dresses then,' he said.

'It was gorgeous. Can we have a coffee sometime soon? We have a new head of sales and marketing and she's done a survey on the brands our viewers wear. It's a small sample but I did say I'd show it to you.'

'Happy to meet but with the caveat that I have to stay clear of endorsing any particular brands; it's part of my deal with *The Gloss*.'

Guy was the kind of man who could spot a bear trap at ten paces.

'Understood and I told her that already.'

'Shall we get together on Thursday after my slot?' he said.

We agreed to meet then. I held back on mentioning my idea about a competition with a fashion college as it needed more work. Lori Kerwell had rejected it but the concept had been growing on me. Harriet had good relationships with several fashion colleges, maybe we could find one local to the station and make it a community tie-in. And Ziggy could help Harriet with it because they worked well together.

I went down to the Hub and got in the queue. Lori and Bob were sitting at a table, deep in conversation. Had that been going on since the end of the morning meeting? If so it was a long encounter and I wondered what they could be discussing at such length. Lori glanced up and saw that I was looking at them. Our eyes met briefly before I turned to the counter and ordered my coffee. I felt uncomfortable and realised that somehow I needed to reach out to her. She was a new member of staff and I didn't want to make an enemy of her.

Back in my office the phone rang and when I heard Douglas Pitlochry's distinctive voice my spirits soared.

'I've been doing some digging and I've found you a tracing company that I'm told is reputable,' he said.

He had been as good as his word and had followed up. He gave me the details of the company he recommended, which was called Brennan Investigations.

'Thank you so much. I'll look into them.'

'And would you let me take you out to dinner?'

'I'd like that very much.'

'I work most nights but I'm off on Thursdays. I wondered how you were fixed this week?'

It was absurd but I felt breathless. Douglas Pitlochry was asking me out. I managed to say: 'Thursday would be great.'

'Do you live north or south, Liz?'

'My flat's in Chalk Farm.'

'Then we're almost neighbours. I live in Camden.'

'Which bit of Camden?'

'Do you know those new flats by the canal?'

'You mean the metal ones?'

'Yes, my son refers to it as my pod.'

'I've seen them, and often wondered about them,' I said.

'Mine is minimal and easy to keep tidy, which suits me fine. I know somewhere we could go on Thursday. I've found this place tucked away behind Camden Road station. It has an odd fifties feel to it with booths to sit in but the chef is young and brilliant.'

'What's it called?'

'The Lizard Lounge,' he said.

I laughed. 'My dad used to call a man you couldn't trust a lounge lizard. You don't hear that phrase any more.'

'I like that. It's descriptive.'

We arranged to meet at the Lizard Lounge at seven-thirty on Thursday. As I put the phone down I was as fluttery as a teenager who had got noticed by the classroom heart-throb. I've got a date with Douglas Pitlochry! I googled the Lizard Lounge. It was all battered leather booths and red and white lino squares on the floor and the menu looked interesting. Then I googled the flats by the canal in Camden Town. They've been written up in architectural journals and they do look like pods with their rounded metal façades. They have balconies over the canal and the windows are shaped like portholes. His comment about living in a flat he could keep tidy pointed to a man living alone. I told myself to stop behaving like an adolescent and called the team in for our ideas meeting, even though I felt like doing a cartwheel.

Harriet was the first to suggest a story. She said an internet dating site had caused a row by implying that red hair and freckles were imperfections.

'They had all these posters in the Tube showing a woman

with red hair and freckles and their slogan was: "Someone will love your imperfections".'

Harriet has light red hair, the colour of apricots.

'Oh yes, I saw one of those,' I said.

'There's been loads of complaints to the Advertising Standards Authority. They've agreed to take the posters down as soon as possible.'

'It's a good peg for a story. We could do some vox pops on it, send the crew down to London Bridge and ask men and women with red hair whether they think they're discriminated against,' I said.

'Actually, I was keen to use the crew to interview the wife of a Saudi blogger. She's willing to talk about the agony of watching her husband receive a hundred lashes,' Molly said.

I had read that story too and it was gut-wrenching. Molly is always drawn to serious stories. I like to have a mix of light and shade on the show but Julius's criticism was still front of mind. He might be on holiday in Cornwall but I was sure he would be watching the show from his hotel room.

'Harriet can do the vox pops in the morning and you can do the interview in the afternoon. I'll be holding your story back till September, Moll,' I said.

Molly's face is an open book and she didn't like this. I have given her oversight of our feature camera crew, which we get for one day a week, but it is not for her sole use. She pushed her dark blonde hair behind her ears and sighed in frustration.

'Do we have to wait for transmission?'

'I think we should. It's bound to be harrowing and we agreed to aim for light-hearted stories this month,' I said.

'But everyone does silly season stories in August. Can't we buck the trend?'

Harriet looked offended. 'I don't think my story *is* silly season. It's making a serious point.'

Molly and Harriet do not see eye to eye and there is much that divides them; their backgrounds, for starters. Molly comes from a liberal Dutch family. She is serious, down to earth and likes doing human interest stories. Harriet's background is the media establishment; her father is at the pinnacle of that world. She's interested in fashion and in celebrity lifestyles and loves the party side of television. I've never seen them go to lunch together and Molly is convinced that Harriet got the job because her father is a newspaper editor who pulled strings. There was an atmosphere in the room and Simon the peacemaker stepped in.

'We're doing Beydaan again in a few weeks, aren't we, Moll? Maybe we could make this part of a mini-series on heroic women who speak out in spite of the risk to themselves,' he said.

'I like that,' I said.

I made the right call when I promoted Simon to be my deputy. He gets on with everyone and has a good instinct on how to give context to our stories.

'Can we get Ziggy in now, please? I want to discuss an idea.'

Ziggy joined us, sitting down next to Harriet on the sofa and wrapping her arms tightly around her slim frame, which is something she does a lot. I think it's a desire to protect herself against a hostile world. Ziggy is rarely comfortable in group meetings.

'OK. I want to see if it's feasible to run a Young Fashion Designer of the Year competition.'

'Oh yes, I'd love that,' Harriet said at once.

'The idea appeals to me and I'd like you to lead on it, Harriet, with help from you, Ziggy. We need to find a reason for doing this and I like the community angle, finding a college close to the station. And it will hinge on Guy Browne agreeing to be the judge.'

'I think he'd like it,' Harriet said.

'Why don't you creative lot go and brainstorm it,' I said.

They left my room and I clicked on the link to the Brennan Investigations website. There was a form where you put in your details and the service you required. I didn't feel quite ready to start the ball rolling. I would call Ron Osborne tonight and give him one last chance to come good and build me some new French doors.

Chalk Farm flat, 7.30 p.m.

Flo was lying in a heap on her bed, stroking Mr Crooks and being listless at the thought of packing for Portsmouth. All she could talk about was her hair and how dreadful it looked.

'Come on, I'll help you pack.'

She got up reluctantly and I plonked her case on the bed, scooting Mr Crooks off.

'Can I borrow some of your scarves, Mum?'

'Really?'

'I need them to cover my hair.'

'Darling, it doesn't look that bad.'

'Please.'

We went through my scarves and she took the white one with black polka dots on it. She stood in front of her mirror and spent ages trying to tie it so that her hair was completely covered.

'I'd hate to have to wear a scarf all the time. Granny called,' she said.

I was laying out her jeans and skirts on the bed.

'She said we're going to the Isle of Wight to stay in a hotel for a night or two.'

'Lucky you, that will be a treat.'

'Not looking like this it won't,' she said.

She sighed and packed the jeans and her favourite black miniskirt and fetched her two bikinis.

'There is a pool at the hotel. I'm going to have to wear a swimming cap though cos the chlorine will make my hair *even worse.*'

I dug out her school swimming cap from the bottom drawer and her Speedo costume.

'And I WhatsApped Dad about my hair but I didn't Skype him because I don't want him to see me looking like this.'

No amount of comforting words from me was going to shift Flo from her tragic stance and I remembered that at fifteen I had been just as obsessed with my appearance. I zipped up her case.

'All done, and now I've got a difficult call to make,' I said.

I went to my bedroom and dialled Ron Osborne's mobile. I don't know if he recognised my number and is ignoring me but it went to answer machine on the eighth ring.

'Hello, Ron, Liz Lyon here. We need to talk tonight. We need to set the date for the job as a matter of urgency. Please call me on my mobile as soon as you get this. Thank you.'

Later, I made mugs of tea and carried one through to Flo.

'Did you put sugar in, Mum?'

'One level spoon, like you always say.'

'Rosie's given up on sugar altogether and I'm going to try.'

I sensed she might want to talk but all evening I'd been looking forward to watching Douglas Pitlochry do his bulletin. I sat on our sofa and put on the television. He has this way of raising his eyebrows as he finishes linking into a story as if to say 'take a look at this, it's so interesting.' I noticed again what good shoulders he had and how well his jacket fitted him. Flo wandered in and joined me on the sofa.

'You don't normally watch this channel,' she said.

It was true, I didn't, but I hadn't expected her to notice and could feel my face getting hot. I wondered whether to tell her about my date. She is fiercely loyal to her dad and usually hostile at the idea of me dating anyone. I had always kept Todd well in the background and decided not to say anything now. At the end of the bulletin Douglas looked into camera and said thanks for watching and gave a crooked smile and I found myself smiling back at the screen foolishly.

CHAPTER NINE

StoryWorld TV station, London Bridge

I'd left Flo in bed and reminded her to leave herself plenty of time to get the noon train from Paddington. As I walked to the Tube I realised I'd got ten days ahead of me completely on my own and a date on Thursday. It was a good feeling and there was a spring in my step.

Julius was due back tomorrow and I kept the meeting as short as possible. Fizzy rang me as I got into my office. She sounded excited and asked me to come over to hers, preferably that evening, as she had an idea she wanted to discuss with me as soon as possible. She wouldn't be drawn on what her idea was but urged me to come over so I said I'd pop round after work. With Flo away I could go out every evening if I wanted to.

I went down to get a coffee from the Hub and saw Henry, our senior floor manager, queuing in front of me.

'Got a minute, Liz?'

We took our coffees outside to the back of the studio because Henry wanted to smoke. He is one of the last smokers left in the station and occasionally I will bum a cigarette from him. He offered me his packet.

'Oh, go on then,' I said, and he lit my cigarette.

Henry is tall, well over six feet, and has a solemn almost severe face, but when he smiles his face is transformed and becomes wry and mischievous. He's in his mid-forties and I always think he looks like he should be in a Western; the kind of seasoned man who would ride into a town and sort out the bad guys, like Gary Cooper in *High Noon*, my dad's favourite film. He doesn't say a lot but he is someone you can trust in a crisis. He wasn't smiling as he took a deep drag of his cigarette and squinted at me as the smoke escaped from his lips.

'What's eating Ledley?' he said.

'What do you mean?'

'This morning he complained that I didn't bring the guest in early enough.'

'No?'

'Yes, chewed my ear off, in the studio too.'

Henry is our most experienced floor manager and an absolute rock. I've never known him bring a guest in late unless we've had a problem getting them out of make-up. I could see why Ledley's rebuke had rankled. And the fact that Ledley had done it in earshot of the camera and sound crew was not on.

'Bad move! That's not like Ledley.'

'Not like the old Ledley,' Henry said wryly.

'Don't let it get to you. You're the best,' I said.

We smoked in silence and drank our coffees. There was an outside broadcast truck parked in the yard and we watched an engineer working on it, lying on one of those trollies on wheels that go under cars. He wheeled himself out and stood up.

'It's buggered,' he said.

He started talking to Henry about suspension and engines and they might have been talking Klingon as far as I was concerned. I said goodbye and headed back in.

★

As I had expected, the crook builder Osborne did not call me back last night nor did he call me this morning. He's avoiding me and I've had enough of his games. At lunchtime I logged into my home account and got up the form on the Brennan Investigations website. I typed:

> I would like to trace the address of a builder called Ron Osborne. I paid him a deposit of £1,000 in February to build new French doors. He has failed to undertake the work. His company is called Ron Osborne Maintenance UK Ltd. I need his address so that I can serve legal papers on him.

I typed in his mobile number and his email address and ended my message:

> Can you help me with this?

The cavalier way he kept postponing my job had made me feel helpless and now I felt elated to be taking some action. Two hours later I got a response from Brennan Investigations:

> Thank you for your email. I have made some preliminary enquiries and believe we will be able to locate the subject in question.
>
> The cost for this trace would be £125. If you wish to proceed then I can pass you over our bank details and invoice for payment and then we can proceed to locate the subject.

My heart started to beat fast at the words 'proceed to locate the subject'. It sounded all very skulduggery and thrilling. Was it worth spending a hundred and twenty-five pounds to get back my deposit? I wrote back.

> Please do send me your bank details.
>
> I am happy to pay the fee of £125 if this is the final figure. And can you please confirm that this fee only becomes liable if you successfully trace the subject?

Back came an email immediately.

> I can confirm in the unlikely event we are unable to locate the subject I will give you a full refund.
>
> As soon as the transfer is complete we can proceed with the trace. I would hope to return the info before the end of this week, all being well.

He had listed their sort code and bank account number.

The deed is done. I have transferred the amount and hired a private detective to do a trace. I felt so excited that I wanted to call Douglas Pitlochry and tell him there and then. But I stopped myself; I would tell him on Thursday when I met him.

I left the station at five and headed for Fizzy's house in Pimlico. Loida opened the door and Fizzy was standing in the living room rocking Zachary in the crook of her arm. She smiled when she saw me and as I bent over to kiss her on the cheek Zachary grabbed my necklace and wouldn't let go. His little fingers clung to the beads – he had a strong grasp for a small baby. Fizzy was laughing at his antics.

'What a boy I've got,' she said.

Loida stepped in and extricated my necklace and Fizzy handed Zac over to her.

'Time for his bath,' Loida said fondly as she carried him out.

'Would you like a glass of prosecco, Liz?'

'Are you having any?'

'No, sadly, I'm sticking to elderflower and rose pressé. Alcohol gives me an appetite and I've a way to go yet.'

She put her hands on her waist and squeezed.

'Several inches still to shed by September.'

Fizzy is a person who sets great store by how people look and she needs constant reassurance about her appearance.

'You look fabulous, Fizz. You should have seen me two months after having Flo. I was a zombie in a dressing gown. I'll have the same as you.'

She poured the pale pink sparkling drink into champagne flutes and we clinked glasses. I took a sip. The bubbles fizzed in my mouth and the taste was perfumed, like a scent caught in a drink.

'Now I know I said there'd be no photos of Zac shown on screen but I've been thinking about it. It's not unreasonable for the viewers to want to see Zac, is it? I mean, they sent me all those toys and bootees and shawls,' Fizzy said.

As well as all the toys, we had received loads of hand-knitted baby clothes after Fizzy had announced her pregnancy on air. Looking into camera, she had confessed to the viewers that she was going to have the baby as a lone parent as the father was married. She had said she deeply regretted her mistake in getting involved with a married man and that part of her life was over for ever. Her on-screen act of contrition, which had infuriated Julius, had done the reverse with our forgiving and generous audience and the knitted baby clothes had started to arrive from all corners of the UK. We had donated these to refugee camps in Calais and further afield and we were still getting a trickle in to the station.

'They have been amazingly generous. They love you,' I said.

'So I had this brainwave. I'm going to hire a top portrait photographer to take a mother and baby shot of me and Zac. I want the man who did Prince George.'

'Wow...'

'I want something *extremely* tasteful. And I'm willing to share the best shot on StoryWorld – only one photo and it won't be broadcast anywhere else.'

'That's a great idea,' I said.

'I'm glad you like it. I think it gives the viewers something back without anyone being able to accuse me of cashing in on my baby.'

'Absolutely; the sooner the better, as far as I'm concerned. There is tremendous interest in Zachary.'

'Maybe we should hold it for my first day back?'

'Good plan. We could get the photographer in too,' I said.

It amused me that Fizzy wanted the royal photographer for this but then Zachary had been born into the mad world of celebrity royalty. Fizzy took a sip of her drink.

'There's something else...'

She hesitated and gave me a thoughtful look as if she was weighing up how much to say. I waited.

'I've also come to the realisation that Bob has a right to

see Zac. He's been a total shit, of course, but Zac is his son. I can't let him near the house for obvious reasons.'

'No, I can see that.'

She put her glass down delicately on the coffee table and turned her body towards me.

'Liz, would you do me a *huge* favour and host a meeting between us at your flat? He could go there incognito, you see.'

I was startled at her suggestion and reluctant to go along with it. Being the go-between would make Bob hate me even more. It would reinforce his view that I had influence with Fizzy and easy access to Zachary which he was being denied. I gave her a brief rundown of what had happened at the awards ceremony.

'What an idiot. Blabbing about me at a place heaving with TV folk,' she said crossly.

'That's what I thought. And I think this would be like throwing petrol on the flames.'

'I know you have issues with him. I know he's been rude to you, but I thought you'd see that he does have a certain right.'

I was casting around for a diplomatic way to say I couldn't host their meeting when I remembered that Fizzy's birthday was coming up soon.

'I've got another idea which might work better. Let's get you in on your birthday and we'll have a small party in the meeting room. We'll invite staff to come along and see Zachary. All the teams have been asking about him. We'll lay on tea and cake and it would be the most natural thing in the world for Bob to drop by. There would be safety in numbers.'

'Maybe. Yes, I guess it could work, but not on my birthday. I'm taking Zac to Burnley on my birthday. Granny's on her last legs.'

Fizzy came from Burnley and her family still lived there. Her grandmother was a fearsome Baptist who was now in the last stages of dementia.

'We're leaving for Burnley on Saturday. Let's do it this Friday,' she said.

'Fine by me.'

'I'm sure Martine will help you organise it. And champagne with the cake, please, not tea; after all, it is a celebration,' Fizzy said.

From another room we heard Zachary start to cry and as his wail got louder Fizzy got up.

'Don't go. Stay and have some supper.'

I have the impression that Fizzy does not have many women friends and must feel lonely at times. Her life has revolved around her career and her men. She has the money and the celebrity but few friends and no privacy and she relies on Loida a great deal.

I called Flo who told me she had arrived safely in Portsmouth and had installed herself in what used to be Ben's bedroom. She sounded reasonably cheerful. The trip to the hotel on the Isle of Wight was still on and they would be going on Friday and staying till Sunday.

'Did you know that's where Granddad proposed to Granny, in the garden there?' she said.

'No, I didn't. How lovely.'

Fizzy came back after five minutes.

'Loida is so much better than me at getting him off to sleep,' she said.

Supper was a small salad with goat's cheese drizzled with balsamic vinegar but no oil. We ate this off pretty plates in her dining room. This was followed by low-fat frozen yoghurt with a handful of blueberries. The yoghurt tasted thin to me. I was missing the dairy richness of ice cream. The whole supper made me think of the sacrifices on-screen presenters have to make every day to keep their figures and to live up to a camera ideal. Fizzy was a new mum yet she was making herself eat a low-calorie diet. Not for the first time I was grateful that I was a behind-the-camera person. We could hear Loida moving around the house but there was no further sound from Zachary.

'Does he sleep straight through already?'

'Oh no, he'll wake up some time before midnight for another bottle. Then he will sleep for about five hours.'

'That's pretty good, you know. How will you cope with that when you come back to work?'

'Loida's staying on and she'll do the late and early bottles. When I'm back at work I have to be in bed at ten at the latest to get my seven hours' sleep.'

'I'm sure. And you feel OK about coming back in two weeks?'

'I have to, and I'm ready for it.'

We moved back to her sitting room and after a while we agreed we should open the bottle of prosecco after all. By our second glass we were drifting into more confessional territory.

'Are you on your own now, Liz? Didn't your man go back to Oz?'

'Todd, yes, last autumn and he won't be coming back. He's hooked up with an old girlfriend in Sydney.'

'Shame, he was an attractive man.'

I nodded and drank some prosecco which I was enjoying more than the elderflower and rose pressé.

'He was never my man in the full sense of the word. We dated for two years but he never got fully involved in my life. He never got to know Flo, for instance.'

'That was your choice though?'

'Yes. She's loyal to her dad and I don't see the point of introducing men into our lives unless it's the real thing,' I said.

'Ahh, the much talked about "real thing"...' She leaned back against the sofa and tucked her knees under her. 'I'm not sure I believe in the "real thing" any more.'

There was wistfulness in her voice and as I looked at her I thought she's about to be thirty-nine and she's on her own, with a baby, working in a fiercely competitive industry. We have more in common than we did before Zachary was born.

'They never leave their wives, you know,' she said.

She was thinking about Bob but also about Geoff. I wondered why she was attracted to married men if she wanted to have someone more permanent in her life. Perhaps that was the point. Perhaps what she really wanted was to have the attention but not the commitment.

'It's strange, but when you're a teen or in your twenties you really think that meeting the right man is going to complete your life. But it doesn't work out like that, does it? Well, it didn't for me. You have to be prepared to create your own life,' I said.

'What you're saying is that men are a disappointment,' she said as she drained her glass.

I laughed but it was a sad laugh.

'Definitely a disappointment; the only man who never disappointed me was my dad and he died when I was twenty-three.'

The image of Douglas Pitlochry's face flashed into my mind and I knew I wouldn't mention him.

Chalk Farm flat, 11 p.m.

It was late but the prosecco and our conversation had had its effect and I made a mug of tea, opened a packet of ginger nuts and googled Douglas Pitlochry. He has a Wikipedia entry and I munched my way through the biscuits while reading that he is forty-seven and was born in Perthshire in Scotland. His family had a small farm there which was sold when he was seven years old and the family moved to England, to Norfolk, where his father became a farm manager. I know Norfolk because my dad's last job was at the university there and I thought it seemed a strange move from Scotland to East Anglia, from mountains to flatness and fenland. I wondered what the story behind that was. He went to school in Norwich and the first newspaper he worked on was the *Eastern Daily Press*. He made the switch to broadcasting via local radio followed by a stint at Anglia Television where he was spotted and elevated to his role on News Nine. He had been married for twenty-one years to a Claire Cooper-Pitlochry. They were now separated but not divorced. They had a son called Stewart who was twenty years old.

I clicked onto the images button and photos of Douglas filled my screen. I spent a lot of time looking at these, thinking, What sort of a man are you? I have always thought him clean-cut and wholesome-looking rather than handsome but I liked the openness of his face.

Next I looked up Claire Cooper-Pitlochry – that name was a mouthful. There was less about her, no Wikipedia entry, but a few references and I gleaned that she ran an online business called Claire Cooper Interiors. There was a link to a Mail Online article which claimed that she had left Douglas to go off with a man who ran a safari park, of all things. I clicked on her images link and several pictures of a thin blonde woman with straight hair and a long fringe looked out at me. She was attractive but it wasn't the friendliest of faces. She's nothing like me at all, I thought, as I made myself put the biscuits away and finally got ready for bed.

CHAPTER TEN

StoryWorld TV station, London Bridge

Wednesday, and Julius was back from his holiday though he showed no sign of a post-vacation glow. He chaired the morning meeting and was not in a good mood. He was short with Lori and he was short with me. At the end of the meeting he said: 'Liz, a word' in a peremptory tone. I followed him to his office with a sinking feeling, knowing that a rebuke was coming my way. I had made a point of keeping the features light all week and couldn't work out from what quarter the rebuke would come. I hate how he can still make me feel like a naughty child. He closed his door but did not sit down.

'I don't appreciate being phoned by Saul the moment I'm back from holiday to be told that you and Lori can't work together,' he said.

'Sorry?'

'Saul said there's a problem. That you two had a meeting and you were dismissive of her ideas.'

'She said that to him?'

'Yes.'

'I wasn't dismissive!'

Had I been dismissive? I thought that perhaps I had been. Her ideas had been so dull and predictable. So she had left our meeting and gone and snitched on me! I took a deep breath to steady myself.

'She wants to do in-store promotions and a roadshow with Guy Browne.'

'And...?'

'I tried to explain that he can't be linked to any one brand. You remember that problem we had with Ledley and that cooking oil he kept using. You said it damaged his slot and you were right.'

He gave a curt nod.

'So I said we'd have to think carefully about how to use Guy. Rather than tying him to a brand I suggested a young designer competition that he could judge. And as I recall she was pretty "dismissive" about that!'

'I'm not interested in a bitch-fest between you and Lori Kerwell,' he said.

'That's not fair.'

I felt my face flushing and was furious that he'd described what was happening as a bitch-fest in that high-handed way, as if he was above such conflicts. As if it was some petty competition between rival women who couldn't work together. But was I being unprofessional? Could I have handled things differently? He looked irritable and glanced at his watch. One of his pet sayings is: 'Don't bring me problems, bring me solutions.'

'How do you think we should proceed? Do we need a meeting with the three of us to clear the air?' I said in a more conciliatory tone.

'I'll think about it. I wanted to hear your take on what happened.'

'Well, thank you for that, Julius. I would like to do the young designer competition, though, and it could have sponsorship potential.'

Julius is the master at getting sponsorship deals for StoryWorld and one bit of station gossip is that he hadn't wanted to relinquish this task to Lori Kerwell. He gestured with a flick of his hand that the meeting was over and that I should go.

'Something else,' I said.

'What?' He was barking at me now but I plunged on.

'I saw Fizzy last night. I suggested we hold a small celebration in the meeting room to introduce Zachary to the teams. She loved the idea and would like to do it this Friday. We thought champagne and cake – can I do that out of my budget?'

'OK, but prosecco not champagne; we're not made of money,' Julius said.

I went straight downstairs and out of the station towards the river. I was incandescent that Lori had reported me. I knew that if I'd gone into my office I would have exploded and ranted to Simon, and the team would have known something big was up. I needed to calm down and get things in perspective. It was windy, clouds scudded across the sky and the river was choppy. It was a particularly sore point that she had complained to Saul Relph. He and I had an uneasy relationship because last November I had finally screwed up the courage to make a confidential complaint about Julius's behaviour towards me at a work event years before. Julius had crossed a line with me at a StoryWorld Christmas party. My complaint had come to nothing. Saul Relph wasn't interested in challenging his trusted lieutenant and I'd dropped the complaint. It had left me feeling exposed that I'd shared a shaming secret with our cold and remote MD. I'd seen him several times since and had to assume that he had never shared my complaint with Julius but it hung in the air between us whenever we met. Lori Kerwell was Saul's appointment, though, and he had been quick enough to listen to her complaint about me and to raise it with Julius.

I sat on a bench and considered my next steps. The River Walk is a popular spot and I watched tourists wander past pointing out the London landmarks and looking light-hearted. I felt the reverse, very down-hearted. I don't know how to deal with Lori. It had only been a few weeks and we were already squaring up to each other. And now she had involved the bosses. Do I confront her today? Do I go back to the station and ask her outright why she complained about me? Or do I play a longer game? I think she is building an alliance with Bob. He would see mileage in supporting her on the principle that my enemy's enemy is my friend. Here I was, thinking about Lori as my enemy. Was I overreacting?

A man who looked rough approached me. He was unshaven and was wearing a dirty grey tracksuit. He bent forward and asked me if I could give him ten pounds so he could have somewhere to sleep tonight. I rooted in my purse and found two pound coins which I gave him. The skin on his hands was red and grimy and he smelled sour.

'I need ten quid,' he said urgently.

'I haven't got a tenner, I'm sorry.' I gave him the rest of my loose change. 'That's all I've got.'

'It's not enough.' His voice was angry.

I stood up and hurried away from him as fast as I could, alarmed that he might follow me and even attack me. It added to my feeling of desolation. How horrible everything was.

I did not confront Lori. I spent a couple of hours holed up in my office feeling anxious and low. Around three, Harriet and Ziggy knocked and came in. They had worked hard on a specification for a fashion competition and they gave me a sheet of points I could talk through with Guy.

'To keep the cost down we wondered if Ziggy could do some of the shooting and editing?' Harriet said.

'If we proceed. It's only an idea at this stage,' I said.

They both looked crestfallen and I knew that I was projecting my gloomy mood which wasn't fair on them.

'You've both made an excellent case for it. If Guy is as keen as I am I think we can make it happen.'

They brightened at that.

'And yes, I'd like to set Ziggy loose on a camera,' I said, smiling at them both.

I watched them leave together and head towards the staircase chatting happily. Harriet and Ziggy are close because of something horrible that happened to them last year; something that always sits at the back of my mind. Julius had persuaded them to act out a sex scene in the small studio, telling them it was a screen test. It was a vile thing to do and an abuse of power. I have the only copy of the screen test locked in a box at home and his voice is on the tape giving them instructions to take off their clothes and make out. I look on it as my insurance should he ever try to make serious moves against me.

Brooding on Lori Kerwell was a waste of time and I had to pull myself together and get on with things. I joined Martine at her desk and we discussed the party for Fizzy which we're holding this Friday. I'd suggested Martine come to my office but she does not like to leave her station outside Julius's office when he is in the building.

'In case he needs me at short notice,' she said.

There never was a more loyal assistant than Martine. She opened her pad and made notes.

'I know lemon drizzle is her all-time favourite. She likes Eccles cakes too, her childhood, you know, though she rarely indulges in either of them, bless her,' she said.

Martine is close to Fizzy. They both worked as PAs at StoryWorld until Fizzy's meteoric rise to become the Queen of Live TV.

'I know she likes those little cat's tongue biscuits,' I said.

'Oh yes, she loves those.'

Martine added *langues de chat* to her list.

'And sausage rolls for the men, I think. They're not as into cake as we are,' she said.

'Julius has approved prosecco,' I said.

'I think we should have tea too. I don't know about you but I'd much rather have a cup of tea with my cake.'

'Agreed.'

'And I'm going to bring in my embroidered tablecloth to make the table look pretty.'

It had cheered me up doing this with Martine because we've had some difficult times in the past. Whenever I fall out with Julius it means that I fall out with her too. Last December, when Julius and I clashed on an epic scale, Martine was furious with me. But loyalty is a rare trait in our industry and I respect Martine for hers.

Chalk Farm flat, 7.30 p.m.

With Flo away I bought myself a ready-made prawn salad. I opened the French doors and surveyed my little plot and ate the salad from the plastic box without even putting it on a plate. I was still brooding about Lori Kerwell. Fenton was back from Barcelona and I called her. First I asked her about her week with Bill because it's not fair on her that every time I ring it's to unload my problems. Their holiday had been everything she had hoped for. They had walked around the city for hours looking at the buildings and eating late at small cafés they found tucked away from the tourist routes.

'We talked as we walked. It's easier to talk about difficult stuff when you're walking, isn't it? He opened up and I feel our relationship is deepening,' she said, sounding happy. 'And how are things with you, darling friend?'

'Well, I've got some good news and some bad news,' I said.

'Tell me the bad stuff first.'

I told her how Lori Kerwell had complained about me to the MD.

'She might have soft poodle hair but her eyes are hard, shark-like. I really don't need this rift with her. It's bad enough that Bob hates me, but I don't know how to deal with her.'

'Is there any way back, do you think?'

'I don't know. She's so hard and money-driven and not my sort of person at all. She's definitely making an alliance with Bob. I've seen them together. Oh God, I'm sounding paranoid, aren't I?'

'You sound worried. I've found that with people like her there is often a reason why they've put on that armour.'

'You mean she may have a softer side?'

I thought about Lori and found that idea hard to credit.

'Yes, that's exactly what I mean. It may be a protective shell. You need to find out who she really is.'

'You always look for the good in people, Fenton. Not everyone has a redeeming feature and my hunch is that Lori is hard as nails all the way through.'

'I'm sorry if she is because there's nothing worse than having a difficult colleague.'

'Two difficult colleagues,' I said gloomily.

'Be careful around her and try to keep Julius onside.'

Fenton knew well how my relationship with Julius went through good and bad phases.

'I'll try.'

'So tell me the good news now.'

'I've got a date tomorrow with Douglas Pitlochry, *the* Douglas Pitlochry!'

Fenton and I ended up giggling about my imminent date before she rang off. I made myself a hot chocolate and sat down with Mr Crooks on my lap to watch Douglas do his bulletin. This is becoming an evening ritual with me, and without Flo around to observe me I can luxuriate in watching him and listening to his distinctive voice. When he interviews a pundit he swivels round in his chair and you see his profile. I like his profile less. His nose looks too blunt from the side. I chided myself for being so superficial and went to bed feeling better about things. Fenton had reminded me of my many years of experience at StoryWorld and said I could hold my own against the newcomer Lori. I often wonder what I'd do without her in my life. Since Ben and I split up she has become even more important as my sounding board, my confidante and my cheerleader.

CHAPTER ELEVEN

Chalk Farm flat, 6.30 a.m.

I was up early trying to decide what to wear for my date with Douglas. It had been almost a year since I'd been on a date and I was as nervous as a kitten. I knew I was being idiotic, worrying so much about my outfit when men are notoriously poor at noticing what a woman is wearing. But he had seen me at my best in that marvellous beaded dress and I couldn't stop myself from obsessing. I laid out three dresses on my bed and tried each one on. The one that looked best was my red linen dress with its flirty skirt – I love the colour red – but if I wore it all day it would be a creased mess by seven-thirty. I decided it had to be the red one, though, so I put on a black shift and carried my date dress into work with me.

StoryWorld TV station, London Bridge

Our main guest this morning was a famous author, a grande dame of the literary scene who had produced her first novel in six years. She was more highbrow than our usual guests. More *Guardian*, Julius would have said. I had reservations about the booking but Molly, who had secured her, said her publishers were keen to get maximum exposure for the new novel and that she had been briefed on the nature of our show and told she needed to be accessible. But she wasn't. She came over as cold and elitist. Ledley asked her what she thought of the current passion for psychological thrillers. There was a froideur in her manner as she dismissed the summer blockbusters as plot-driven books that were more concerned with delivering a twist at the end than with creating believable characters. She and Ledley did not connect at all and he looked seriously out of his depth. I watched the interview from the gallery with a sinking heart and told the director to come out of it early. It was the first time I had seen Ledley struggling with a guest; Fizzy would have handled it better, would have found some common ground. We get tweets from our viewers during the show and during the ad break I scanned these. One viewer had tweeted:

> What a snob! You write stories. You don't do brain
> surgery. #StoryWorld #author

At the morning meeting, Julius was critical as I knew he would be.

'That didn't work, Liz.'

'I agree. She's a major name but her manner was awfully off-putting.'

'She's a snob and is well out of touch,' Ledley said.

I was waiting for Bob to pitch in with a critical comment but on this occasion he stayed silent. Lori was not at the meeting today which, frankly, was a relief. I was still burning with the fact that she had reported me to Saul Relph.

'I'll make a point not to book literary writers in future. They might be big in the publishing world but they don't work for us,' I said.

'But I liked the piece on how red-headed people feel they

are treated. It was light-hearted but made a point too. That's one of the things we aim for,' Julius said.

Harriet had produced this item and I resolved to pass his compliment on to her.

I was meeting Guy Browne straight after. He had changed out of his studio clothes into cycling gear and I suggested that we have a coffee off the premises. I find that the Hub can be such a goldfish bowl. We were walking across the forecourt and he was wheeling his racing bike when I spotted Lori Kerwell approaching us. This was the first time I'd seen her since I knew she'd snitched on me and I felt my body tensing and my heart starting to speed up. She was wearing an orange suit with a large gold brooch on her lapel and it was not the outfit for a warm August day. She is a thin woman and maybe she feels the cold. Her appearance is always smart and hard and bright, like a uniform she puts on to face the world. I recalled Fenton's comment that her hardness might be an armour protecting something vulnerable that was hidden deep inside. I still found that hard to believe. I stopped and introduced her to Guy.

'Pleased to meet you. I'm a big fan of your slot,' she said.

'That's good to hear, thank you,' he said.

She reached in her bag for a business card and presented it to him.

'It would be good to work on something together.'

Guy took her card and looked at it. He must have noticed that I was cut out altogether from this exchange.

We walked along by the river where there was a pleasant breeze. He was wheeling his bike and asked if we could find a café with tables outside where he could lock it up. Certainly his bike, made of titanium he had told me, looked like it cost hundreds of pounds. We passed several places till we found one with a terrace and he secured his wheels. We sat at a table under a rainbow-coloured parasol and Guy asked for Earl Grey tea. I ordered a pot for him and a cappuccino for myself. I handed him Lori's presentation, being scrupulous to keep my voice neutral.

'Here's the survey I mentioned and a few of Lori Kerwell's marketing ideas.'

He flicked through the pages quickly and I watched him. At the table next to ours a couple of women spoke in fervent Spanish as they consulted a guide book. The sunlight through the parasol cast a pink glow on his thin and sensitive face. He wears his hair shaved close to his skull and he has freckles over his nose and cheekbones and a full mouth. He also favours black clothing. One of my more embarrassing duties six months ago was to ask him not to wear black shirts on set. Telling a renowned style expert that our director of programmes would only allow pastels on the sofa had been excruciating. He hadn't been difficult about it; had merely raised an eyebrow and muttered 'when in Rome' and since then has worn cream shirts on camera.

'Thanks, Liz, but this is not for me,' he said. There was a finality to his tone of voice as he pushed her presentation back towards me and poured more tea from his pot. The mean part of me was pleased.

'There is something else,' I said.

I sketched out our idea to run a young fashion designer competition and went through the points Harriet and Ziggy had drafted. 'We thought the community angle was worthwhile,' I said.

'Now that *is* something I would be interested in getting involved with.'

I was delighted. Guy would make an excellent mentor to young fashion students and it would be thrilling for them to get guidance from such a respected expert.

I hurried back to the station and called in Harriet and Ziggy.

'Guy is up for being a judge so the competition is a goer,' I said.

Harriet, who doesn't usually show much enthusiasm for things, actually clapped her hands and Ziggy grinned at her.

'And you two take the credit for doing the legwork on this. Thank you both very much. The next step is for me to work this up into a sponsorship document and share it with Julius.'

'When can we launch it?' Harriet asked.

'It will take at least two months to get this off the ground, maybe longer,' I said.

After they'd gone I opened my home email account and there was a message from Brennan Investigations. They had attached a photo and a simple query:

Is this the subject?

I downloaded the photo. It showed Ron Osborne in what looked like a holiday snap. He was standing on a sunny terrace with bougainvillea trailing on the white wall behind him and a bright blue sky above. He was wearing shorts and a shirt that was undone halfway down his chest. I was ridiculously pleased to see it. Gotcha, I thought, and emailed straight back:

Yes, that is Ron Osborne.

They emailed me his address in Bedfordshire. It might have

cost me a hundred and twenty-five pounds to get hold of it but I am cock-a-hoop. And it's all thanks to Douglas.

Later, I changed into my date dress, reapplied mascara and lipstick and squirted perfume onto my hair. At the top of the staircase I met Julius and we walked down to the exit together.

'You weren't wearing that dress this morning,' he said.

'I changed because I'm going out tonight.'

'Going anywhere exciting?'

He was the last person I would tell that I had a date with Douglas Pitlochry. For a man who valued his own privacy, Julius could be probing at times.

'Supper with a friend in Camden.'

'Nice dress,' he said as he walked out of the building.

The Lizard Lounge, King's Cross, 7.35 p.m.

When I entered the Lizard Lounge my stomach was all a-flutter. I scanned the room and saw Douglas sitting in a booth. Even in that dim lighting I could see that he didn't look well. He stood up awkwardly as I slid into the seat opposite him.

'Liz, I'm so sorry, we're going to have to pass on dinner. I've been throwing up all afternoon.'

'Oh no! You should have cancelled.'

'I didn't want to cancel. I took something for it but, well, it's not helping.'

He sat down again as the bartender came over and asked us what we wanted. Douglas was wearing a white linen shirt open at the neck and his face was almost as white as his shirt.

'Umm, I'll have a tonic water and what would you like, Liz?'

'A gin and tonic would be nice but...'

Douglas ordered our drinks.

'But… I think you need to go home. You're awfully pale,' I said.

I felt a crushing disappointment that our evening would be over before it had started but he looked in a bad way.

'Excuse me one minute, please,' he said.

He hurried to the gents' toilet and I noticed that he walked as if his back was hurting him. I imagined him throwing up in the toilet bowl. He had chosen not to cancel our date, which was gallant of him, but he must have been regretting it now. The bartender returned with our drinks and a bowl of pretzels. Mine was a double gin and I added a splash of tonic and took a large gulp to steady my nerves. Douglas came back and sat down gingerly.

'Sorry about that. I think it's best I go in a minute but tell me, is there any news about the crook builder?'

He took a sip of tonic while I filled him in on the developments as fast as I could.

'When they sent the photo through it was so exciting and now I've got his address. Brennan Investigations were great, so thank you so much.'

'It was my pleasure.'

'Now I think you should go home.'

'I feel awful leaving you to finish your drink.'

'Please don't.'

'I'm away this weekend but can we do a rerun next Thursday? Let me make it up to you.'

'With the greatest pleasure. Now please go.'

He paid the bartender and left the Lounge. I drank my gin and tonic and ate all the pretzels and considered ordering a second drink. The first few times I went into a bar on my own

I felt self-conscious, but I don't any more. As first dates go it ranked as a bit of a disaster and I was disappointed at how it had turned out, but he had seemed keen to meet again and I hugged that feeling to myself as I left the Lizard Lounge and headed for home.

CHAPTER TWELVE

Julius opened the morning meeting by praising Bob's lead story. The news team had done an in-depth piece on the collapse of a high street chain. Not only had thousands of shop workers lost their jobs but their once robust pension scheme had been raided by the men running the chain. It now carried a huge deficit and their pensions were in jeopardy. Bob's report had been scathing about the conduct of the bosses but had stayed on the right side of libel.

'I liked your use of the term "vampire capitalism". I've not heard that before,' Julius said.

'They've been complete bastards. If they were normal folk they'd be behind bars by now,' Bob said.

'It made my blood boil. How do they sleep at night?' Ledley said.

Lori turned to Bob.

'Have you ever thought about running a dedicated business slot?'

Bob shook his head.

'Wouldn't work. There's too many out there already. We can't compete with *Wake Up To Money* or the Bloombergs.'

'Fair point, but I was thinking of a softer business slot, one that profiled UK success stories, good news rather than bad news,' she said.

'We do those stories as and when they come up. There's not enough to justify a regular slot,' he said.

I thought Bob had got that right. Good news stories were few and far between. Ledley pitched in:

'What about running some stories on UK food companies, you know small businesses that are doing well and changing what we eat? I'm thinking here of UK vineyards; English cheeses, artisan breads, that kind of thing.'

'That could work as a feature series,' I said.

'I'm more interested in us profiling bigger companies, FTSE 100 companies,' Lori said.

There was a pause in our discussions. I'm sure Bob felt what Julius and I felt, that profiling FTSE 100 companies were not, nor ever would be, box office. Lori was no programme maker. Julius pulled his papers together.

'That's a wrap,' he said.

Lori looked put out that her idea had been snubbed. She pressed her lips together so that they went pale, then clutched her lever arch file to her chest like a shield.

We are holding Fizzy's party at four o'clock today and after the meeting Martine and I went through her list to check we had thought of everything.

'I got Fizzy's dressing room cleaned in case little Zachary needs a nap. And Loida is coming with them,' she said.

'Good call.'

'I think we need some orange juice. Some people like it with their prosecco.'

'Ziggy can get a couple of cartons from the Hub.'

I had ordered a lot of prosecco from a wine warehouse on a sale-and-return basis; because it was a Friday I had a feeling the party might run on.

Mid-morning I received an email from Ledley's agent Angela Hodge. She had attached a list of marketing ideas, mainly related to food but not exclusively, which Lori Kerwell was keen for Ledley to front. As he is a features presenter and is paid out of my budget it was up to me to clear them. Angela Hodge made the point that Ledley was keen to do all the events listed and she had added notes under every idea.

Some of the suggestions were outlandish. One required him to judge a best pie competition for League One football clubs. This would entail him travelling to far-flung stadia to sample the pies on offer on match days. His agent had written under this: *As you know, Ledley is renowned for his Jamaican patties and we think this is a good match with his brand.* Then there was a request for him to be part of a panel of judges for an ice-sculpture contest. This was being run in the Midlands to launch a dancing on ice show at a major venue in Birmingham. Angela's comment here was: *Ledley thinks this will be a lot of fun and they are paying well.*

I guessed that he was being paid well for all these appearances. I decided I would agree to the full list of ideas, however outlandish. Ledley only had two weeks left of being the main anchor at StoryWorld and if he wanted to make the most of it and earn some cash who was I to stand in his way? None of these ideas required a tie-in with our programme content, only the presence of Ledley to give the events some star appeal. I thought I should keep Julius in the loop and rang Martine.

'Pop down now, he's going out in ten,' she said.

I hurried to his office and presented the list to Julius.

'These all came from Lori. She wants Ledley to front them and I'm minded to say yes but I wanted you to see the list,' I said.

He took the sheet from me. As I'd walked in he was putting the phone down and he looked tense.

'Ice Extravaganza? Hell's teeth! You sure you want him to go so downmarket?' he said.

'He wants to make the most of his last two weeks on the sofa and who can blame him? If you don't mind I don't mind. It won't impact on our programming.'

Julius was looking uncomfortable and he ran his left hand round the back of his jacket as if he was easing the collar. Usually he is the one who favours the more populist end of the spectrum and I couldn't understand his discomfort.

'And meat pies... really?'

'Nothing wrong with a good meat pie, as Bob would say.'

Like Fizzy, Bob came from Burnley, but unlike her he had clung to his northern identity and frequently derided the effete taste in food and drink which we southern softies favoured. Julius handed the sheet back to me.

'OK, they sound ghastly but you can approve them,' he said.

'And Julius...?'

'Yes.'

'Please let Saul Relph know that I am being cooperative with Lori.'

Martine and I did a last check of the meeting room. It looked festive with Martine's embroidered tablecloth covering the prosaic meeting table. Platters of cakes and sausage rolls were arranged around a central posy of flowers in a jug and we had laid out the champagne flutes and the tea things on a side table. Fizzy, Loida and Zachary arrived at ten to four in a taxi and Martine and I met them in reception. Loida was carrying a load of baby equipment and we helped her carry this to Fizzy's dressing room. There were fresh flowers in there too and I guessed that Martine had done that. Fizzy stood in front of her full-length mirror and surveyed her reflection.

'God, it's good to be here again.'

'We've missed you so much,' Martine said.

Fizzy hugged Martine while Loida unpacked the changing mat and baby wipes and disposable nappies.

'Best I change him before you take him upstairs,' she said.

Zachary was dressed in a sailor suit and looked adorable.

'Could Ellen take a quick look at my make-up?' Fizzy asked.

I went to get Ellen and then headed upstairs and tapped on Julius's door.

'Fizzy's in her dressing room and it would be a nice gesture if you brought her up,' I said.

'I'll do that,' he said.

I went into the meeting room and told everyone that Fizzy was in the building and she would be with us soon. The room was filling fast. Friday was the day of Gerry's slot so I had expected him to be there. He was standing by the window talking to Harriet. Betty had made a special journey in and was chatting to Ledley. Henry the floor manager and two of the directors were sitting at the end of the room. A crowd of the news team had come along and were clustered by the table where the food and drink was laid out. There was no sign of Bob. I asked my team to hand out glasses and pour the prosecco so that we could toast Fizzy when she made her entrance.

Julius came in with Fizzy carrying Zachary and there was

a spontaneous outburst of applause. We had kept a seat for Fizzy at the top of the table and Martine directed her there with Ellen in attendance. Once Fizzy was seated with Zachary on her lap and a glass in her hand, Julius made a toast.

'To our queen of StoryWorld and her little prince; to Fizzy and Zachary,' he said.

'To Fizzy and Zachary,' we all repeated enthusiastically as Bob walked into the room. Even though he and I are now foes I felt for him at that moment. He must have been under intense pressure, desperate to catch his first sight of his son but also feeling exposed. Simon offered him a glass of prosecco but he shook his head and moved around the table so he could get nearer to Zachary. I went over to join Henry and the directors.

'Nice idea to do this, I heard it was yours,' Henry said.

'Well, a baby *and* cake, what's not to like?' I said.

People were queuing up to get close and to compliment Fizzy on her baby son. I saw Betty chatting with her for a while, no doubt giving her lots of advice. My team had graduated to handing out slices of cake and sausage rolls and Martine was allowed to hold Zachary while Fizzy accepted a small sliver of lemon drizzle cake which she ate daintily with a fork. Bob was working his way towards her with Ledley behind him. Finally, he was standing in front of her.

'He looks a great little lad,' I heard him say in a strangled voice.

'Thank you, I'm told he's big for his age,' Fizzy replied.

His eyes had locked on Zachary and there was such a hunger there. I was struck by the sadness of the moment. Here was a father seeing his son for the first time and it should have been an intimate moment, not a moment shared with a crowd of colleagues. He was probably longing to hold Zachary but of course he could not. He could not give himself away as the secret father. I thought then that my reaction had been wrong. Perhaps I should have laid my grudge aside, however justified it was, and allowed a private meeting to take place at my flat. I tried to push the feeling down but a knot of guilt had lodged itself. It made me feel ill at ease as the prosecco continued to be poured and the party continued well past our usual leaving time.

Scissor Sisters, Chalk Farm, Saturday morning

The salon was in a miserable parade of shops with a betting shop on one side and a doner kebab bar on the other. The white plastic sign above the window had a pair of scissors between the two words. I spent a moment looking at the price list which was stuck in the window. Flo was such an innocent to have gone into this place. One glance had told me it was a no-go area. On my walk to the salon I had been formulating what I would say to the hairstylist. Seeing the shop now I knew any chance of getting a refund was remote. I pushed open the door. One woman was painting the nails of a client and there was that acrid smell of varnish remover in the salon. Another client, who looked like a pensioner, was sitting under one of those old-fashioned hair-dryers, like a beehive. A tall blonde woman came over to the desk and the appointment book. She must have been six feet tall and her hair was pulled back tightly into a high ponytail.

'You need an appointment?'

She had a strong Russian accent.

'I need to speak to the manager,' I said.

'I am the manager.'

'Then I have to tell you that you caused major discomfort to my daughter. You dyed her hair blonde last Saturday and you did not do a skin test. Her scalp was on fire.'

Her chin had flown up at my accusation.

'You are wrong,' she said.

'I am not. Her name is Florence Lyon. She'll be in your book.'

She slapped the appointment book shut and placed her hand on it.

'You are wrong,' she repeated.

'You didn't do a skin test. Her hair is ruined and I would like a full refund.'

Her face was like a mask but two spots of pink had formed on her cheekbones.

'You leave my salon now. You are a very rude woman,' she said loudly.

The woman having her nails painted and the other stylist had turned their heads to look at us. The old lady under the hair dryer was oblivious to the drama. I wasn't going to get Flo's money back but I was going to make my point.

'You make a habit of it, do you? Taking money from young girls and ruining their hair?' I said it loudly too.

'You go now or I call my brother.'

She picked up the white phone on the desk and was punching in numbers. I could imagine a burly Russian brother pitching up. It was time to go.

'I'll be reporting you,' I said as I pulled the door open. I had sounded confident but I hurried away expecting the arrival of Russian mafia-types at any moment. I was glad when I reached the familiar shops of my high street.

Chalk Farm flat, Saturday evening

The flat was so quiet without Flo's chatter, even if her chatter was not usually with me but to her friends on FaceTime. She was on the Isle of Wight with Grace and Pete and there had been no word from her. This was a good sign as it meant that she was content but I was missing the sense of purpose that I get from her being around and needing me. I would do something useful; a major sort-out of my clothes was required. A friend had told me about doing that declutter thing where you hold up an item of clothing and ask yourself 'does this bring joy into my life?' If the answer isn't a yes then it goes straight into a bin bag for the charity shop. I opened my wardrobe which was overfull and tried the formula on several pieces. The joy question just wasn't working for me. Instead I made a pile of the clothes I hadn't worn for the last five years and bagged them up. I then spent an age colour-coding my remaining clothes and shoes and getting a sense of satisfaction from this task. I thought about Douglas Pitlochry a few times, wondering where he was spending the weekend and whether his son lived with him or with his wife.

Chalk Farm flat, Sunday evening

It was a hot thundery evening and I wrestled with the French doors to shut them. They were sticking again and I cursed Ron Osborne as I pushed them closed and locked them. If he hadn't messed me around I would have had the new doors by now. I turned on my laptop and studied the instructions on the small claims court website. It made clear that before instituting legal proceedings you were expected to show that you had made every attempt to resolve the situation. Now that I had Ron Osborne's address, which he was clearly cagey about sharing, I could send a letter to him by recorded delivery. I drafted a legal-sounding letter which gave him seven days to return my deposit or I would commence legal proceedings. I hoped this would shock him into returning my money. I felt pleased with myself as I printed and signed it with a flourish.

But later I suffered from a bad attack of the Sunday night blues, brought on by my spending the whole weekend on my own. I thought about it. Had I got the Sunday night blues while Ben and I were living together? Probably not, but we might have been arguing instead. I put more lamps on and rang my mum in Glasgow for a long catch-up. Mum has retired from teaching and in December she'll be off to Kenya for a two-year work placement with Voluntary Services Overseas. Since Dad died Mum always has to be doing something useful. Once she sets off to Africa Flo and I will see her, at best, once a year. I am proud of her, though, for her courage and her resilience.

There was a sudden flash of lightning and Mr Crooks belted through the cat flap. I stood at the French doors and watched giant raindrops bouncing on the ground and my hollyhocks rocking against the wall.

CHAPTER THIRTEEN

StoryWorld TV station, London Bridge

A story on our news bulletin this morning had me crying in the gallery. A fifteen-year-old girl had gone missing last week. Her distraught parents had made urgent calls for information, saying she wasn't the sort to run away and pleading with the public to help them find her. There was something about the mother that I connected with and yes, the missing girl was the same age as Flo. I imagined how terrified I would be if she had gone missing. We have been running updates on the search ever since. Her body was found late last night in a lock-up garage. The thought came to me that the girl would have cried out for her mother and her mum wasn't there and I couldn't stop tears rolling down my cheeks at the sheer bloody horror of it.

After the morning meeting Harriet popped her head round my door.

'How's Flo? She told me about her hair.'

'Really? Then you are one of a select few. I've been forbidden to mention it to anyone. Come on in.'

She perched on the arm of my sofa.

'She WhatsApped me but wouldn't send a pic even though I told her I did something similar when I was at school. I dyed the front of my hair blue.'

'Blue?'

'Yes, dark blue, almost black. I was aiming for a goth look. My mum was beside herself and I was grounded for weeks.'

I couldn't imagine the stylish Harriet as a goth, ever.

'How old were you?'

'Fourteen.'

'And you were into goth?'

'I had a major thing about this boy. He was into goth and I was into him.'

'Well, I'm seeing a whole new side of you, Harriet.'

She laughed. 'Anyway, I wanted to cheer her up so I mentioned Guy's idea for a teenage makeover slot.'

'I don't know about this?'

'He got this fantastic letter from a sixteen-year-old who asked why he never discussed fashion for her age group. So he'd like me to find three teenage girls to do a fashion makeover. The letter-writer is going to be one of them and I thought Flo could be one too. She'd be ideal.'

'It's sweet of you, Harriet, but won't it smack of nepotism if we use Flo?'

Harriet looked blank.

'You know, me using my position to favour my daughter.'

'Oh, I'm sure that won't matter at all,' Harriet said breezily.

As the daughter of a newspaper editor she was used to privileges coming her way and couldn't see any conflict of interest. Her impulse had been a kind one, to cheer up Flo. I wished she had mentioned it to me first though. I could imagine how thrilled Flo would be at the idea and I knew she would brook no opposition.

'Would this be a studio item?'

'No, Guy thought we should shoot it on location, maybe

at a street market, and do a montage of the girls before and after,' she said.

I could see that working and it was a perfect August story. But Flo as one of the models, the idea made me uneasy.

I had lunch in the Hub with Martine and Ellen. I like my new-found friendliness with Martine. The Hub was having an Italian week and red, white and green bunting was strung along the food counter. The room smelled of oregano and baking pizza dough and there was a different pasta dish on offer each day. I had toyed with the idea of a salad, as I'd like to shed a couple of pounds, but in the end we'd all gone for the linguine carbonara which was lovely and creamy. We discussed Friday's party and how sweet Zachary was and what a marvellous job Loida did in supporting Fizzy. Ellen was struck by how keen Fizzy was to get back to work.

'He's still so tiny. I hope she's not rushing it. It's only been three months and I took eight months off with Tara,' Ellen said.

'I was off for nine,' I said as I twisted the linguine onto my fork.

'But she loves her job. She gets such a buzz from connecting with the viewers,' Martine said.

'She does. She actually gets energy from them, I think. And she's not the stay-at-home kind, is she?' I said.

Ellen added black pepper to her pasta.

'I guess not. And even though Ledley is doing a good job, Fizzy *is* StoryWorld.'

'It will be great to have her back,' Martine said.

Lori was sitting on her own at a corner table with a half-eaten pizza and a newspaper spread on the table before her. Ellen glanced in her direction.

'She didn't come to the party, did she? I've only exchanged

words with her once and I'm not sure what to make of her,' she said quietly.

'She's stand-offish and I never knew a woman who worked as hard as her. "Driven" doesn't even begin to describe it,' Martine said.

The two women looked at me, waiting for me to say something. It was interesting how they too had found Lori disconcerting.

'I think she's a woman in a hurry. She wants to prove herself,' I said.

It was mid-afternoon when Ledley appeared at my threshold.

'You got a minute?'

'For you, always,' I said.

He smiled and closed the door. He was looking smart again in a pale grey linen suit and he hung his jacket over the back of the chair before he sat down. The jacket was lined with apple green silk and looked expensive. Ledley is handsome and could almost pass for a male model these days, but I still preferred the scruffy street-style Ledley.

'Angela called me. Thanks for approving all the ideas,' he said.

'My pleasure, but you've signed yourself up for a whole lot of travelling.'

'That's fine with me. I like trains. Can we keep what I'm about to say between us?'

'Of course.'

He tapped his fingers on my desk and without looking at me said: 'I was watching Bob at Fizzy's party.'

My stomach plummeted because I knew what was coming.

'And the feeling has been growing on me that Bob is Zachary's father.'

He had raised his eyes to my face and somehow I managed to make my expression look incredulous.

'What on earth gave you that idea?'

'The way he was with Fizzy, the way he looked at the baby, the way he talked. He was unbelievably tense.'

'Oh, come on,' I said.

I was relieved that he had nothing else to base this on.

'I know how to read people, Liz.'

'I'm sure you do, but Bob and Fizzy? No way. They're good friends because they both come from Burnley.'

'He's married with two kids, you know.'

'I know. I've met his wife, Pat,' I said.

'So have I. And she's a nice lady. And wasn't that Geoff she was involved with married too?'

He was being uncharacteristically righteous on the issue and I tried to tease him out of this.

'I didn't have you down as a guardian of morals,' I said.

He would not be deflected and repeated his conviction that Bob was Zachary's father.

'They had plenty of opportunity to meet up. I often saw them in the Hub together.'

'As friends... having a coffee,' I said, hoping I wasn't protesting too much.

'It was more than that. I know it was. You could call Zachary an in-house production!' he said.

I felt a strong need to protect Fizzy. I had to stop Ledley from voicing his suspicions to anyone else in the station.

'You're basing this on what, Ledley? On body language? My strong advice is to let this go.'

'The truth always comes out in the end,' he said.

It occurred to me that he was trying to stir up trouble against Fizzy and why would he do that? Was this burst of moral outrage tied up with his wish to retain his position as the anchor? I feared that it was. Being on camera does something to people. I've noticed it before. It has a corrupting influence and I felt less fond of Ledley than I had before. Should I say something to Fizzy about Ledley's suspicions? I didn't think I would. It would only get Fizzy into a state.

Chalk Farm flat, 8 p.m.

Flo called me from Portsmouth and although I asked her about her weekend on the Isle of Wight all she could talk about was the teenage fashion makeover and how Harriet had told her she had the opportunity to be a model on TV.

'We can get my hair done in time. Please, Mum, I really, really, really, want to do this.'

I tried to explain my reservations.

'I'm worried it will look like favouritism,' I said.

'You *have* to let me do it.'

Later, I had settled down to watch Douglas do his evening bulletin when my landline rang. I felt irritated but turned the sound down on the TV and picked up. It was Ben calling me from Dubai, which was a rare enough occurrence. There was no preamble, he launched straight in.

'Please let Flo do this fashion thing,' he said.

'Did she ask you to ring me?'

'What's the harm? She's been miserable because of the hair fiasco and it will give her a boost.'

'I know it will. But I feel uncomfortable about it.'

'Why?'

'Oh, you know, the producer pushing her own daughter forward.'

'Flo said she'd be one of three models,' he said.

'Yes, that's true, but...'

'This is a one-off, for God's sake, let her do it.'

'I'll have to clear it with Julius, but I guess it will be OK as long as she gets no financial benefit from it,' I said.

'It's commendable that you're so squeaky clean about your work but honestly, Liz, you need to lighten up,' he said.

'Goodnight, Ben.' I clicked off the phone.

He had made me furious. Telling me to lighten up when I looked after Flo ninety-five per cent of the time, was there for all her crises and paid most of the bills. Of course he could be the relaxed, good-time dad on the rare occasions he saw her. I grabbed the remote and turned the sound up and went back to watching Douglas read the news but was still feeling angry when the bulletin ended. It was ten-thirty but I took all the mugs out of the cupboard and wiped down the shelf. Next I went through the spice jars and packets and threw out any that had passed their use-by date. I swept the kitchen floor and finally felt ready for bed.

CHAPTER FOURTEEN

Camden Town, 9.30 a.m.

Tonight I've got my second date with Douglas. I've been thinking about it all week and it's kind of pushed my worries about Lori's hostility and Ledley's suspicions out of my mind. In fact, the date has loomed far too large in my consciousness. Earlier this week, Douglas emailed to say I needed to dress for sitting outside as he'd got us tickets to an outdoor concert at Kenwood Gardens in Hampstead. It was going to be light classical and he had chosen it because of the setting and he would bring a picnic. Yesterday he called saying would I bring a large umbrella if I had one as the weather forecast wasn't brilliant. I thought a picnic and a concert was a romantic gesture and I wanted to look good, which meant getting my hair done.

So I asked Simon if he would sit in on the morning meeting for me today as I needed to do something near home. I walked down to the salon in Camden Town to get my hair washed and blow-dried. Most of the time I pay Ellen in make-up a small fee to cut my hair but I do like the stylist at the Camden salon, Mark. He's been doing my hair for years when I have a special occasion and he has become a friend. He brought me a cappuccino and I told him about Flo's bleaching disaster. He was horrified.

'That's actually quite dangerous, you know?' he said.

'That's what I thought.'

'There are strict guidelines about how much peroxide you can use. Poor love, what a horrible thing to happen.'

'It was about two weeks ago and she's desperate to get her hair dyed back to its natural colour. Can you do that?'

'We can, Liz, but it won't come cheap, I'm afraid.'

He told me the price and it was a heck of a lot of money. I booked her in though and I'll ask Ben to pay for it.

StoryWorld TV station, London Bridge

At twelve noon I got a call from Martine who said I was needed at once in Julius's office. She sounded flustered and when I reached her desk she said:

'Sorry for no notice, it's an unscheduled meeting.'

I knew something was up the minute I walked in because Saul Relph was sitting there, as was Lori Kerwell. Saul is rarely seen in the building as he delegates programming matters to Julius. I still felt resentful that Saul had spoken to Julius about me and seeing the three of them sitting there made me anxious. They looked like a cabal who were hatching some plot. The charged atmosphere was further heightened when Julius closed the blinds at his windows so that passing staff could not look in.

'Good to see you, Liz,' Saul Relph said. 'We want to share our latest thinking with you.'

'Which is speculative and confidential at the moment,' Julius added quickly.

Julius indicated I should sit facing the large screen on his wall and Lori, who had her laptop open, flashed up a slide. I wondered if she ever did anything without first preparing a PowerPoint. She talked through her presentation. It was full of graphs of viewer reactions to specific features we had carried over the last two months since Fizzy had been on maternity leave. The response to Ledley had been enthusiastic, she said. She clicked up another graph. Her detailed study of viewer comments and of the demographic breakdown of the StoryWorld audience had led her to the conclusion that Ledley and Fizzy should be a double act on the sofa from September.

I was stunned. Fizzy had been the solo star of StoryWorld for years and I had thought her position was unassailable.

'What do you think?' Julius asked once Lori had clicked the last slide and shut her laptop.

'My first thought is that it's so conventional to go with a male–female pairing. One of the things that makes us stand out is that we have a solo woman fronting our show.'

'Yes, but Ledley's presence will open up new markets for us. His status as a chef will help us get food advertising on board. And there's a wide range of male products, including fragrances, which we could tap into and the advertising spend on this area is substantial,' Lori said.

'My second thought is that this is a bear trap,' I continued.

'A bear trap? What do you mean?' Saul said.

'A bear trap is when we do something which bites us back and harms our reputation. Fizzy returns from maternity leave to find that she has essentially been demoted for going off and having a baby. How do you think that will play in the media?'

I saw straight away that this angle had not occurred to Saul. His eyebrows drew together and he looked over at Julius.

'It would need careful handling, of course. We are well aware of that,' Julius said.

'It's not a demotion if Fizzy is on the same salary and she will be, won't she?' Lori added.

'It really isn't about her salary, Lori. Surely you can see that? This will be seen as a demotion by the industry. Up till now she got to do *all* the interviews. Now she'll have to share them with a co-host,' I said.

'But my research shows overwhelmingly that Ledley will help us achieve more advertising,' she said, as if this trumped any possible objections to her plan.

'It will also help our diversity profile,' Julius said.

I looked over at him. 'If you do proceed, who is going to do this *careful handling*?'

'I take it you're not in favour?' he said.

'I've had ten minutes to absorb the idea, but my instinct is that this could backfire badly. What if Fizzy cuts up rough, which I think she's bound to do?'

'You know we all think the world of Fizzy. We were wondering that with a young baby to look after she might welcome the added support,' Saul Relph said in a subdued voice.

I knew he had always been a big fan of Fizzy but I was amazed at how little he knew her. She is fiercely ambitious and driven. Julius knew her, though, and was well aware how she would react. This was a high-risk change and would be a nightmare to manage. The great irony was that this was exactly what Fizzy had feared when she went on maternity leave. She'd thought I was plotting to replace her with Ledley and we had fallen out over it. I had never wanted any such thing. But Ledley's star had risen and it was the newcomer Lori Kerwell who was promoting him. This was Lori's way of making her mark but she also appeared confident about her figures. She was a woman who did not suffer from self-doubt. Saul, who does not like to be thwarted, or even argued against, had moved into irritable MD mode.

'We have to secure additional advertising. We have no choice. You want to hang on to your team and your guest presenters, don't you, Liz?'

I was startled at such a direct question. Were the finances of the station in such a parlous state?

'Well yes, of course.'

'We have to do this and it's your job to make this work in programming terms,' he said.

So that was it. If it backfired I would get the blame. Wonderful! And I had the impression that the role of breaking the news to Fizzy, and of placating her, had been intended for me and that my reaction had scuppered that. I left the meeting shortly afterwards having been reminded by Saul Relph in a stern voice that our discussion had been entirely confidential. Lori stayed behind with Julius and Saul, the cabal. Martine shot me a look but did not ask what the meeting had been about so I was spared having to lie to her. My head was spinning as I went back to my office. This was going to be a major challenge.

It was only later that I recalled that Julius had been uncomfortable when he and I discussed the downmarket PR events that Lori had lined up for Ledley to front. At the time I hadn't understood his reaction. Now it was clear. Julius must have known they were planning to keep Ledley on as the co-host with Fizzy. I wondered if Ledley knew this too. I felt belittled that they had only thought to share it with me once their decision was made, and my sympathies were all with Fizzy.

Kenwood House Picnic Concert, Hampstead, 7.15 p.m.

I had arranged to meet Douglas outside the main entrance of Kenwood House. It's an elegant building sitting in landscaped gardens. I spotted him standing under the Ionic portico and he was laden. He had a bag of picnic food, a bottle of champagne and was carrying two cushions under his arm. We greeted each other and he kissed me on the cheek awkwardly, with the bags getting in the way.

'Let me help you carry some of that,' I said.

He handed me the two cushions which were firm rather than decorative ones.

'Clever of you to think of bringing cushions,' I said.

'Oh, the cushions are kind of essential. I'm plagued with a back problem I've had since I was seventeen. I'll tell you the whole sorry story some day. It's a completely self-inflicted injury. Now, we need to get to the Pasture Ground.'

I followed him. It was a lovely setting with a lake and ancient woodland stretching beyond the landscaped vista. Rows of seats had been set up in front of a temporary stage and Douglas manoeuvred us to our places. He arranged one of the cushions carefully at the base of his spine and handed me the other one.

'Why don't you use them both? I'm perfectly comfortable,' I said.

He put the second cushion into place and it was clear that back pain was a part of his life. He looked up at the sky and the darkening clouds which were gathering.

'The forecast said rain is on the way but we may be lucky.'

As asked, I had brought a large StoryWorld golfing umbrella along and I pushed this under my seat. I was finding him desperately attractive in his open-necked shirt and jeans as he leaned forward and drew out a bottle of champagne, nicely chilled, and two plastic flutes.

'I think a drink would be pleasant,' he said.

He opened the bottle expertly so that it gave a satisfying pop but no champagne frothed out, poured, and handed me a flute before serving himself.

'I've got some smoked salmon sandwiches here if you fancy one?'

'You've thought of everything. Yes, please.'

I had looked up the programme before I'd set off and there were some glorious and familiar pieces of music listed.

'This is such a wonderful idea for a summer evening. Thank you for organising it,' I said.

The orchestra opened the concert with Bach's 'Sheep May Safely Graze'. This was particularly apt as we were sitting in the Pasture Ground and I whispered this to Douglas.

'Yes, kind of perfect, isn't it?' he whispered back.

This was followed by Tchaikovsky's stirring 'Sleeping Beauty' waltz and then the mood became tranquil again with the 'Canon in D' by Pachelbel. It was lovely and I felt happy in a fluttery kind of way and as if tears were close to the surface, but then music can do that to me.

In the interval Douglas and I finished the bottle of champagne and the sandwiches. As the orchestra was walking back onto the stage we felt the first large drops of rain on our arms and within a minute the sky had opened and dumped a barrel of rain on our heads. My dress was stuck to my body and my fabulous hairdo was flattened as I struggled to get the umbrella out from under the seat. Douglas was soaked through and he was trying to stuff his cushions into a plastic bag. He started to laugh and that set me off and we were both hysterical, unable to stop laughing as the rain hit us in the face and pelted the grass. He grabbed me by the hand.

'Let's go and find shelter in a pub,' he said.

We ran through the rain to the gates of Kenwood Gardens and stood under a tree to get our breath. Finally, we managed to stop laughing.

'That orchestra... and us running out on them like that,' I said.

'Oh, there'll be plenty of diehards who'll sit till the end and not let the rain stop them,' he said. 'I know a pub near here. We need to dry out.'

The rain was less fierce now and we walked out on to the road sharing my umbrella. We turned left and arrived at the Spaniards Inn within five minutes. This was all uneven flagstones and low beam ceilings, the sort of place that would have a log fire burning in the winter. We found a table and I went to the Ladies while Douglas went to the bar. I looked in the mirror. Some mascara had run beneath my eyes so I wiped the smears away. There was nothing I could do about my hair so I combed it back and tucked it behind my ears. And I was wet down to my bra. I joined Douglas at our table. His hair was wet and tousled and looked rather attractive. He had bought a bottle of Chablis which was in an ice bucket. We sat close and drank the wine and I asked him if he would tell me the story about his self-inflicted back injury.

'What a young idiot I was, seventeen and reckless. We were living in Norfolk and had gone to Sheringham for our summer holiday.'

'I know Sheringham.'

'Funny little place, isn't it? Mum and Dad didn't have a lot of money then and we were camping. It's not got much of a beach.'

'It's all pebbles, isn't it?'

'Exactly. But it did have the great attraction of sandy cliffs which I could climb. My parents had warned me that they were soft and known to crumble. That didn't stop me. I set myself more and more daring challenges. I used my penknife to make footholds in the cliffs and these footholds would crumble away as I climbed.'

'How high are these cliffs?'

'Some are up to eighty feet.'

'Scary,' I said.

'Not to me. I found it thrilling and got kind of addicted to the adrenalin rush. But at the end of the week it started to rain and it didn't stop for two days. Mum wanted to go home early but I was desperate to do a last climb. The rain stopped and I went down to the beach and did a climb and this time I was unlucky, or maybe the rain had softened the cliff, because my foothold gave way and I fell badly onto the pebbles and hurt my back.'

'You could have been killed!'

'I didn't fall that far.'

'Poor you and your poor mum. She must have been beside herself.'

He gave me a rueful smile.

'A dog walker found me and called an ambulance. I was in hospital for a while and I still have to see my osteopath regularly.'

He poured me more wine and topped up his glass.

'And it's had a long-term impact on my life. It's the reason I'm a newscaster behind a desk and not a reporter out in the field.'

He sounded regretful and I reached over and squeezed his hand.

'Liz?'

I looked up and Amber was in front of our table. I hadn't seen her for ages though I knew that she was back with Julius. She looked over at Douglas and I could tell that she recognised him.

'Amber, hello. Um, this is my friend Douglas.'

He got to his feet and shook hands with her. She looked immaculate, as she always did, in a Burberry raincoat. No smeared eyes or flattened hair for Amber.

'We got caught in the rain,' I said.

'It was quite a storm. Well, good to see you. I have to dash. There's a taxi outside.'

Douglas gave me a quizzical look after she had gone. He must have noticed that I looked uncomfortable.

'That's Amber. She works in fashion and she is currently dating my boss.'

'Ahh, Julius Jones,' he said.

'You know him?'

'I've met him a few times. A tough boss, I would think.'

'Tough but talented,' I said.

When we parted outside my flat two hours later Douglas got out of the taxi and kissed me. It was a very nice kiss and there was a part of me that wanted to invite him in. Flo was in Portsmouth and I would feel much freer with her away. But it was too soon. This was only our second date. He waited until I had unlocked my door and gone in and then I heard his taxi chugging away.

'Well, that was extremely nice,' I told Mr Crooks as I got out of my still-damp clothes and pulled on a long T-shirt. I lay in bed and went through the whole evening again, recalling how closely we had sat next to each other in the pub. And there was that delicious goodnight kiss.

CHAPTER FIFTEEN

StoryWorld TV station, London Bridge

I was in the gallery with the director as Ledley discussed Gerry's topic of the week which was superstitions and star signs. Ledley has grown into an assured performer and I wondered again if he knew anything about the plan to keep him on as Fizzy's co-presenter. I used to think that Ledley was a straightforward person to deal with. He had seemed to be someone who did not have the monster ego that comes with so many on-screen personalities. My doubts about him have been growing and that conversation we'd had about Bob being the father of Zachary had shown him in a different and nastier light. He was capable of stirring things up if he thought it would advance his interests.

'So you see Pisces, my sign, is the most superstitious of all. We will devise all kinds of rituals to avoid ladders and Friday the thirteenth, whereas canny Capricorns think this is the height of foolishness,' Gerry said.

I recalled that Gerry had wanted us to have dinner and I reminded myself to book in a date with him. He's a good man and I was in need of an ally.

Later, we were all seated in the meeting room to discuss the show and I looked around the table. At least three of us – Julius, Lori and I – were in on the bombshell that Fizzy would not be returning as the solo presenter in September. Bob was there but he didn't know, nor did the director sitting next to him. I saw Ledley exchange a glance with Lori and I thought, He knows, he must know. I was finding it hard to focus on the discussion, thinking instead about the ramifications if the change went ahead. It would mean that with every guest we booked I would have to make a decision about who would do the interview. It was going to be a minefield. Fizzy would insist on the big interviews. But, more to the point, how would she and Ledley work on camera? No matter what private feelings they had about each other on camera they had to present a united front. I saw nothing but conflict ahead. At the end of the meeting I asked Julius if I could have a quick word and I followed him to his office.

'I wanted you to know that I've agreed that Flo can be one of the three subjects of Guy's teenage fashion makeover shoot.'

'OK.'

'It's not a studio item, it will be a short digital package and she won't get any pay for it,' I said.

'It's fine by me.'

'Thank you. I didn't want you to think there was a conflict of interest.'

'Of course not. You worry about the wrong things, Liz.'

There was a pause as he placed his papers on his desk before he turned back to me.

'I heard you were dating Douglas Pitlochry?'

Blood rushed to my cheeks. How on earth had he heard that? Of course, it would be Amber. She had seen us at that Hampstead pub, but that was only last night! To my consternation my face was on fire and my blush was deepening.

'We've been on a couple of dates.'

'Be careful there. I've heard that since he split with his wife he's been playing the field.'

Julius was telling me to be careful in my love life. I was astonished. I needed to change the subject fast.

'Are there any further developments on the Fizzy situation?'

He looked grim.

'I'm driving up to Burnley tomorrow. She has to be told face to face.'

'You're really going through with it?'

'We have little option. The numbers stack up and we need the advertising Ledley can bring in.'

'Are you sure that Lori's figures are robust? You can do a lot by manipulating figures.'

'I know: lies, damned lies and statistics,' he said.

'Exactly.'

'She may not be the easiest person to work with but I will say this about her, she knows her stuff. I got her analysis verified by a number-cruncher and her forecast stands up.'

'But the first rule of broadcasting is look after your talent. Fizzy is our greatest asset. Saul and Lori are money people. They only see the bottom line.' I said this with more force than I intended. Did I still hope that I could persuade Julius to go against the decision? I could see Martine sitting at her desk outside and consulting her watch. It was clear she wanted Julius for his next meeting.

'And Martine has no idea?' I asked.

Usually Martine knows what is happening in the station before any of us. She adores Fizzy and we both knew she would take this development badly.

'No. And we're going to keep it that way,' he said.

'How on earth will you tell Fizzy? She's going to be devastated.'

'I'm working on that and I could do with your help. It

is part of your job, you know, to carry out our policy on presenters.'

'I've done some tough conversations in my time, but I wouldn't know how to break this to her.'

Martine had grown fed up with waiting and she tapped on the door and pointed to her watch. Julius held up his hand to indicate he needed five more minutes with me.

'I was going to ask you to come to Burnley with me but I know weekends are difficult for you with Flo,' he said.

'Thank you. She's been away and I need to spend time with her this weekend.'

He seemed genuinely perturbed and I noticed that his left eyelid was twitching, a sure sign of stress. I looked down and tried to think how I would break this to Fizzy.

'I guess the best thing is to be straight with her and say it's got *nothing* to do with her appeal which remains sky high. Think of all those toys that got sent in for her. Say it is purely a commercial decision because Ledley can draw in another section of viewers.'

'Yes. I'll say that because it's the truth; economic necessity. Saul is cut up about it too you know, even though he is a money man,' he said.

'And Julius, please tell Fizzy that this decision had nothing to do with me. She's going to take this hard and she'll need support. I want to be there for her.'

I went back to my office thinking that I had rarely seen Julius looking so ill at ease. This had to be a decision that had been imposed on him by Saul against his instincts. Yet Saul had always been Fizzy's biggest fan. I remembered the huge bunch of flowers he sent her when she was in hospital last year, and the way he had talked to me about her when she revealed her pregnancy on camera. He had stood by her then and said that she was very important to StoryWorld's continued success. It must be that the company finances were in a parlous state and they were desperate to bring in more advertising. This enhanced Lori's position still further as she was seen as the key to increasing revenue. And a by-product of this would be that Ledley would now see Lori as his patron. I didn't like any of these developments or what it would mean for me and my features team.

I told Harriet that it was fine for Flo to take part in the teenage fashion shoot. Then I rang Flo in Portsmouth and confirmed that she was going to be one of the three models. She whooped with joy at the prospect.

'I can get my hair changed back before the shoot, can't I, Mum?'

'Yes. I've talked to Mark about it and I want him to do it. We can trust him. I'll see you in a few hours. Can't wait, I've missed you, darling.'

It's the late summer bank holiday on Monday and we won't be broadcasting again till Tuesday. Fizzy is due to return on Thursday. I had suggested she come back the following Monday but she is determined to be back on the sofa on the first of September. Would this still be the case? Julius is breaking the news to her tomorrow and I have a slightly sick feeling that everything will be thrown into turmoil. As Flo is back tonight I decided I would leave early. I'd get some treat food in and we can do our Friday night veg out. I was looking forward to it. I locked my office door, just after five, and heard Harriet ask the team if any of them fancied going to the opening of a new sushi bar that was introducing the 'sushi doughnut'. She had a spare invite and it was at a cool venue in Bermondsey.

'Sushi doughnut? That sounds a truly vile combination,' Simon said.

'It doesn't have any dough or sugar in it. It's sticky rice shaped like a doughnut with the usual sushi toppings.'

'What's the point then?' Molly asked.

'Well, doughnut hybrids are the thing, aren't they?' Harriet said.

'But it's not a doughnut,' Molly persisted.

This turned out to be another of Lori's invitations from her marketing contacts. Considering she doesn't like her I've noticed that Harriet is quick to accept Lori's freebies.

'Have a good bank holiday,' I said and headed gratefully for the staircase and the exit.

Chalk Farm flat, Saturday afternoon

I'm so pleased to have Flo back and she has been more affectionate than usual. Last night as we ate pizza and watched rubbish telly she told me she'd had a good time in Portsmouth but had felt ready to come home a couple of days before. We snuggled up on the sofa with Mr Crooks between us. She was stroking him and I looked at her face in profile, my beloved daughter. She had scraped her hair back into a ponytail and seemed less obsessed with its colour. She fumbled in her tote bag.

'Oh, and Granny gave me this.'

She held out a brooch and I took it from her. It was a vintage brooch, diamond in shape, with three dried orange flowers embalmed in plastic.

'They're real flowers,' she said.

To my eyes it looked old-fashioned; the sort of brooch grannies wore decades ago.

'That was kind of her.'

'She said to look through her jewellery box and pick something. It's from the nineteen seventies. Isn't it great?'

Flo is out now, with Rosie, and she went out without tying a scarf over her hair, which is progress. I'm planning an afternoon of cooking but I can't stop thinking about how Julius is getting on with Fizzy in Burnley. What excuse would he have given for driving up to see her? Surely she would have suspected something if he told her in advance. But would he pitch up unannounced at her parents' house? I did not envy him his task and he had seemed genuinely rattled about it.

I decided to make apple crumble with cinnamon and sultanas. I had bought a large bag of cooking apples from the market and was peeling these and listening to a play on the radio when my mobile buzzed. It was a text from Fizzy and my heart gave a weird tumble as I read:

I'm in pieces. Please call me now. Fx

I washed my hands and called her and she answered on the first ring.

'How long have you known about this?'

'They told me on Thursday,' I said.

'They? Who's they?'

'Julius, Saul, Lori Kerwell...'

'That evil bitch! I hear this is her big idea.'

She sounded furious rather than tearful and that was a relief because I felt I could handle her anger better than her sadness.

'He's just gone. Drives up here and tells me my career is on the skids and then buggers off. Treacherous bastard...'

'Your career is *not* on the skids,' I said.

'Liz, we're friends, aren't we?'

'Yes, we are.'

'Well, don't bullshit me then. You know how this will play in the industry: Fizzy Wentworth no longer able to carry a show on her own. I feel so insulted.'

I wondered what words Julius had used to break the news to her.

'But you know it's purely about money, about advertising,' I said.

'That's the line he used. But no one will believe it's about that. They'll all think it's because I'm not as good as I was. I told you this would happen if I had a baby. The total bastard! I wanted to slap his face and I nearly did.'

This conjured up a vivid image and part of me wished she had slapped him.

'From what they said to me they're desperate to get more advertising and Ledley's there purely to bring in male product advertising,' I said.

'That talentless, disloyal creep! He's so vain. Thinks he's the cat's whiskers these days. He's a bloody chef, for chrissakes.' Her voice wobbled as she said: 'Granny's dying and Zac is teething and Julius ruined my birthday get-together. I'm devastated.'

'Oh, Fizzy, I'm so sorry. When are you back in London?'

I heard her blow her nose and when she resumed her voice had hardened.

'On Monday, and I'm seeing my agent the minute I'm back. We're going to play hard ball on this.'

We all knew Fizzy's agent Jonny Hammond. He had a lot

of clout and was feared in the business because he had been known to pull his clients out of deals when he didn't get his way.

'Can I do anything to help you?'

'You can ring that bastard Julius and tell him that he'll be hearing from Jonny,' she said.

'OK. Keep in touch. I can come over to yours Monday afternoon if that would be any help.'

After she had hung up I went back to peeling and coring the apples. I was relieved that she hadn't blamed me for the decision. After all, I was the one who had suggested that Ledley sit in for her. I'd said Ledley was a chef and what he cared about was building up his food business. I had been wrong on that score. I was grateful that Julius had said the idea came from Lori. She was now the arch-villain in Fizzy's eyes but in truth it was Julius and Saul who had been the ones to make the final decision. What cowards men are. Fizzy needed an ally at the station and I was going to be that. My mobile rang and Fizzy's number flashed up again.

'A quick one: does Bob know?' she asked.

'No, he doesn't.'

'And Martine?'

'No, Julius was adamant we keep it confidential.'

'OK, thanks. I'll call you soon.'

Would she be back on the StoryWorld sofa on Thursday? I couldn't call it.

Chalk Farm flat, Saturday evening

Flo and Rosie had spent three hours going through the stalls at Camden Market and arrived home hot and happy. I invited

Rosie to stay the night and fed them omelettes and apple crumble. They each had two helpings of the crumble which was gratifying. It was after nine when my mobile went again and this time it was Julius.

'Has Fizzy been in touch?'

'Yes, she called me.'

'How was she?'

'Devastated. And furious. Did you give her any warning you were coming?'

'I said I was on my way to a football match, that I was passing through and wanted a word.'

'I see. It must have been difficult.'

'It was awful. I draw up outside this row of terrace houses and Fizzy was standing there, waiting for me on the doorstep. She looked glamorous and out of place in that funny little street. She knew something big was up. She said they were going out for a big family meal and I had only just caught her. Then she ordered her parents to take Zachary out in his pram and we went into the living room. She wouldn't sit down so I had to tell her standing there like a cop with bad news.'

It was unlike Julius to go into this much detail. I wondered if he was finding it cathartic to talk it out.

'Anyway, I told her this had nothing whatever to do with you. I took your point that she needs someone at the station she feels is completely on her side.'

'She does.'

'So what did she say about it?'

He expected me to be the go-between between Fizzy and him. It felt disloyal to be talking to him about our conversation but she had asked me to pass a message on.

'She's angry and insulted. She's seeing her agent on Monday and said you should expect to hear from him.'

'Jonny Hammond. He's a right bastard. But she's not leaving?'

'I don't know.'

'What's your hunch?'

'She didn't say she'd go to the media or take on StoryWorld legally,' I said.

'The nuclear option,' he said.

'My hunch is that she'll stay on, but you can't always predict how Fizzy will behave.'

I knew this from bitter experience. Last December I had moved from being her confidante to being seen as her enemy in the space of a weekend.

'We can't afford to lose her,' he said.

It was the Bank Holiday weekend but he would be working, trying to manage the fallout. He was the one who discovered Fizzy and moulded her into the queen of morning TV and this must have made his task even more difficult today. He and Fizzy come from similar modest backgrounds. His parents had run a small post office in Essex and he was born and raised Nigel Jones. He only invented himself as Julius Jones when he got into television. Well, he's the director of programmes and he gets paid a great deal more than me. I had two more days off and I intended to make the most of them. I ran myself a bath, adding my favourite rose oil, lit two candles and slid into the fragrant water.

CHAPTER SIXTEEN

StoryWorld TV station, London Bridge

Martine knows. She caught me on my way into the station and she looked tired and miserable.

'You need to get Simon to watch the show from the gallery and do the morning meeting. You're needed off-site at a breakfast meeting with Julius and Jonny Hammond.'

'OK, where is this meeting?'

'At Soho House; you'd better get a taxi – Julius wants you there asap.'

We looked at each other for a long moment and she shook her head sadly.

'Has Fizzy spoken to you?' I asked.

'Yes. She called me on Sunday. She's devastated and my bank holiday was ruined. I'd planned to take Milo for a long walk in the country. Instead I've been holed up at Julius's place the whole time going through bloody contract clauses and typing papers for the board!'

I had expected her to take the news about Fizzy hard but it was the first time I had ever heard Martine complain about Julius.

'That Lori Kerwell was there too, throwing her weight around. She expected me to make her a coffee but I didn't budge,' she said.

I took a taxi to Soho House thinking that Lori had alienated Martine as well as me and that wasn't a wise move.

We reached the club and I was shown into a private room upstairs. Julius was already sitting in there. It's the club where Jonny Hammond hangs out so we were meeting on his territory.

'I'll do the talking. You're here to be the friendly face of StoryWorld,' Julius said.

'Is Fizzy coming?'

'No. And it's better that she isn't here.'

I sat down next to Julius at a table with a tall salt and pepper mill and a menu stuck between them. It was hot and stuffy in there and the thought of eating anything did not appeal at all. I was feeling nervous and slightly sick.

'Can we open a window?' I asked.

Julius stood up and pushed the sash window as far as the locks would allow. No breeze stirred the curtains. The door opened and Jonny Hammond came in. He's an old Etonian, the sort of man who would say 'Were you at school?' and that could only mean 'Were you at Eton?' No other school mattered. Julius, the grammar school boy, despised him. Jonny was wearing a sharp black suit and pale grey suede brogues. He is known for his impeccable manners, his drawling voice and his killer instinct when it comes to securing deals.

'You've met Liz before, I think,' Julius said.

'Indeed, hello, Liz.'

We shook hands.

'They do good smoked salmon and scrambled egg here if you're minded?' he said.

'Nothing for me to eat, thanks,' I said.

'Julius?'

'Coffee and water would be good.'

Jonny placed the order and sat down opposite us.

'I have an unhappy client,' he said.

'Then we need to address her key issues and make her feel better about this change. It in no way reflects any less esteem from us for Fizzy and her many talents. It is driven by commercial need alone,' Julius said.

'You are fixed on making Ledley her co-host?'

'We are.'

'No room for negotiation?'

'None,' Julius said.

The coffee arrived, a cafetière for six, jugs of hot and cold milk and sparkling water. We waited while the waiter moved everything from his tray to the table and exited the room. None of us spoke while we did the business of pouring the coffee and adding the milk. Jonny Hammond drank his coffee black and he let the silence build. I filled a glass with water and gulped it. I looked down at Jonny's shoes. They looked expensive; they looked handmade. I was glad that I was not required to take part in this duel between the two men.

'Fizzy is concerned how this will play with the media. If she is to agree to stay with StoryWorld she and I will want to draft the wording of any press statement,' Jonny Hammond said at last.

'Of course.'

'She requires that she sit on the left-hand side of the sofa,' he continued.

Julius looked over at me and I gave a tiny nod. I understood Fizzy's demand. The left-hand side of the sofa is seen as the power side. In most dual set-ups in TV news and features it is the male presenter who gets the prestigious left-hand spot. There had been a row about this very issue six months before when an inexperienced male presenter had joined an established female presenter on the BBC. He had automatically been given the left-hand spot and this has generated charges of sexism.

'Agreed,' Julius said.

'She also requires that all interviews of the day be conducted by her,' Jonny said.

This was more difficult. Ledley would be sidelined if Fizzy got to do all the big interviews and it would make the show look one-sided too.

'Liz, what is your view on that?' Julius asked.

He had said I was not to say anything so the only reason he could have been asking me this now was because he wanted me to argue against this demand. I put my glass down on the table.

'While this would not be a problem in the majority of cases and we would be happy for Fizzy to interview our major guests, there will arise situations where Ledley would be the more appropriate interviewer,' I said, knowing I sounded verbose.

'Such as?' Jonny queried.

'Such as a top chef, for instance. Ledley would be better equipped to ask questions in that area and we would like to retain the freedom for him to do that,' I said.

Jonny Hammond moved his eyes from my face to Julius's and his drawl got slower. He has what people describe as a cut-glass accent and he oozes effortless public school boy poise.

'Julius, your argument is that Ledley is there in order to generate male product advertising. He does not have the presenting and interviewing track record of Fizzy, or anything like her profile. He is therefore there in a supporting role.

We would be fine with him interviewing a top chef but Fizzy gets to do the big interviews.'

'Don't push it, we're the programme makers,' Julius said.

'We see this as a key point to agree and we would like to use the words "supporting role" in the press release,' Jonny said.

Julius agreed to this wording. We had little choice. But Jonny Hammond was not finished. For the first time in the meeting he consulted a small Moleskine notebook, flicking it open and reading a page of tiny writing.

'If you agree the above, Fizzy is prepared to return this Thursday the first of September, as always envisaged. She would like the opening item to be an interview with the photographer who took the portrait shot of her and Zachary and she will allow StoryWorld to use this shot in subsequent publicity.'

Jonny addressed me.

'I believe you were consulted on this item, Liz?'

'Yes, I was. And that's fine.'

Fizzy had not managed to secure the royal photographer but she had commissioned a celebrity photographer to do the shot and he would make a perfectly reasonable guest for her first day back. Jonny Hammond returned to his notebook.

'The next item is Guy Browne's weekly fashion slot and Fizzy will conduct this interview.'

Fizzy was getting him to tie our hands. It is usual for presenters to alternate interviews. However, I knew that Fizzy would want to hang on to the fashion slot. I would have to think of a short item to sandwich before it which Ledley could do. I hoped Jonny Hammond wasn't going to go over our entire running order, stipulating which slots Fizzy would do. As Julius had said, we were the programme makers and that would be a concession too far.

Julius and I shared a taxi back to the TV station.

'That shit Hammond. He's obsessed with wealth and celebrity and power but what does his job really entail? He does contracts. That's his only output,' Julius said.

He stared moodily out of the window. There's a saying, 'If you spot it you've got it', and I wondered if the reason Julius hated Jonny Hammond was because both men were chasing the same things. Julius likes power and hates having it taken away from him and Jonny Hammond had got the better of the encounter. Our taxi got too close to a cyclist who wobbled on his wheels. At the next red light the cyclist drew up, banged on the window and shouted abuse at our driver. Julius and I exchanged glances.

'Nothing would induce me to be a cyclist in London,' I said.

Guy Browne came to mind. He goes everywhere on his racing bike. We were drawing up outside the station when Julius spoke again.

'I need to put a statement out to staff by the end of today; same time as the press release. Can you draft it for me? You'll have to clear it with that shit Hammond.'

'I'll get on to it at once. Shall I use that "supporting role" phrase he insisted on?'

'Yes,' Julius growled.

I was holed up in my room drafting the press release and the statement to staff for the rest of the day. I worked hard to get the wording right but predictably this had to go through multiple drafts from Jonny Hammond and Fizzy poring over every single word and nuance. Julius had finally conceded that we would have to announce the change on Wednesday morning. This was giving staff like Ellen in make-up, Henry the floor manager and the technical crew only twenty-four hours to prepare for the change in camera settings and lighting that having two presenters on the sofa would entail. It was late afternoon by the time Simon finally got into my office and briefed me on what else had been going on.

'Ledley's gone all Hollywood on us,' he declared.

'What do you mean?' I asked with a guilty start. Could news of Ledley's promotion have got out?

'He's had his teeth done, the full orthodontist works. God, he must have spent the whole bank holiday in the dentist's chair. You should see him, Liz. When he smiles the light pings off his teeth and ricochets around the room!'

I smiled for the first time that day.

'That sounds well over the top. Personally, I find the American celebrity smile off-putting. Give me crooked English teeth any day,' I said.

'And Molly and Harriet had a tiff this morning.'

'What was it about this time?'

Simon rolled his eyes. 'That hoary old chestnut editorial integrity; Harriet was sent a discount voucher by a company who want Guy Browne to mention them and Molly said she should return it as it compromised the slot.'

'Was it worth a lot?'

'A twenty per cent discount which all the press get. It goes deeper than that with those two. They're chalk and cheese. They'll argue over anything,' Simon said.

Harriet and Molly would never be close friends but I needed them to rub along. In such a small team any kind of rift can fester and make the atmosphere at work unpleasant. It was another issue that would need addressing but it would have to wait. At the moment all my energies were focused on how we were going to get Fizzy on to the sofa with the appearance, if not the reality, of a good partnership between her and her new co-host. I would need a session with Ledley tomorrow, once the statement had gone out, and then I'd have to call Gerry, Betty and Guy to make sure they were in the know before the news hit the media. Simon was still hovering and I wondered if he sensed that something was up. He is good at reading my moods and seems to know when something is worrying me.

'We need to work as a team, now more than ever. Let me know if you think I need to get them in here and have a clearing-the-air conversation, though I'd rather we parked it till next week,' I said.

After Simon had left I tidied my desk and shut down my PC. Damn Lori Kerwell. Her intervention was causing so much conflict. Julius was irritable, Martine was shaken, I could see a lot more work ahead for me, and as for Fizzy... well, she was an unknown factor.

I looked at my team sitting outside. Molly wasn't there and Simon, Harriet and Ziggy were in a huddle discussing something intently and Ziggy looked tense and unhappy. I watched the three of them as Harriet leaned in to her and said something and Simon reached over and patted her hand several times. He's a kind man and is cute-looking in a Harry Potterish way. Ziggy continued to look stricken and I wondered what was up.

Chalk Farm flat, 7.30 p.m.

As soon as she heard my key in the lock a beaming Flo with brown hair opened the door to me.

'What do you think, Mum?'

She spread her arms wide, did a twirl and swished her hair back and forth. Her hair looked lovely.

'Oh yes, it looks great.'

'Mark is brilliant. I'll *never* go to a cheap salon again,' she said with another swish of her head.

'I'm glad to hear that.'

I checked my mail. Ron Osborne has had a week to respond and yet again he has ignored me. Sod him! Anger galvanised me and I sat at the kitchen table and made my claim. There was a form on the Small Claims website where you had to explain the dispute. I typed that he'd had my thousand pounds deposit since February and no work had been undertaken. You can ask for interest to be applied but I wrote that I didn't want any interest, just my deposit back so I could pay someone else to do the job.

Douglas called me around nine and asked if I was free to go out on Thursday. He suggested a drink at his flat and supper around the corner at a small French bistro he liked. This will be our third date and they have always been on a Thursday evening, which is his day off from presenting the bulletin. He doesn't seem to be free at the weekends and I wondered why that was. Perhaps the weekend was when he spent time with his son. I felt a tremor when he suggested we meet at his flat in Camden Town. What did that mean? And should I get Flo to do a sleepover that night?

I called Fenton and updated her.

'Is it acceptable to sleep with a new man on the third date?'

'I slept with Bill on our fourth date and it was something of a fumble and a let-down,' she laughed.

'Don't! I'm nervous even thinking about it. It's been a while and I don't know if I feel confident enough to undress in front of Mr Sexy News.'

'It got better with Bill, much better. Try to be light-hearted about it. First shags are nearly always a let-down,' Fenton said.

'I've been asking myself why I'm so nervous. I think it's because deep down I want this to become a relationship too much. You can only be light-hearted when you don't care. I approached sex with Todd light-heartedly, didn't I? But I never expected Todd and me to be a big relationship. I wish I didn't want this. When I want something too much I nearly always mess it up.'

There, I had told Fenton what I really felt. Underneath my nervousness was a dread of rejection. I felt that Douglas Pitlochry was too well known, too much the media figure to be really interested in me. Ben and I split up eight years ago and although I've had dalliances since then I haven't had a partner. Part of me feels safe in my single status because it means I am in control of things. Another part of me has such a strong yearning to reach out and connect.

As I lay in bed I thought about how Flo will have to negotiate all this dating stuff soon enough and what a cyclone of emotions it can stir up. She talks about boys a lot with her friends. I've heard her mention an Ethan a couple of times. There's this all-boys school in Highgate and after school Flo and her gang often go up to Highgate and sit on the green there in the hope of talking to the boys. I had done the same thing at her age but we had hung out in a skate park. It doesn't get easier. Dating is as much a minefield in your forties as it is in your teens.

CHAPTER SEVENTEEN

StoryWorld TV station, London Bridge

Straight after the morning meeting, Julius summoned me to his office. He was standing at his window looking out at the river and I went over to his side. Great white clouds were rolling across the sky and we watched the traffic moving through the water, the barges and the river buses, a calming view, but he was tense.

'We're putting the press release out at noon. We've agreed there'll be no comment from Fizzy or Ledley.'

'I'm surprised Fizzy doesn't want to say anything,' I said.

'I spoke to her last night. She's still furious and said under no circumstances would she talk to the press. She said they always twist what you say and they'll try to paint her as a victim. She insisted Ledley stay shtum too. She almost spat out Ledley's name.'

'That bodes well for tomorrow,' I said.

'She'd better not flounce on set,' he said.

'She's too professional to do that but off-air it's going to be tough to manage.'

He didn't reply. I looked at his profile as he continued to watch the boats moving up and down the river. He is handsome in a bland way with his straight nose and full lips, a clean-cut face which can change from pleasant to menacing in an instant. I was sure that, like me, he had serious reservations about tampering with the presentation which had worked so well for years. He might have moulded Fizzy into a star but he was finding it hard to control her now. And he had never liked Ledley.

'Won't it look odd if we make no comment; as if we're hiding something?'

'If they want a comment you'll have to give one,' he said.

'How do you want me to play it?'

'Treat the whole thing with the minimum of fuss, as if it's a total non-event.'

'I'll say we're delighted to have Fizzy back, the star of our show, and Ledley is there to support her.'

The rest of the morning was a round of meetings and phone calls with my presenters to brief them on the change. Betty had been in to do her advice slot – she was relaxed about the new approach, saying that Ledley was a peach to work with and she was glad he was getting the recognition he deserved. It was Gerry who reacted most strongly when I called him up.

'That's tough on Fizzy.'

'It is.'

'But I take it that we all have to be happy-clappy and pretend that it's no big deal,' he said.

'You got it in one, and we need to help her through it so she doesn't feel she's lost face.'

'Poor love. So Ledley is well and truly on the up?'

'He is, but I wouldn't want to be in his shoes tomorrow,' I said.

'Nor I; Fizzy is a Leo and they hate to share the spotlight. But I'm not surprised. He's got close to Lori Kerwell, hasn't he? I keep seeing them together. Is she behind this change?'

I hesitated before replying. My habit of being the discreet

producer had kicked in but how could it harm to tell Gerry that Lori was the instigator?

'She says Ledley can help us get more advertising for male products,' I said.

'That woman is a force of nature and I wouldn't want to stand in her way!' Gerry said.

Once the media had got hold of the story they were on to me all afternoon and there were a lot of complaints that they couldn't get access to Fizzy for a comment. I repeated, many times, the mantra that Ledley was joining her in a supporting role. One woman journalist, Lou Gibson, who wrote for a popular online news site, was especially persistent. I had encountered Lou before. She is highly opinionated and likes to create controversy. Her copy is hyperbolic and always comes with shouty headlines.

'We'd like to hear from Fizzy directly. I mean, it looks to us like she's being punished for having a baby,' Lou said.

This was the angle I had been most worried about.

'Nothing could be further from the truth. Fizzy is the star of our show and we're so happy she'll be back on our sofa tomorrow.'

I hoped I had deflected Lou but after I'd put the phone down on her I thought I'd better warn Ledley. Lou had pitched up at the station on more than one occasion and doorstepped our presenters. I did not want Ledley being ambushed and talking out of turn. He was still at the stage in his career where he liked to please journalists and wanted to be their friend. I went down to his dressing room. He had been allocated the second largest dressing room which we used to reserve for our A-list guests. The maintenance department had already put up his name on the door. I tapped and turned the handle. Lori was sitting on Ledley's sofa and he was standing by his full-length mirror. He turned as I came in.

'Liz, great to see you. Lori and I are having tea. Would you like a cup? It's rooibos and very refreshing.'

He flashed me a smile and I saw what Simon meant about his teeth.

'No, thanks. I wanted a quick word about dealing with the press, but I can pop by later,' I said, starting to back out of the room as fast as I could.

Seeing Lori sitting there had thrown me. The two of them looked comfortable together. Of course, Lori was Ledley's patron now and she would be a welcome visitor to his room.

'Oh no, do stay and share. I've had several calls but I let them all go to answer machine as instructed,' he said.

I was reluctant to talk in front of Lori but had no choice. I perched on a chair. Ledley sat down next to her. She had taken her jacket off and moved it for him while barely acknowledging me.

'We want to keep it low-key until the new format settles down. But there's this journalist, Lou Gibson, and she's taking a line we don't want to go anywhere near,' I said.

'What line?'

'Kind of feminist outraged and implying that the station is punishing Fizzy for going off and having a baby—'

'That's nonsense,' Lori said.

'We know it's nonsense but she is extremely persistent. If she gets in touch with you, Ledley, please be careful not to be drawn in,' I said.

'I won't say a word. Thanks for the alert. You know I want this to work, very much.'

'I know you do. We all do,' I said, and left them to their tea. I didn't feel any of us had expressed our true feelings for a minute. I could not tell if Ledley was embarrassed or combative or triumphant about his new role. I had an all too familiar sensation that my job meant feeling my way through a maze of different desires and agendas. As I walked through the atrium I saw Henry and he came over to me, looking down at me with his kind, serious face.

'You OK with all this, Liz?'

The technical team had been briefed earlier by Julius. I gave a weary shrug.

'I've spent the day fending off the media, trying to convince them it's a non-story.'

'Fancy a fag break?'

'Oh, go on then.'

I followed him to our usual spot outside at the rear of the studio. He lit one cigarette and handed it to me and then lit a second for himself. It reminded me of a famous scene in a Bette Davis film when the man who is falling in love with her lights two cigarettes for them.

'What's the name of that film, you know, the one with Bette Davis where the man lights her cig? I can see the scene but I can't remember.'

'*Now, Voyager*,' he said.

'That's it. Oh you're good.'

'It was my mum's favourite film.'

We smoked in silence and I looked at the sky. The clouds over the river had darkened to a smoky purple.

'Is Fizzy OK with it?' he said at last.

'No. She's furious.'

'Seems a mistake to me. If it ain't broke why fix it?'

'I'm with you there but it has been decreed from on high.'

I was surprised at how bitter I sounded. Was I taking this so badly because the idea had come from Lori?

'Who gets to do the big interviews?'

'Fizzy gets them,' I said.

I dragged on my cigarette and it calmed my head. Henry looked at me sympathetically.

'It's going to be more work for you, isn't it?'

I nodded. Henry threw his cigarette down and ground it under his heel, then picked up the tip and put it in the bucket of sand by the studio door.

'We'll make it work. And come to me if there's anything I can do to help,' he said.

Henry is a cool head in a crisis and I found his offer of help comforting. I went upstairs and Simon followed me into my office.

'Ziggy's got a big problem,' he said.

I hadn't expected that.

'What is it?'

'Her shit landlord says she has to leave her flat and he's given her a month to get out.'

'A month? Can he do that?'

'It seems he can. It's a basic bedsitter in Camberwell but it's been her home since she left care and she doesn't know where she can go.'

'Poor kid. She's got no family to turn to,' I said.

'We're her family now. Harry and I are looking for a place for her but rents are ridiculous and they all want a big deposit. Harry said she'd do the deposit and Ziggy can pay her back

155

slowly. I thought you should know because Zigg is finding it hard to concentrate on anything at the moment.'

I felt a huge rush of affection for Simon and Harriet for stepping in like this, and a feeling of pride that my team were pulling together. Ziggy had been looking pinched and anxious recently and I hadn't thought to ask her what was wrong.

'I think it's brilliant what you and Harriet are doing. You must let me make a contribution.'

Simon took off his round glasses and polished them, which he does when he's feeling shy or embarrassed.

'It's going to be hard enough to get Ziggy to accept Harry's help. She's proud and feels she should be able to sort this out for herself. And she won't cry, you know, even though she's terribly stressed. She feels she should tough it out,' he said.

'She's a brave girl. She's had more to cry about than any of us. Keep me posted and I'm glad you told me.'

This conversation reminded me that I need to secure a permanent post for Ziggy by the end of the year. There is no way I am going to let Ziggy leave StoryWorld and go back on the job market. The cards were stacked against her at birth and we are her safe harbour. I shut down my PC and checked myself in the mirror before locking my office.

I was crossing the forecourt outside our building when Lou Gibson loomed up in front of me. She was wearing a black raincoat which was flapping in the wind and I spotted the small tape recorder around her neck with its light on.

'A quick word, Liz, if you don't mind?' she said.

I stopped walking. Had she been waiting for me or for Ledley? I was glad I had warned him about her.

'Lou, we've spoken already.'

'I had another question.'

I sighed and crossed my arms. I wanted to get home to Flo. 'Which is?'

'How much notice did Fizzy have about this change? We've heard it was sprung on her less than a week ago.'

How could she know that? She had to be bluffing.

'That's nonsense. Excuse me, I need to get home.'

I tried to walk past her.

'But aren't you offended as a woman working in TV that Fizzy has been demoted in this way? I mean, yours was one of the few shows that gave centre stage to a woman. I would think you would condemn this demotion,' she said.

She was trying to appeal to the feminist in me. I knew I sounded like a cracked record as I reverted to my script.

'Like I said to you earlier, this is not a demotion. Ledley is in a supporting role. I am delighted, as we all are, that Fizzy, our star, is back tomorrow.'

'You're a single-parent mum, aren't you? Must be tough for you and that must be why you feel sympathetic to Fizzy's plight,' she said.

This stopped me in my tracks. I like to keep my family life private. How did she know I was on my own? Several responses leapt to my lips but all of them would have given Lou more information to build her story on.

'There's nothing more to say and I really do have a home to get to.'

I hurried away from her, fighting hard the urge to jog. It looked as if she was planning to accompany me to the Tube and press me with more questions. I put my head down and she peeled off after a minute.

I plunged down into the station. The platform was crowded and I pushed to get onto a northbound train to Chalk Farm.

I held on to a roof strap as we rattled through the dark tunnels. A man who reeked of garlic was standing too close to me. I wanted to move away from him but there was no space to inch into. I turned my head away from his breath. Lou's questions had shaken me. I hated her reference to my personal situation and it made me wonder how celebrities like Fizzy ever got used to the media crawling over every aspect of their lives. Lou appeared to know two things. The first was that Fizzy had been given very little notice about the change. The second was that I was against the change and was Fizzy's champion at the station. Was this her intuition at work or did she have some inside information, and if she had inside information who could be her source? Garlic man finally got off and I could breathe more freely again. He was replaced by a tall youth with earphones whose thumping music I could hear. I didn't think Lou's source could be Ledley because a story about Fizzy's anger and upset would put the spotlight firmly on her and make him the bad guy. It could have been one of the journalists at the station talking out of turn. Everyone had been gossiping about it since the news broke. Molly's face flashed into my mind. Molly is a feminist and she knows Lou Gibson. No, Molly is as loyal as they come. My hunch was it was either idle talk overheard, or guesswork on Lou's part.

Chalk Farm flat, 7.40 p.m.

Janis had cooked pasta for Flo. There was some left and I wondered if I should settle for that. Could I be bothered to cook anything for myself? But cooking decompresses me after a stressful day at work, cooking is my therapy. I opened the fridge and peered in. I had cheese and some lovely fat spring onions. There were six eggs on the counter. I'd make a cheese and onion frittata.

Flo joined me as I was beating the eggs.

'Good day, sweetheart?'

'OK. Harriet WhatsApped me. They want to fix a date for the fashion shoot next week.'

'You're back at school next week.'

'They're suggesting Sunday.'

'That's OK then.'

'But I *must* have some new underwear, Mum. In case I have to undress in front of the other girls. I hope I won't have to, I hope there'll be separate changing rooms.'

She looked anxious. Fifteen-year-old girls are so self-conscious about their bodies, seeing only flaws where I see beauty. I agreed we would buy her some new underwear at the weekend.

'Can we go to Selfridges?'

'I was thinking Primark,' I said.

'Please, Mum.'

'What's wrong with Primark?'

'In case the other girls see it.'

I put my whisk down and turned to face her.

'Give me a hug. I've had a hell of a day.'

She hugged me and sat at the table while I grated cheese and made a salad.

'There was this awful pushy journalist who kind of ambushed me as I was leaving work.'

'Why did she do that?'

I explained the whole Fizzy and Ledley problem and realised I hadn't told Flo much about what was going on at work and that I should probably share it more with her.

'Poor Mum. Sounds awful. Can I make the dressing?'

'Yes, please.'

I got out the mustard, oil and vinegar and she measured each ingredient carefully into our dressing jar and shook the mixture.

'I like your dressing,' I said.

CHAPTER EIGHTEEN

We were about to go live on Day One of the Fizzy and Ledley show and there was palpable tension in the air. I had checked in on Fizzy earlier. She had come in extra early to get Ellen to do her hair and make-up. Then I had gone to Ledley's dressing room to wish him luck. He seemed nervous. The lighting had been changed to accommodate two presenters and I noticed the posy of cream and yellow roses in a vase on the table in front of the sofa. We had dispensed with daily fresh flowers while Fizzy was away but it was something she was keen on and I was pleased that Henry had remembered to organise that for her today.

'End of an era,' the director said as the countdown clock started and he switched through to the opening titles. We came out into a wide two-shot of Fizzy and Ledley both beaming into the camera. Fizzy was sitting on the left-hand side of the sofa, the power position. She looked fantastic and her demeanour was relentlessly upbeat.

'Good morning, Britain. It's brilliant to be back and I must start by thanking you wonderful viewers for all the toys and clothes you sent me for my little Zachary. Oh, Ledley, you wouldn't believe how kind and generous our viewers are.'

'We have the best viewers,' he agreed, smiling widely.

'We do; the very best. And to thank you all I want to share a rather special picture which I had taken of me and Zac by one of Europe's top photographers, Marco Torti, and he's with me now.'

Fizzy turned to Marco Torti who was sitting on her right. He was an attractive forty-something Italian snapper who was the darling of the celebrity crowd and who spoke with a charming misuse of English.

'I am honoured indeed that you agreed to do this mother and baby shot of us, Marco, as I know you don't usually do this kind of thing,' Fizzy said.

'It was my happy pleasure,' Marco said as the director flashed up the image of Fizzy with Zachary on her lap. He was leaning his head back against his mum and it was a beautiful and tender photograph. They were sitting in some kind of greenhouse with a feathery fern in the background and the light was soft. We held the image up on the screen for thirty seconds, which is long in TV time, as Marco talked about the shot and how the image of the mother and baby was iconic in his country. Eventually, the director faded back to a two-shot of Fizzy and Marco who then embarked on a lively discussion about his many other celebrity subjects. We flashed up images of these too. I had given this item longer than usual because it was the welcoming Fizzy back item. Ledley played no role in it at all.

After the ad break we ran an item which Ledley presented on the growth of artisan bakeries and how there was a turn away from the giant supermarket chains. Shoppers were favouring small independent shops, Ledley said. He did the item well and involved Fizzy by offering her the platter of different breads we had prepared as his prop. He asked her if she preferred sourdough or focaccia and did she want to sample them? Fizzy played along and you would have thought she was delighted to have him there, sitting next to her, and that they were the best of friends. What a consummate actor she is, I thought.

The next item was Guy Browne's fashion slot. Fizzy ignored Henry's countdown after six minutes and the item overran by a full two minutes. Guy was talking to her about the current fad for vintage clothes.

'My advice is to look in your granny's attic because crushed velvet, tea dresses, floral prints, beads and brooches are the look to put together.'

I thought of how Flo had chosen that brooch from Grace and how my daughter was more in tune with fashion trends than I was.

'You have to have a good eye to pull it off. Mix it up but don't overload it and maybe pair the dresses with biker boots to make it contemporary,' he said.

Fizzy recalled, at length, the joy of going through her granny's dressing-up box when she was a little girl. I wondered if she was making this up. She had spoken of her granny as a fearsome Baptist. Would she have had a dressing-up box? But Fizzy often made things up and their discussion was animated and entertaining. The director was irritated at the overrun.

'Please wind it up, Fizzy,' he said twice before she brought the item to a close. There had been no opportunity for Ledley to insert himself into this discussion for the whole eight minutes.

'I'm putting this down to first day back nerves,' he said to me off mic so that Fizzy could not hear.

I was relieved when the end credits rolled. Viewers may not have noticed but some items had run too long for comfort and Ledley's items had all been squeezed.

The atmosphere in the morning meeting was sub-arctic

as Julius welcomed Fizzy back and complimented the two presenters on their performance that morning.

'We have some tweaks to make but it was a good start,' he said.

I wondered if that was what he really thought. Fizzy had sat down between Julius and me. Ledley sat opposite with Lori on his right and Bob was next to Lori. The battle lines had been drawn. The director was there too and he delivered his report. All was fine from a technical point of view. I reported that we had had a Twitter surge welcoming Fizzy back.

'And our viewers loved the portrait of you and Zachary. It is a gorgeous shot,' I said.

'Thank you, Liz. I've had photo-cards made which we can send out,' she said.

She did not look at Ledley once and was giving Lori her death stare. Julius, who usually manages by the sheer force of his personality to corral us all into discussing the show, seemed at a loss. He kept the meeting short and asked Lori, Bob and me to join him in his office afterwards.

We sat in a semicircle around his table as Martine brought in a large pot of coffee. The atmosphere was tense as Martine laid out the cups. She flashed a sympathetic glance at me. She would have watched the show and noted how much Fizzy had dominated it. It had not come anywhere near a double act and the expression on Julius's face said it all. We had a problem on our hands.

'We couldn't talk frankly with Fizzy and Ledley present. It's too new and too raw for her. I want to know how the three of you think it went this morning, honestly,' Julius said.

I stirred a little sugar into my coffee. I wasn't going to be the first one to speak. This had been Lori's big idea. Let's see how she assessed it. She was wearing another of her boxy suits and today it was a nasty royal blue. The ever-present brooch glittered on her lapel. She addressed her remarks to Julius.

'Ledley was given hardly anything to do. They are supposed to be co-hosts and for this to work it needs to be a partnership,' she said.

This was true but we had had no choice in the matter. I waited for Julius to explain that the allocation of items had been a contractual obligation but he maintained a charged silence and looked at me to say something.

'Our hands were tied by Fizzy's agent. He pretty well stipulated the running order for today,' I said.

'Do presenters really have that much power? I mean, the station pays the wages and surely has a right to make changes?' she said.

'I'm not interested in talking about contractual issues. We need to discuss this in programming terms,' Julius snapped.

Julius is a brilliant programme maker, he had seen how the show had not worked and it had angered him. In my role as head of features he would expect me to make it come right. I felt a wave of weariness and foreboding wash over me.

'It's going to be difficult. We've agreed Fizzy will do the big interviews so she will inevitably be seen as the senior presenter. We'll need to develop a distinctive role for Ledley, make certain areas his own. Food, of course, but also Betty has gelled with him. We could give him that to do. We need to bring his humour out too; he used to be funny on his cooking slot,' I said.

Ledley's weekly cooking slot had always been an opportunity for him and Fizzy to have a good laugh together. She would tease him about his unhealthy ingredients and he would get her to sample his dishes. There had been no humour on the show this morning. Lori looked less than satisfied at my response and I felt like saying to her 'You fix it then, shark-eyes!'

'We've all got to *want* to make it work,' she said.

I was furious at that. One thing that Julius and I share is the desire to put on a good show at all costs. I sometimes think that I put my drive to do that above my need to be a good mum to Flo. How dare she imply that we, or I, would try to sabotage the programme.

'That's a given,' I said, glaring at her. 'This is a major change and will take some adjusting to. The item with Marco Torti was a great opener and our viewers liked it.'

'The fashion item went on and on,' Lori said.

'Make sure she doesn't make a habit of overrunning, Liz,' Julius said.

He poured more black coffee into his cup and swirled it around before swallowing it with a slight grimace. He had been looking at Lori and me with a sour expression on his face. His comment about not tolerating a bitch-fest came to mind and I hated the fact that the two men were watching Lori and me trying to take lumps out of each other. I couldn't fathom his attitude to Lori. He was being careful around her. He couldn't like the fact that she was close to Saul Relph and I wondered if he too felt her to be a threat to his position, the sales tail wagging the programming dog.

'Bob, you're here because I want to know what you made of it,' Julius asked.

Bob looked more cheerful than usual and he had had his hair cut. I wondered what he had to feel chipper about. Was he glad that Fizzy was back? He had been obsessed with her last autumn, could hardly drag his eyes away from her, but their affair was over.

'I agree with Lori that Ledley looked like a spare part this morning. It was awkward. I guess it will get easier as they both adjust to the new set-up.'

It was predictable that Bob would support Lori. My sense of foreboding deepened. If this failed as a double act and we lost ratings it would be me, not Lori, who would get the blame because I am the one who produces the items.

'We're going to have to keep a careful eye on it and track ratings and viewer comments,' Julius said.

'I'm on it,' Lori said.

I bet you are, I thought. We trooped out of his room and I was heading for my office when Martine called me back. I stood at her desk, noting the new framed photograph of her beloved Jack Russell Milo sitting in pride of place. She was watching Lori and Bob walk down the stairs together.

'They're thick as thieves,' she said.

'They are.'

Martine must have picked up my despondent tone and she gave me a penetrating look.

'Is she making life difficult for you?'

Usually I put a brave face on things but I felt tired of always having to conceal my true feelings at work.

'Yes, she is.'

'She's an operator and she's got Saul Relph eating out of her hand.'

'I know, and that's a big problem,' I said.

Martine is astute and keeps a close eye on what is going on at the station. She could see that a shift in the power balance was happening. Lori was in the ascendant because she had won the argument about Ledley and I had lost power.

'I'm glad Fizzy's got you on her side. She said could you pop down and see her?' Martine said.

Fizzy was seated at her dressing table. She had changed out of her studio clothes into jeans and a soft grey jumper. She stood up and brushed her hair vigorously.

'Where does Lori Kerwell get her hideous suits from?' she said.

I shrugged, feeling too disconsolate even to join in the abuse of Lori's taste.

'I know what you're going to say,' she said.

'What am I going to say?'

'That I overran on the two main items.'

'Well, yes, you did, but—'

'That prick Ledley needs to know that he's the junior partner,' she said.

I pulled up a chair. Fizzy sat down again, reapplied some pink lipstick and blotted her lips on a piece of tissue. She looked every inch the TV star in relaxed mode.

'He *is* the junior partner but the show comes first,' I said firmly.

'Of course. Now, Liz, I've got to leave in a minute but I need your advice. Bob's seen Zac the once and he's *determined* to have more contact.'

'What did he say?'

'That he's willing to pay towards Zac's upkeep and he wants to see him from time to time.'

'But not to play an active role in his life, surely? I mean, Pat could find out.'

I had met Bob's wife Pat once at a StoryWorld Christmas do. They had got together in Burnley when she was seventeen years old. She worked in the health service and wasn't part of the TV scene at all. In fact, she was the antithesis of TV people. She had struck me as a strong woman and someone you should not underestimate.

'He knows it's a huge risk but he said he's desperate not to be shut out of Zac's life altogether.'

I wondered if Fizzy was exaggerating. Would Bob say he was desperate?

'It's a very difficult situation,' I said.

'I have no idea what to do about it.'

She was fiddling with her bracelet which was gold and delicate. Again, I held back from offering any answers.

'What are your options?'

'God, I don't know! I can tell him to get lost. That it would be easier all round if he stays out of Zac's life for good. Or I can let him have limited access on my terms.'

'Do you have any preference?'

'I had it in my head that I would do this by myself. But it's lonely, isn't it, not being able to share the responsibility of your baby with anyone else?' Her voice had taken on a plaintive note.

She had had three months of lone parenthood and was already finding it a burden. I felt for her but could see nothing but trouble and heartache ahead. Bob had so much to lose. His urge to see his son must be strong indeed.

'OK. Let's try to think this through. What's the worst-case scenario?' I said.

'That he sees Zac regularly and it gets out that he's the father. The tabloids would have a field day and I can't afford any negative publicity at the moment. That prick Ledley would love that to get out, wouldn't he?'

She crossed her arms and looked at her reflection. She had

frowned at the mention of Ledley's name. She smoothed her eyebrows with a brow comb and I felt a tremor watching her, remembering that Ledley had voiced his suspicions about Bob. The new ambitious Ledley was not above using this to his advantage and I felt Fizzy was walking on thin ice. Should I alert her to Ledley's suspicions?

'You need to be careful. Don't give him any ammunition,' I said.

'I know. If we do meet it will have to be in a safe house,' she said.

Fizzy loves to dramatise things and the notion of a safe house made me think of spies and John le Carré novels, which I read avidly. I wanted to ask her where the safe house was, whose place it was, but Fizzy had wanted my flat to be a safe house for her and those two words hung in the air between us. I didn't enquire further.

I went upstairs and called my team together and Ziggy joined us. I was veering between lowness about the show and excitement about my date with Douglas tonight. I asked them what they thought about the programme. Molly was the first to speak and the most blunt, as she usually is.

'I much preferred it when Fizzy was solo. I mean, what's with this always having to be a male–female pairing? It's so conventional,' she said.

'It could work because Ledley can be funny and good to watch, but he looked the junior one today, didn't he?' Harriet ventured.

'They were trying to look like they were the best of friends but if felt forced, and forced is not good. The show works when the presenters are being genuine, well, as genuine as TV presenters can be,' Simon said.

'What did you make of it, Ziggy?' I asked her gently. Ziggy is bright and comes at most subjects from a different angle from the rest of the team, but she is shy and rarely volunteers an opinion. She wasn't looking well and had dark circles under her eyes. When Ziggy is upset her face takes on a pinched look and becomes the face of a much older woman on her young body.

'I liked the item about the different breads,' she said.

'Good, we should build up Ledley's role around food. He's on strong ground there. Can we please think up interesting food stories and make this a regular feature,' I said.

'Is Fizzy going to interview *all* the celebrity guests?' It was Harriet.

'Most of them, and she'll do Guy and Gerry, but I thought Ledley could interview Betty. Would that work, Simon?'

Betty adored Simon and he always produced her item and shortlisted the letters she discussed on air. She had even invited him out to her house in Windsor for a Sunday lunch once.

'Yes, I think so. Betty gets on with Ledley, better than with Fizzy, actually. They could be prickly with each other sometimes,' he said.

It was true that there had been an occasional coolness between Fizzy and Betty. Betty was a middle-aged, comfortable and deeply conventional woman. After Fizzy had announced her pregnancy on air and said she would be bringing up her child as a lone parent, this coolness between them had grown. Betty thought children should be reared by two parents and she and I had crossed swords on this issue.

'We're going to have to find some really strong, hard-hitting issues for Betty to discuss with him. Ledley needs some items of real substance or he will look like a spare part,' I said.

We had to make it work but it was clear that my team shared my reservations about the new set-up. They left me and I went back to scrolling through our viewers' comments about that day's show.

Around five-thirty I started to get ready for my date with Douglas. He had asked me to get to his place as near to seven as I could. He wanted to show me his pod, he said, and he'd booked us a table for eight. Flo was staying over at Rosie's and I could stay at his if I wanted to. I had prepared for that by bringing a change of clothes into the office. And I was wearing my prettiest bra under my shirt. I wondered if tonight would be the night Douglas and I took things to the next level. As I freshened my make-up and squirted perfume on my hair I brought his face to mind. I was attracted to him, but I still hardly knew him. The thought of staying with him was both exciting and agitating. Molly burst into my room.

'Have you seen Lou Gibson's piece?' she said.

She looked alarmed.

'No, I haven't.'

'She's just posted it up. You need to read it. She mentions you.'

I was straight to my desk and googled the news site and there was her piece with the headline: *Sofa Wars at StoryWorld!* I speed-read the article and my stomach plummeted three floors. Lou had painted a picture of open hostilities at StoryWorld over the imposition of Ledley as Fizzy's co-host.

She had made much of Fizzy going off to have her baby, only to return to find her role seriously diminished. She said viewers were disgusted at this treatment of Fizzy Wentworth who was a much loved presenter and who had managed to present the show very successfully on her own for years. Lou laid on her feminist outrage with a trowel. But the killer bit came near the end:

> It is believed that head of features, Liz Lyon, who has herself come up against the macho and bullying culture at the TV station, is horrified at the change in presentation arrangements. One source said that Liz Lyon is working tirelessly behind the scenes to get Fizzy returned to the solo spot.

This appalled me and made me feel quite sick. Simon came into the room. He had seen the piece too and he looked as worried as Molly.

'She made it all up. I said nothing like that. How could she do that?'

Simon closed the door.

'Did she speak to you?'

'Yes. She called me here. She was insistent but I held the line. Last night she was waiting outside the building. That's when she tried to put words into my mouth, but I said nothing, nothing at all, only the line we'd agreed. She's invented all this.'

'She's written it carefully, she said "it is believed" rather than saying it's a direct quote from you,' Simon said.

I read the article again and I felt even more shaky. The article was like a rock hurled into a pool and its ripples would spread and spread.

'This will play badly with Julius and with Saul Relph. Very badly indeed. They'll think I'm stirring things up.'

'Go and speak to Julius now. Tell him what happened,' Simon said.

'I think you should call Lou Gibson and tell her she's lying and that you want an immediate retraction or you'll report her,' Molly said.

I looked from Molly to Simon, trying to get my thoughts in order. I was on the edge of panic.

'I need to speak to Julius.'

I got up and hurried to the door. Simon opened it for me and he patted my arm as I walked past him.

'It will be OK. Tell him what happened,' he said.

When I reached Martine's desk I saw his office was empty and when I tried his door it was locked. She was nowhere to be seen but had not gone for the day as her shopping bag was by her desk. I sat and waited for her, trying to control the fearful feelings that were building in me. I needed to speak to Julius before he saw the article. At last Martine walked back from the Ladies.

'Are you OK, Liz? You look pale.'

'I need to contact Julius at once. A bloody journalist has written a really inflammatory piece.'

'About Fizzy?'

'Yes.'

'You won't get him now. He's meeting a major sponsor and he told me no calls. You could try him after eight.'

'Damn. I won't be able to ring him then.'

'Leave a message?'

'I wanted to talk to him, to explain.'

We were closer these days and I could confide in her.

'Can I show it to you?'

I sat down next to her and tapped in the name of the site. She saw the headline and read the article.

'It's a complete fabrication. She accosted me outside the station but I did not say one word of that to her.'

'I hate journalists, they've got no morals at all,' Martine said.

She stood up and unlocked the door to his office.

'Call him in here.'

I dialled his mobile. Martine stayed in the room with me and closed the door. She knew this was serious as I stammered out to his answer machine what had happened.

Thursday evening, Camden Town

It was six-forty when I took the Tube to Camden Town. From the Tube I walked quickly to Douglas's flat, my heart still beating too fast from the stress. I was clutching my mobile in case Julius called me back but I would have to turn it off before I met Douglas. He couldn't overhear any conversation Julius and I might have. Douglas's block of flats overlooked the Grand Union Canal and were approached by a flight of steps at the side of the bridge. I went down the steps and checked my phone for one last time before I turned it off. I was late. I took a deep breath to steady myself and punched in the number of his flat on the electronic keypad. His voice, slightly distorted, came through the grille.

'Hi, Liz. Take the lift to the first floor.'

He met me at the lift.

'Sorry, I'm later than I intended.' I was breathless.

He led me into his flat.

'Welcome to my pod,' he said, spreading his arms wide. 'Do show me around.'

I tried to focus and sound normal. It was a three-bedroomed flat, two doubles and one single. One double room looked like it was his son's, judging by the sports equipment lying on the floor and the posters on the wall. The other double, the master bedroom, had a good view of the canal but it was strangely impersonal, as if he hadn't the time, or the inclination, to add his touches. He was using the single bedroom as his office and this was messy with books and papers piled on the desk and the floor. The flat had two bathrooms and there was a nice smell of his aftershave in one but otherwise these too felt impersonal, like hotel bathrooms. His kitchen was modern with state-of-the-art equipment. There was a shortage of utensils and I noticed a single recipe book, the *Delia Smith's Complete Cookery Course*, on the shelf. It was rather touching that he didn't have more stuff. It was the kitchen of a single man starting out again.

The sitting room was the nicest room and looked more lived in. It was a good size and had three large porthole windows looking out over the canal. The floor was black and white ceramic tiles. There was a red leather chesterfield with a footstool in front of it. A chaise longue upholstered in pale yellow taffeta was placed by the windows. Both pieces of furniture looked broken in and I guessed that they had come from the family home, as had the table lamps placed around the room, probably. I remembered the whole process of dividing our furniture, our music and our books when Ben and I split up, and how for a while our furniture, bought hopefully as a couple, felt tainted by the failure of the marriage. I wondered if Douglas felt that way. I stood at the middle window and looked out. On the other side of the canal stood a terrace of elegant townhouses with long windows and high ceilings and I thought that I would prefer to live in those more traditional spaces. Then I blushed. Why was I even thinking like that?

Douglas brought out a bottle of wine from the kitchen.

'White OK?'

'Lovely, thanks.'

I sat down on the chesterfield and he joined me there, placing a cushion at the base of his spine. He poured us each a glass of pale-straw coloured wine.

'I like the way you've put the red and yellow together,' I said.

'Me too, though I'm sure I'm breaking all interior design rules. These pieces used to be in different rooms, properly colour coordinated rooms,' he said, handing me a glass.

I recalled that his wife ran an interior design company. We clinked glasses and I took a large mouthful of the wine which was cold and delicious. I was still feeling stressed and thought I must be sounding strained. I took another mouthful.

'Are you making any progress with the crook builder?'

'Oh, him! I wrote this legalistic letter giving him seven days to return my deposit or I'd take action. I sent it special delivery and I know he got it. He ignored it, of course. So I've made my claim with the small claims court.'

'Good for you. He sounds an arsehole.'

We drank our way through the wine far too fast but it helped me to relax. Douglas wriggled up the sofa closer to me and we started to kiss, shyly and awkwardly to begin with, then getting more passionate until we were both half reclining on the Chesterfield and my shirt was unbuttoned. I could have had sex with him at that moment. Eventually, he pulled away from me and his face was flushed. I was sure mine was bright pink too.

'I'd better tell the restaurant we're running late,' he said.

He called them and I adjusted my clothing and we both left the flat reluctantly.

La Bougie Bistro, Camden Town

We held hands as we walked to the bistro which was on a side road near the Camden Road railway bridge. A train thundered over our heads as we crossed underneath. Douglas had his back cushion tucked under his arm. The bistro had a discreet brown exterior with the words *La Bougie* written in faded gold letters above the door.

'Another place I didn't know about,' I said.

'It gets its custom through word of mouth.'

Douglas pushed the door open and we were met by a wonderful smell of roasting meats and herbs. He had reserved us a table away from the window and he put his cushion in place as he sat down. A thought flashed through my head: did Douglas have problems with sex because of his bad back? I found myself blushing again like a schoolgirl. The waiter presented us with handwritten menus. There was a select list of dishes and I saw that steak tartare was on offer.

'I'm sure I'm unsophisticated but the idea of eating raw meat with a raw egg on top revolts me,' I said.

He laughed.

'It doesn't revolt me, but it's not my first choice, for sure.'

We both chose the French onion soup which came in brown tureens and was rich, dark and sweet with a lovely cheesy crouton floating in its centre. It was a meal in itself and I needed it after all the wine I had drunk. Our main courses arrived, both beautifully presented on our plates. I had chosen sea bass with crab bisque and Douglas had ordered grilled calf's liver. We were on another bottle of wine which was slipping down beautifully. I was enjoying being with him and had almost buried my anxiety about work. It was Douglas who raised the issue of our exes. He said one of the things he and Claire had always clashed about was how their home looked.

'She drove me mad with her obsession about having the perfect home. Interior design is her thing, you see, and she could never relax until the house looked immaculate. We could never relax either, or leave anything lying around!'

'And now you can be as untidy as you want but your place looked pretty neat to me,' I said.

'Except for my office... *and* I tidied up before you came. How long ago did you split up with your ex?'

'Eight years ago. My little Flo was seven and she took it hard.'

I was waiting for him to ask me why we had broken up, but he didn't go there and I was grateful for that. I would not have wanted to talk about Ben's gambling addiction; it would have felt disloyal.

'How do you manage it now? Are you civil with each other?' he asked.

'Civil, yes; you have to be when there's a child involved. The first two years were horrible. He was furious with me because I had initiated the break-up and we didn't talk to each other, we snarled. It settled down eventually. Ben lives in Dubai now. It means he sees less of Flo than he used to. I regret that but I have to say it does make things easier.'

I was burning to know more about his separation which was far more recent. The article I'd read implied that his wife had left him. I took a sip of my wine.

'Has your separation been civil?'

There was something in his face as he answered me. Was it pain or contempt? I didn't know him well enough and couldn't read his expression.

'There's still a lot of anger and blame, so much blame. We are barely civil but, like you, we have to keep communicating because of Stewart.'

'The whole blame thing is miserable, isn't it?' I said.

'Miserable and petty,' he said.

He wasn't over it. I could see that he was still in the thick of separating from her, untangling the ties that had bound them. It takes years to get over the break-up of a marriage and his had lasted far longer than mine. Go carefully here, I told myself as he leaned forward and poured more wine into my glass.

'Where does your son live?'

'Some of the time with me and some of the time with Claire. At weekends Stew and I go down to my mum's in Norfolk when Norwich are playing. We're both die-hard Norwich fans.'

He grinned at me and I fancied him so much at that moment and wished we were back at his flat on the sofa kissing even if he was still on the rebound. I didn't really need this meal of rich food, delicious though it was.

'I've stayed on good terms with Ben's parents. That's helped and Flo sees a lot of them,' I said.

'You're lucky there. Claire's mum detests me. Always has. She probably popped a bottle of champagne when we split up!'

I wanted to know more. I would have thought that Douglas as a successful news journalist would be seen as the model son-in-law.

'Why didn't you get on?'

'Because Natalie Cooper is convinced I'm a pinko. She's a true blue Tory from the Shires, the sort of woman who has a loud voice and is rude to waiters and cab drivers.'

I didn't have Douglas down as a leftie but then, like most news journalists, he was careful to appear neutral when covering politics on television.

'And are you a pinko?' I smiled at him.

I knew from my researches on Wikipedia that his father had been a small farmer who had had to sell up and become a farm manager; Douglas had implied on an earlier date that money had been short when he was a boy.

'I hate the whole privileged entitled thing, you know. But enough of our exes. Tell me, how has Fizzy taken the change in her role?' he said.

I did not want to talk about work at all. I had just about got my anxiety under control. Was it possible that Douglas had seen the Lou Gibson piece? I had to remember that he worked for the opposition and I couldn't allow myself to open up to him.

'You noticed? Do you watch our show every day?'

'No, I read about in the trades. Maybe they were making too much of it but they implied that Fizzy was taking it hard?'

I felt myself clamming up. This change of direction in the conversation was a definite passion cooler.

'Fizzy is a pro to the tips of her toes so we'll make it work,' I said slipping into my work-Liz voice, the capable TV producer who sorted all the problems the programme threw at her. Ben had hated it when I used that tone with him and would say, 'Don't talk to me like I'm one of your team.'

'I'm sure she will but won't that put more pressure on you? I mean presumably you have to allocate the stories?'

'Yes I do.'

'Won't that be a cause of conflict? I know how pushy presenters can be!'

I didn't understand why he was persisting with these questions. Couldn't he see how uncomfortable it was making me feel?

'It's what I'm paid to do,' I said.

Douglas sensed the change in the atmosphere between us.

'Sorry, we should probably have a rule that we don't talk shop when we meet,' he said.

I was being touchy but I knew that if I started talking about work I would reveal far too much: how worried I was about the new double act, how I felt threatened by Lori bloody Kerwell and behind it all lurked the secret that oppressed me, that Bob was Zachary's father. They were all things I couldn't share with him. I tried to reach out to him again, to recreate the warm feeling we'd had earlier.

'It's difficult, isn't it, because our work is such a big thing in our lives,' I said.

'Too big, I've been told, more than once,' he said with a rueful smile.

But our mood of intimacy had gone and I was panicking at the thought of going back to his flat. I felt too anxious and vulnerable to have sex with him. So I lied and told him that I needed to get home for Flo. We left the bistro and he hailed a taxi and opened the door for me.

'Thank you for a wonderful evening,' I said.

We kissed quickly and I got into the cab. I was miserable as the taxi chugged along back to Chalk Farm. I was returning to an empty flat and tonight was not, after all, going to be the night I slept with Douglas Pitlochry. The driver tried to start a conversation but I gave him one-word answers and he gave up. I looked out of the window. Litter was piled around the Camden Town Tube entrance, empty hamburger boxes, greasy paper and crushed cans. I saw a man who was out of it on drink or drugs staggering down the steps of the Tube and nearly falling on his face. I pulled my mobile out of my bag and looked at its black screen. Could I bear to turn it on and listen to the message from Julius that I was sure was waiting for me? Douglas had invited me to his flat and taken me for a lovely dinner and I had scuttled away. Why did work always have to spoil everything?

CHAPTER NINETEEN

StoryWorld TV station, London Bridge

They say attack is the best form of defence and I was determined to have my say about the Lou Gibson piece. We were seated for the morning meeting in the same configuration as yesterday, Fizzy and her allies opposite Ledley and his. Lori was wearing a purple suit and her expression was grim. She and I exchanged icy looks and I could see that she thought I'd been stirring the media up against Ledley. I wondered if she had complained to Saul Relph about me again or if that was yet to come. Our rift was becoming a chasm. Julius entered the room and went to his chair at the top of the table, the place no one else ever took. The atmosphere in the meeting room was as tight as a drum. Julius cleared his throat and was about to start but I spoke up.

'Julius, before we begin I would like to say something about the Lou Gibson piece which I'm sure you will all have seen.'

He nodded his assent. He'd got my message and we'd spoken briefly early this morning about the poisonous article. I had told him again exactly what had happened.

'I said *nothing* of what was reported by Lou Gibson; *not one word*. She called me on Wednesday and I gave her exactly the same script I gave all the other journalists. But she had it in her head to write the story she did. I warned Ledley about her that afternoon.'

I was grateful when Ledley backed me up.

'Yes, you did,' he said.

'As I was leaving the building she doorstepped me and tried to put words into my mouth. All I did was repeat the lines-to-take that we had agreed.'

I took a breath and looked over at Julius.

'I think it's possible, however, that she picked up some intelligence from the station, possibly from one of the journalists.'

'Are you accusing my team?' Bob barked at me.

'I'm accusing no one specific. What I am saying is that there was a lot of chatter and gossip in the station on Wednesday afternoon, after we issued the statement. Journalists know each other. There could have been some idle talk that she overheard.'

Lori had the article printed out in front of her.

'But she is very specific.' She put on her glasses and read it out: '"It is believed that head of features, Liz Lyon, who has herself come up against the macho and bullying culture at the TV station, is horrified at the change in presentation arrangements." You are saying she invented that point about your opinion?'

'Yes. I have no idea where she got that from. I said nothing at all about the culture here. For heaven's sake, do you think I would be so crass or so stupid? All I said was that we were all thrilled that Fizzy was returning and that Ledley was in a supporting role, as per the agreed script.'

'Of course Liz wouldn't have said that. She's a highly experienced producer and she knows how this business works.'

It was Fizzy and she addressed her remarks directly to Lori, emphasising *knows how this business works*, her implication being that Lori the newcomer did not.

'So she invented that bit?' Lori was not going to let it go.

'Journalists invent stuff all the time,' I said.

'Yes, they do. I've had lots of experience of that,' Fizzy said with a toss of her head.

Finally, Julius said something.

'But you think something might have come out of the station, Liz?'

'It's possible. There was a feverish atmosphere here on Wednesday.'

'Wherever it came from it is damaging and has been picked up by other outlets,' Julius said.

A moment of quietness descended on the room as each one of us thought about that. The room was thick with suspicion and hostility.

I was meeting Gerry for lunch off-site. He had done his best this morning to include both Fizzy and Ledley in his discussion of compatibility and the zodiac. He had pointed out that they were both fire signs, Fizzy a Leo and Ledley a Sagittarius, and this meant that they were compatible. Both had played along and seemed, as with yesterday, to be the best of pals. Only those of us who knew them well might have spotted the tiny signs of strain: a minute tightening of a lip here, a dropping of the voice there.

Gerry had booked us a table at a Thai restaurant and was already there when I pushed the door open. He stood up and kissed me on both cheeks.

'Darling, it's a car crash,' he said as I sat down.

'I know. I saw how you tried to make it work this morning, thanks for that,' I said.

'Of course, we have to make it work, but you should feel

the atmosphere in the studio. Tense doesn't even begin to describe what it's like in there. When we went to the ad break she blanked him completely. They loathe each other now and it's poisonous. All the crew know what's going on.'

I glanced around the restaurant to check that we weren't being overheard. Our table was away from the occupied ones.

'It is hugely difficult,' I said.

'I hope it's worth it, Liz. It's an unhappy show at the moment.'

'Only time will tell,' I said and picked up the menu though I had little appetite.

We waited for our food and I pointed at the orchid in the vase on our table. It had a flat white face and a dark pink speckled centre.

'Have you noticed how orchids have a front and a back? I mean, most flowers are kind of in the round, aren't they, but orchids are directional, aren't they?' I said.

He laughed at my observation for some reason. We had both ordered pad thai with prawns and our plates arrived. I like the peanut taste and I squeezed a lemon over the noodles.

'I saw Lori Kerwell out with Saul Relph last week,' Gerry said.

'Where was this?'

'At that big travel show in Olympia. I was there doing a book signing on the Yoga Holidays stand and I saw the two of them walk past with a couple of men. They stopped and said hello briefly but didn't say who the men were. I wouldn't have thought it was the kind of event that Saul Relph would attend.'

'No, nor I,' I said.

That was an interesting piece of intelligence.

Chalk Farm flat, 9 p.m.

Flo is interested in a boy! This came out tonight while I was on my knees in front of the washing machine sorting out the whites from the coloureds. I overheard her discussing a boy called Ethan. His name has come up before. He's at that school in Highgate and yesterday Flo and Rosie had bumped into him in Camden. He was with a mate and the four of them had walked to the Roundhouse together. Cue for huge excitement on Flo's part and a reprise of what he had said, what she had said back, how she wished she had looked better when she met him, how she couldn't wait to see him again and that she was glad that school was going back next week because they could go up to Highgate green and seek him out. I sat back on my heels recalling the joy and intensity of those first adolescent crushes. There was a boy I used to look for at the bus stop every morning. He went to the school near mine and if I saw him my day was made. I have no idea if he was aware of my devotion.

I stood up and added fabric conditioner and selected and pressed the wash cycle. I put the kettle on. I was feeling angry with myself for my reaction to Douglas last night. Why had I pulled back because he had asked me a couple of questions about work? Have I really got to the stage where I don't know who I can trust any more?

Chalk Farm flat, Saturday

I start cooking again in September. There is something about the beginning of autumn, about that nip in the air and the shorter days, that makes me want to make casseroles and soups and puddings.

While Flo slept on I did an early visit to our local market and bought onions, carrots, parsnips and a bunch of parsley. I treated myself to a cappuccino. The café was full and the hiss of the coffee machine was a constant refrain. I had agreed we would go to Selfridges later to buy Flo a bra and panty set for the great teenage fashion makeover shoot which was scheduled for Sunday week. I've already been told by Flo that I am *not* to accompany her to the shoot. The location they are using is the Lock Tavern pub in Camden which has a roof terrace.

Selfridges, Oxford Street

Selfridges on a Saturday was a bad idea. We took the bus to Oxford Circus and had to push our way through the crowds to get to those famous doors. Once inside the store we worked our way through the cosmetic and fragrance section, swerving the hectic saleswomen who were clutching perfume bottles ready to spray us. We reached the lingerie department upstairs. Flo was measured up and told her cup size and she must have tried on a dozen different bras.

'Harriet told me she only ever wears matching sets,' Flo said.

'You mean she has as many bras as panties? Surely not.'

'Oh yes, she has about thirty sets and wears a new one every day. She has her favourites but she *never ever* wears non-matching underwear.'

'If she bought several pairs of the matching panties she wouldn't need as many bras,' I said.

'But she likes choosing a new set to wear every morning. She said she lays them out in her drawer by colour.'

Flo spoke as if this was great and something to be emulated.

'And when she goes on holiday she packs fourteen different bras and panties,' she added.

'That's bonkers!'

I had found a chair in the changing room and had to draw on my reserves of patience when Flo couldn't decide between her two favourites and kept going back and forth on which one she should choose. The implication was that I should buy both sets and I flatly refused to do this. Finally, she made her decision. I was grumpy at the inflated price for matching pieces of lace and satin prettiness until I recalled that I had treated myself to a pricy red bra and panty set when I started dating Todd. Nice underwear does give you a boost and my girl was growing up fast.

'Now I need some tea,' I said.

We went to the coffee shop. As I was standing in the queue I spotted a woman in the line in front of us who looked familiar. I watched her as she reached the cash register and, even though I had met her only the once, I thought she might be Pat, Bob's wife. She had two girls with her and I knew they had two daughters. She paid and turned with her tray.

'Pat?' I said.

She stopped and peered at me.

'It's Liz from StoryWorld,' I said.

'Of course. How nice to see you. Do join us. Girls, go and find us a big table,' she said.

I bought a pot of tea for me and a Coke for Flo and we joined them at a table by the window.

'I haven't been here for ages and it's exhausting isn't it?' she said.

'It's a scrum,' I agreed.

I poured my tea and Pat leaned back with her mug of hot chocolate and took a sip. She was a nice-looking woman, simply dressed in a linen shift and with a trace of pink lipstick on.

'It was a last-minute decision to come because of Bob having to go in to work,' Pat said. 'I know it comes with the job but it does bug me when he's called in on a Saturday, even if it is for a news scoop. We'd planned a visit to Hampton Court today.'

I wasn't aware that there was any big news scoop. Nothing had been said at the Friday meeting about weekend working and as that entailed overtime rates Julius would have had to approve it. I looked down at my cup as the strongest suspicion grew in me that Bob had lied to Pat and that he was off meeting Fizzy and Zachary at the safe house, wherever that was. I didn't know what to say but muttered something about it being a shame.

'You're on the features side, aren't you?' Pat asked.

'I am, so thankfully it's rare for me to have to go in at the weekend. Just as well, as I see little enough of Flo as it is,' I said.

'Bob doesn't see nearly enough of the girls either. Hannah's off to uni in October and we'll only have her back in the vacations. Television is a demanding business, isn't it?'

She sounded fed up. We looked over at our girls. They were chatting happily and examining each other's purchases. Her elder girl had Bob's features, including his angry eyes. The younger girl looked softer and more like Pat.

'It is extremely demanding and it kind of sucks you in,' I said, and then I tried to think how I could change the subject and get away from such dangerous territory as the TV station and Fizzy Wentworth.

'Does your work entail shifts?' I asked.

'Yes, it does, but we know well in advance about weekend working so I can plan ahead,' Pat said.

She told me about it. She's the administrator of a Well Women clinic that runs checks for breast and cervical cancer. She liked her work and it kept her grounded, she said. I found myself liking her and feeling uncomfortable about what I knew. Bob had cheated on her for months last year. He might even at this moment be cheating on her again.

'You know Bob has always been restless at work, usually moving on after two or three years, but he seems to have settled at StoryWorld and that at least is a relief,' she said.

She was a nice woman who deserved better. Fifteen minutes later I said we had better be making tracks as I had a pile of housework to get through. The girls had exchanged their Instagram details and promised to follow each other.

CHAPTER TWENTY

StoryWorld TV station, London Bridge

The conflict started early today, even before the morning meeting. Ledley grabbed me as I was heading for the stairs, after the credits on the show had rolled.

'Liz, a quick word in my room, please.'

I followed him reluctantly along the corridor to his dressing room. It had to be something difficult if he wanted me out of earshot of the others. He opened the door and I looked around. His room smelled of a man's cologne. He has made himself more at home over the last few days. There was a whole series of framed photographs on the wall. One showed him standing outside his restaurant, The Caribbean Shack, and there was another with Ledley and a well-known footballer. His sofa was covered with a brightly coloured throw in green, black and gold. He shut the door and stood opposite me with his arms folded over his chest, his face a picture of hurt outrage.

'She did it again this morning and you've got to tell her to play fair,' he said.

I knew what he meant. This morning we had booked in another food story for Ledley to present and Fizzy had overrun her item so that his interview had had to be cut short.

'She does it on purpose. Cuts into my time and I get little enough to do as it is.'

'I'm sorry, Ledley. It's still early days and she's feeling raw about the change. Give it time and I'm sure things will settle down.'

I hoped this would happen but wasn't sure it would. Ledley saw straight through my weasel words.

'She needs to be told *now*, before she thinks she can get away with it. She's deliberately messing up the timings to push me out. It makes life hard for the crew as well as for me.'

That was true. The director was finding it a nightmare to hit the ad breaks to schedule and Henry was having to hold guests back in the green room because Fizzy was deliberately ignoring their countdowns.

'I'll have a word with her after the meeting, but we need to remember that she's had a baby and she may be tired and not at the top of her game.'

'Sorry, but that's bullshit. She's at the top of her game and knows *exactly* what she's doing.'

As I looked at his angry face I wondered where the laid-back Ledley had gone, the one who used to be the easiest of all my presenters to work with. His complaints were legitimate but I hardly recognised this new, pushy Ledley.

'Will I get to do any of the big interviews or has she put a ban on that too?'

He needed to know he was the junior partner so I told him straight.

'Her agent was tough when we negotiated the change. Julius had to agree a contractual obligation to give the big interviews to Fizzy. I'm sorry about that, but we have to live with it.'

'My agent Angela Hodge might have something to say about that,' he said.

'Come on. We need to get to the meeting. You know Julius hates to be kept waiting.'

'You go ahead. I'll be up in a minute.'

That was significant, I thought, as I headed to the stairs. He did not want to be seen arriving at the meeting room with me because I was no longer his patron. Lori Kerwell was his patron.

The mood at the meeting was horrible. Fizzy said nothing. She sat and examined her nails as if they were the most fascinating thing in the world. I sensed she was waiting for one of us to mention how she had overrun her items again. Julius was subdued and brooding. Ledley was fuming and Lori was glaring at me. I glared back at her. Martine tapped on the door and there was a palpable sense of relief when she told Julius he was needed for a call from Sweden from Saul Relph. I put my papers into my bag and turned on my mobile. I was hoping that Douglas would get in touch soon but my screen was clear. When I looked up, Bob was standing in the room. The others had gone. He was staring at me and I felt a prickle of apprehension down my spine.

'What did you say to Pat on Saturday?' he said.

'Sorry?'

'You heard me.'

I stayed seated so that I could keep the table between him and me. Since our rift over Fizzy all my lone encounters with Bob have been threatening and I wanted to get away from him.

'What did you say to her?' he repeated, his hands balled into fists on the table.

I knew then that he must have been with Fizzy on Saturday and that his overtime story to Pat was a lie. He was sweating about what I might have revealed to his wife.

'I don't like your tone of voice but I said nothing incriminatory, if that's what you're worried about.'

'You keep your bloody nose out of my business and keep away from my family,' he snarled.

'You're a fool, Bob. I have no intention of saying anything about your affair because I care about Fizzy. But if you keep making me feel threatened you might tip me over the edge.'

I stood up.

'So back off!'

I snatched up my bag and strode to the door and was out of there before he could say anything else. My heart was in full gallop. I'd decided to fight aggression with aggression but now I needed a breather before I saw my team. I went downstairs to the Hub, bought a cup of tea and took it outside. It was a bright day and sunlight was bouncing off the river. I sipped my tea and took deep breaths as I watched some gulls circling above the boats that moved through the water. There has always been conflict at work and it's inevitable when you work on a live TV show with presenters and their big egos. Up until now I have been able to manage it but it was starting to look like there would be battles every single day. Bob hating and suspecting me and Fizzy and Ledley fighting over every slot and how much time they would get. I hoped I had the strength to deal with it. I headed back in and saw Henry standing in reception. He walked over to me.

'How are you coping in the nut house?' he said.

'Nut house? Snake pit would sum it up better, I would say.'

We smiled at other sympathetically and nothing else needed to be said.

★

As I passed Ziggy's desk I took a good look at her. She was bent over her keyboard, her face pinched and her body language defeated.

'Simon, a quick word,' I said.

As soon as he came in I asked him for an update on Ziggy's search for a place to live.

'She hasn't found anywhere yet. Harry and I are scanning the estate agents every day. Anything suitable is out of her price range. We suggested she should do a house share.'

'That might work.'

'But she wants to live on her own. She'd rather be in a grubby little bedsit than in a room in a better house. You know, I think all her years in care has made her guard her privacy so strongly. She says she'll do a house share if all else fails.'

'Well, keep me posted. She looks beaten at the moment.'

This reminded me that I have yet to secure a full-time position for Ziggy. I'd speak to Julius about it but I would need to choose my moment. With money tight at the station there was a reluctance to make staff permanent. Simon handed me a script.

'And Betty's doing eating disorders with Ledley tomorrow.'

I scanned the script and the three letters they had chosen to discuss.

'Good choice and hard-hitting. Thanks, Simon.'

It was four o'clock when Julius wandered down to my office. It used to be a regular event for him to drop in on me. Ever since the screen-test incident he has kept away and his appearance now caused a frisson of alarm from Harriet and Ziggy. He stood at my threshold.

'Have you got a minute?'

'Of course.'

'And I'm parched.'

'Will water do?'

He sat down on my sofa and I poured him a glass of water. I noticed that his left eyelid was twitching, a sign of stress with him.

'Lori has just been to see me. It appears that she has secured a large sponsorship deal with WayToGo airlines.'

As Julius mentioned the name of the company his lips had curled. WayToGo was a budget airline with a reputation for long queues, cutting corners and losing luggage. He was the sponsorship expert at the station and had brought in some quality deals over the years. He would have been mortified that Lori had secured this deal and with such a cheapskate company. He drained his glass as if washing a nasty taste from his mouth.

'She's already shared this news with Saul, who is apparently delighted. What WayToGo want for their cash is a dedicated weekly travel spot and they've asked for Ledley to front it,' he continued.

'That explains it,' I said.

'Explains what?'

'Gerry spotted Saul and Lori at some big travel show in Olympia.'

'When was this?'

'Last week.'

Despite our personal differences I knew that he and I felt the same about this. Neither of us liked how close Lori had got to Saul Relph or that she had gained power at the station. Not to mention having to work with a company like WayToGo. They were the kind of company that would expect a lot for their cash.

'We've never done a travel slot because producing one that looks good costs too much. We need footage of locations and you know how pricey that can be. Without proper footage the item will look cheap,' I said.

'I agree, but she doesn't get any of that. She is adamant that there has to be a travel slot to secure the sponsorship cash. I spelled out the problems but she said why can't it be a sofa item with graphics and viewers sending in their holiday footage?'

I groaned.

'Really? She wants to reduce everything to the lowest common denominator.'

'Saul says the travel spot goes ahead from next month and you'll need to make a pilot for WayToGo to approve,' Julius said.

Julius would have hated it that Saul had insisted on a specific programme item.

'Well, the only silver lining is that it will give Ledley something to do,' I said.

He left my room. This had not been the moment to mention a permanent role for Ziggy. For all his faults Julius is first and foremost a programme maker who cares about quality. He was as unhappy as I was that the show was being bent out of shape.

Chalk Farm flat, evening

It had been a wretched day at work and was a miserable evening at home. Flo had period pains and was snappy all evening. I retreated to my bedroom. There had been no word from Douglas and I hated myself for continually checking my mobile for texts or missed calls. A watched kettle never boils and a watched phone never texts. Douglas usually called early in the week to suggest a date for Thursday night; well, he had three times before. Maybe this was it and I wouldn't hear from him again. Julius had warned me that he was 'playing the field' and Douglas could not have missed how I pulled away from him at our last date. I couldn't believe how low this made me feel.

I went into the kitchen to make a cup of tea and could hear Flo talking to one of her friends. I caught the words 'went to fourth base'. I moved closer to her door, which was open just a crack.

'She isn't someone you'd think would do it,' Flo said.

I wondered who she was talking to and about whom.

'I know. And Justin said she was a skank and Ryan called her a sket, but they would, wouldn't they.'

A long pause while Flo listened to her caller.

'She's made a big mistake. It won't make him like her for long.'

I was sure that Flo was still a virgin and this exchange confirmed it. I recalled the girls in my year who had 'gone the whole way' as we called it then and how they had been subjected to abuse for being an easy lay. So it was still going on; boys pushing to have sex and then deriding the girls who did it. Fifteen-year-olds can be cruel and the thought of that probably insecure and vulnerable girl being verbally abused was upsetting. I crept away from her door and put the kettle on noisily, rattling the mugs so she would know I was in the kitchen. A minute later she got off her bed and clicked her door shut. She did not want to talk to me. This added to my feeling of lowness and when I got into bed I had a good cry. The tears were a release. After a while I blew my nose and sternly reminded myself of my blessings. I got up, tapped on Flo's door and went in. She was lying on her side hugging a pillow.

'Feeling any better, darling?'

'A bit,' she said drowsily.

I leaned over and kissed her cheek.

'Sleep now.'

Even if she was grumpy sometimes, I had a good kid.

CHAPTER TWENTY-ONE

StoryWorld TV station, London Bridge

Fizzy and I left the morning meeting together and she asked me to join her downstairs. I sat in her dressing room as she changed out of her TV clothes.

'I've sorted the access problem with Bob.'

'OK.'

'We're meeting at Loida's flat in Kensal Rise.'

So this was her 'safe house'. Loida, of course, would go to any lengths to help Fizzy and it was a discreet place to meet.

'I'm glad you managed to sort something out,' I said.

'He told me I was not to tell you under any circumstances.'

I wondered why she had told me. It was another secret for me to carry.

'Are you OK, Liz?'

'I'm feeling under pressure. And Bob hating me is part of that.'

'I think he fears you rather than hates you,' she said.

'Whatever, it's still very uncomfortable. But one thing I can do is keep a secret,' I said.

'I know that. He's a difficult man but he's actually rather sweet with Zac.'

Sweet was not a word I would ever have used about Bob.

'And I'm sure we can make it work,' she said.

I think she wanted me to reassure her and I searched for words that I could say and mean.

'You can count on my support,' I said.

She was ready to go and we walked to the exit and waited for her taxi to draw up. She gave the driver an address and put one finger to her lips as I waved her goodbye.

With everything that had been going on, my plan for a Young Fashion Designer competition had slipped down my list of priorities. But now would be a good time for Julius and me to secure a quality sponsorship deal for the station. We would show Lori Kerwell and Saul Relph what we could bring in. Having Guy Browne as our front man might tempt a good brand on board. I worked on a proposal, printed copies and took these out to Harriet and Ziggy.

'Can you research good brands who may be interested in sponsoring this? I'd like to add a list before I show it to Julius.'

Harriet looked interested but Ziggy still seemed subdued. Losing her base was hitting her hard. She had lived her whole life thinking the world was a hostile place and that you couldn't trust people. I wondered if she would ever feel safe.

I was called by the agent of Bethany Burton. She is the UK's hottest young actor and wanted to come on our show on Friday to discuss her new TV series. Normally I would be cock-a-hoop at having her as a guest. But there's a major wrinkle: her agent was insistent that Bethany wanted Ledley to interview her. Apparently Bethany is a big fan, loved Ledley's cooking slot and had only agreed to come on the show in order to meet him. But our contractual obligation was to give the big interviews to Fizzy and this was one of the biggest. I went down to Julius's office because I wanted him to help me deal with it. Martine was at her desk.

'I hope it's not bad news, he's having a difficult day,' she said.

'I'm afraid it could be.'

'Oh dear. Well, you'd better go in.'

Julius was sitting slumped at his desk.

'Our first big issue,' I said.

'What now?' he said.

I explained the Bethany Burton dilemma.

'Well, we have to have her on the show. She's too big a star to turn down,' he said.

'I agree, but this calls for a word with Jonny Hammond, doesn't it?'

'It does my head in having agents dictating our running orders. Who's Ledley's agent?'

'Angela Hodge,' I said.

'She's a tough nut too.'

'The only idea I've had, which might mitigate it, is to conduct the entire interview in the kitchen. Bethany was a big fan of Ledley's cooking spot so we could ask her to join him in the kitchen while he cooks something for her. It might make it a little easier for Fizzy to bear.'

'Yes, that's a good idea. You better call Jonny Hammond. If I do I'll get abusive,' he said.

Julius and I have been working together more closely recently, which is one positive development.

I went down to the Hub to get a drink. Ledley was sitting at a corner table with Lori. He waved at me and beamed and I guessed that he had already heard about the Bethany Burton booking. If he already knew then Fizzy needed to know and I hurried back upstairs without anything. I kept trying to get through to Jonny Hammond but his phone went to voicemail each time. I called Fizzy and Loida said she was out with Zachary and wouldn't be back for a while. So that was where she was going in the taxi; to a meeting with Bob in Kensal Rise.

At six o'clock I left a message for Jonny Hammond explaining that Ledley would be doing a cooking spot with Bethany Burton on Friday. I shut down my PC and headed for home, knowing this would not be the end of it.

Chalk Farm flat, 8 p.m.

I had the ironing board out and was working my way through Flo's school shirts when my landline rang. My heart sank that there would be a furious Fizzy on the line. It was Douglas.

'Sorry I've not been in touch. We've had major stuff going on at work and I haven't had a moment,' he said.

'It's fine,' I said.

It hadn't been. I had been in pieces but I managed to sound airy because my heart had lifted the moment I heard his voice.

'This is a long shot but I wondered if there was any way you could get away this weekend? A good friend of mine has been refurbishing a small hotel in Sussex and he's having his opening this Saturday. There's going to be a rather good dinner and an overnight thrown in for invited guests.'

'That sounds lovely. Where is the hotel?'

He was suggesting a weekend away with him and I was filling up with joy. And then I remembered that Sunday was the day of Flo's teenage fashion shoot. Oh God! Could I really go away on Saturday and leave her to do that without me?

'It's in West Sussex, near Arundel. Do you know the area?'

'No, I don't.'

'It's lovely countryside round there. He's a good mate and he's worked flat out for months to transform the place. I thought weekends might be difficult for you because of Florence. But if you could get away I think it will be a lot of fun. I'd drive us down there, of course.'

He wanted to spend the weekend with me, the whole weekend, at a country hotel. I knew I would be wretched if I said no to this.

'It sounds great and I'd love to. The only thing is I'd have to be back early afternoon on Sunday. Flo is doing a fashion shoot. She doesn't want me there. In fact I've been banned from attending, but I need to be on hand here, you know, for afterwards. It's a big thing in her life.'

'Of course, it would be. Is it for your station?'

I was silly to feel defensive whenever Douglas asked me about StoryWorld. It was the obvious question to ask and I had to be able to deal with this if we were to have any hope of a relationship.

'Yes, with Guy Browne and it's his first foray into teenage fashion. He's doing a makeover with three fifteen-year-olds.'

Douglas laughed.

'Brave man! Look, I can get you back to your flat by the afternoon. Do say yes.'

I said I would go. I put the phone down and punched the air in joy. A weekend in the country and a hotel opening; I was thrilled. And I'd meet his friend too and get an insight into how other people related to Douglas. I skipped over to the fridge and poured myself a glass of wine and called Janis. I asked if as a huge favour she would sleep here on Saturday and get Flo off to the fashion shoot on Sunday morning. I had to tell her why; that I had been invited on a rather special date.

'About time you had some fun in your life, Liz. I'm pleased for you and I'll do it,' she said.

Now I have to tell Flo about Douglas. I was feeling stupidly nervous and decided to make some flapjacks. She loves eating them warm from the oven.

As I predicted, the aroma of warm flapjacks drew Flo out of her bedroom. I put the baking tin on the table and started to cut them into squares, handing her the first piece.

'Do you want some milk with that?'

'No, ta. Mmm, they're yummy.'

She reached for a second piece.

'Darling, I've arranged for Janis to sleep here on Saturday night because I'm going to be away at a special event in the country.'

She looked incredulous.

'You're going away this weekend? But it's my shoot.'

'I know, sweetheart, and I'll be back here by Sunday afternoon to hear all about it. You don't want me anywhere near the shoot, do you?' I said, already feeling a mountain of guilt that I had agreed to go away.

'But where will you be?'

'In West Sussex.'

I told her about the date with Douglas.

'He's the one you're always watching on the telly,' she said in an accusing voice.

'Yes, that's Douglas.'

'So you're going to sleep with him then? If you're staying in a hotel. That's why people go to hotels, isn't it?'

She sounded amazingly resentful. I nodded. There was no point in denying that we were going to sleep together.

'How long have you been seeing him?'

'This will be our fourth date.'

'Your fourth date? Why didn't you tell me before?'

'It all happened while you were away in Portsmouth,' I said.

This wasn't true.

'And you didn't say a thing! I think it's *really mean* of you to go away this weekend of all weekends.'

'I'm sorry you feel like that but I'm entitled to have a life too.' I said it more sharply than I intended because I felt guilty and she scraped her chair back from the table and stormed into her bedroom. I looked at her closed door and cursed her teenage selfishness and my stupid guilt.

Fizzy called me at nine and she was furious.

'Jonny says you're in breach of contract.'

'Look, it's a glorified cooking spot. He's going to cook for her in the kitchen,' I said.

'Are you kidding? With Bethany Burton! You know how hot she is at the moment.'

'There's nothing I can do about it. She's got a bit of a thing about him, you see.'

'Oh, how he's going to love that! And he'll *adore* making me look small. Why can't we share the interview? He cooks for her in the kitchen and I talk to her on the sofa about her new series.'

'That won't work. She'll talk to him about the series while he's cooking for her.'

'I won't put up with it. It's the thin end of the wedge.'

'No, it's a one-off, Fizz. You'll have Gerry and we can find another good guest for you too.'

I hoped we could. We had one day to find another class guest for her to interview and they weren't easy to come by.

'You know I've a mind to bow out of Friday's show. I will *not* play second fiddle to that amateur. That vain pushy amateur! You can tell the viewers that Zac is teething and I'm needed at home.'

'I don't think that's a good idea. Sleep on it, Fizz, please,' I said.

After she'd hung up I pushed the French doors open and stood in my small garden. Gardens smell good at night. My neighbour has planted nicotiana and I recognised its heady scent. There was the faint sound of a car alarm but it was a street away and didn't disturb the peace of my little plot. It was a clear night and I could make out the Plough in the sky. My father always called that constellation Jack and his Wagon, saying the three stars in a curve represented a horse's head and the other four were the cart. He told me I should look for it wherever I went in the world. And I do.

'The stars are always there, even when we can't see them, and they put things in perspective,' he had said.

How I missed my dad and his calm good sense. I wondered what he would have made of my life now.

CHAPTER TWENTY-TWO

StoryWorld TV station, London Bridge

Thankfully, Fizzy decided to come in on Friday and I went down to her dressing room to give her support. Yesterday, Harriet and I had called all our showbiz contacts and had managed to book in TV detective George Walter for her to interview before the main event. I think he fancies Fizzy because he had said yes at once. He was the guest on the day she revealed on camera that she was pregnant, and he said at the time how much he admired her courage. But he wasn't in the same league as Bethany Burton and she was deeply mortified that Ledley was doing the major interview of the day. She was prickly with me.

'Why didn't you tell me you were dating Douglas Pitlochry?'

She must have heard it from Julius and I felt caught out.

'I didn't want to make too much of it. I mean, it's only been a couple of dates.'

'So how did you meet him?'

'We were seated together at the People's TV Awards.'

She was doing a calculation.

'That was in August.'

'Yes.'

'You're a dark horse, Liz Lyon.'

She seemed annoyed that it was me, a producer, and not her, a presenter, who was dating a fellow TV anchor.

'He hasn't divorced his wife, you know, and I bet he won't. They never do. I'd tread carefully there if I were you.'

Ellen came in to do the finishing touches to her hair and make-up. Fizzy had made a special effort and was wearing a beautiful dusty pink velvet dress that suited her strawberry-blonde hair.

'And watch out if he starts digging about this place. He's the opposition, you know,' she said.

That irritated me. It was like something Julius would have said, suspecting that Douglas was only going out with me to get information, which was frankly insulting. I wondered if they had discussed it, which made me feel more uncomfortable. And now Ellen had picked up on it too. Yet I found myself trying to placate Fizzy, because I had the cheek to be dating Douglas Pitlochry!

'That's a gorgeous dress, Fizz, perfect with your colouring.'

'Guy says velvet is *the thing* for autumn/winter and he picked it out for me,' she said.

I left them and hurried to the green room. George Walter was sitting in there and Ziggy was handing him a cup of coffee. He thanked her nicely.

'Thanks so much for coming in at such short notice. Fizzy is delighted you could join us today,' I said.

'It's my pleasure. She's a favourite of mine. I had to fight my way through the fans outside. Not mine, alas, but Bethany's,' he said cheerfully.

He was a nice man and I was glad we had him on the sofa. It would soften the blow for Fizzy, even if Ledley had the crown jewels today. Henry took George Walter off to make-up and I stood in reception awaiting the arrival of Bethany Burton. The show had begun but I missed the opening and started to get nervous as the minutes ticked away and she hadn't appeared. She finally arrived and was sweet and un-starry, in spite of the large retinue with her. She apologised for being late. She has a pretty elfin face, wears her dark hair short and was dressed in a chiffon skirt with a leather jacket and Doc Martens. I took her straight to make-up and hurried to the gallery. Fizzy had finished her interview with George Walter and was talking to Gerry about star signs and their sense of humour. Gerry said Scorpio did a wicked line in banter.

Ledley was stationed in the kitchen area in readiness for his cooking item with Bethany and you could see that Fizzy much preferred having the sofa to herself. We went to an ad break and came back to a two shot of Ledley and Bethany Burton in the kitchen.

'You take your jacket off, girl, I'm going to make you work,' Ledley said.

Bethany laughed in delight and pulled off her leather jacket. Ledley gave her an apron and she put it on with a giggle. All the cameras were on them as Ledley got her to grate parmesan while she told him about her new series. It was natural and spontaneous and it made me think we should put Ledley back in the kitchen more. This was the relaxed, funny Ledley I liked best.

'It's working great,' I said to the director as we went to the next ad break.

I glanced over at Fizzy. She was scribbling a note and she called Henry over and handed it to him. A moment later Henry's voice came over the sound system, only to the director and me.

'Fizzy says she'd like to join them in the kitchen at the tasting and can we deploy a camera on her.'

'Shit! She wants to get in on the act,' the director said.

The ads were still running and we had two minutes to

decide what to do. In the running order the instructions were clear that all cameras would be deployed in the kitchen for the entire duration of the Ledley and Bethany interaction.

'She's well out of order,' he muttered.

'I need instructions,' Henry said.

'Maybe we should let her walk over, at the end of the item, and join in the tasting. Is it such a big thing?' I said.

'Presenters mucking with our running order...' he said.

'The crew need instructions now,' Henry said.

The director sighed and went on to open mic which all crew members and Fizzy and Ledley could hear.

'Change of camera position. Will Camera One please move to Fizzy two minutes from the end of this item so that Fizzy can join Ledley and guest in the kitchen for the tasting,' he said.

As Ledley heard this I caught a glimpse of his face and he looked furious. He masked it super quick as we came out of the ad break to a shot of him and Bethany in the kitchen and he continued with his cooking and their chat as if he didn't have a care in the world. The viewers would not have noticed but the final minutes of the show, with Fizzy trying Ledley's dish and cooing over it with Bethany, had made uncomfortable watching for the director and me. As the credits rolled he looked over.

'It's open warfare now, isn't it?' he said.

'Yes, and I wish I knew how to deal with it,' I said.

'That goes for all of us.'

He and I headed for the morning meeting. Fizzy had broken a golden rule of broadcasting. You do not allow a presenter to tamper with a running order when a live show is in progress. Late changes can and do happen in a live show but it is always at the director's discretion. I could feel how tense my body was and wondered how Julius was going to react. Would he rebuke Fizzy in front of everyone? Lori walked in with Ledley at her side, followed by Bob. Fizzy made a late entrance, getting there thirty seconds before Julius and looking flushed and defiant. Julius went to his seat at the top of the table and took his time sitting down. He was ominously calm as he asked the director for his technical report.

'Nothing to note, sound and vision both fine,' the director replied.

'And the late change to the running order?' Julius said.

'We coped with it fine, thanks.'

The director did not want to land Fizzy in it and I was grateful for that. We could tell her off but not in this public forum. Ledley was smouldering but it was Lori who pitched in.

'I'm not a programme maker, but wasn't the interview with Bethany Burton meant to be with Ledley alone?'

'We made a late change to the end of the item. These things happen in a live show,' the director said.

'And that is acceptable?' Lori addressed her question to Julius.

He didn't answer her but he looked at me.

'What's your view, Liz?'

We needed to keep a lid on the venomous emotions that were pulsating in that room. I could tell Julius what I really thought later.

'I think it worked. It was a nice inclusive way to end what had been an excellent interview, well done, Ledley,' I said.

Lori sat back in her seat and snorted.

'Well, of course you would say that. You're on Team Fizzy.'

I had been tightly wound up and her taunt infuriated me. I smacked the table hard with my open palm.

'No! That's a very provocative thing to say. There is no Team Fizzy or Team Ledley. There is only Team StoryWorld and we have a programme to put out and we've got to make it work. Stop being so divisive, Lori.'

'I haven't noticed Fizzy sharing her interviews with Ledley,' she snapped back.

I saw Fizzy's eyes flash dangerously at this.

'That's enough. You're trying to stir things up. You're making things worse. The only thing that will happen is that the show will suffer, the viewers will notice and our ratings will slip. This has to stop *now*,' I said.

There was a shocked silence in the room. I had never spoken out with such passion at a morning meeting before. I was the one who was diplomatic, who spent my time soothing egos and making the best of things. After a stretched out pause Julius got to his feet and looked at every one of us round the table, one after the other, and the tension in the room reached breaking point. No one dared say a word.

'Liz is right. The show comes first. Put your petty differences aside. This pathetic squabbling is to stop now.'

He marched out of the room and I hurried after him. I was sure that Fizzy would want to talk to me but I felt too worked up to see anyone so I walked out of the building, along the river walk and hid in the back of a café I sometimes went to. I was grateful that Julius had supported me but I was trembling as I ordered a pot of tea. No coffee today; I was already fired up enough. I hated my job at the moment; hated the constant conflict and the fact that our energy was being deflected from making a good programme to dealing with the civil war between Fizzy and Ledley.

When I got back to the station Fizzy had left for the day. I went upstairs and asked Harriet if she would keep an eye on Flo at the fashion shoot as I wouldn't be there.

'Would you like me to pick her up from your flat? I'm getting a taxi to the shoot and I can get Flo on the way.'

'That would be great. I'm feeling guilty about being away but she's been firm that I wasn't to come along. What time will it be finished?'

'By four, we hope, five at the latest,' she said.

'I'll make sure I'm home by four. Have you seen the outfits Guy has chosen?'

'No, but he says he's come up with three themes that are on trend and he thinks Flo will look great in the gothic, twisted beauty look.'

'Really?'

This was not how I saw my girl at all.

'Oh yes, she's the tallest of the three girls and the most dramatic-looking.'

I couldn't stop myself from feeling like a proud mum.

Chalk Farm community centre, 7 p.m.

Tonight was a taster session for a Boxercise course at our local community centre. Flo had spotted the class and said why didn't we try it out? My reckoning was it would be a good way for her to release some teenage angst. As for me, my usual way of coping with stress is to cook dishes with half a pound of melted cheese in them. Boxercise had to be worth a go.

I met Flo in the reception area and she was already kitted

out. I changed into tracksuit bottoms and trainers and stuffed my work clothes into the changing room locker. The exercise room was high-ceilinged and echoey and the male trainer, well-toned and with a shaved head, ticked us off his list. There were ten of us in the class, all women.

'Now, you are to stop if anything starts to hurt. We'll start slow and build it up,' he said.

He launched us into a vigorous warm-up session. We had to run across the room, squat and then make punching motions with each arm.

'So run, squat and punch, run, squat and punch,' he shouted.

The room rang with his voice and our running feet. He kept the tempo up for ten minutes. So that was his idea of starting slow. He clapped his hands.

'Now please get into pairs.'

Flo and I paired up and collected one pair of boxing gloves and one strap-on pad, like a kind of shield which you put your arm through.

'You're going to take it in turns to punch at the pad, like this.'

He picked a fit-looking woman in the front row and demonstrated the moves with her. He took up a defensive posture with the pad as she punched at him.

'So, ten minutes with your partner and then we'll change over,' he said.

Flo wanted to be the first to punch so I got into position and she laid into my pad with great gusto. Being the defensive partner was harder work than I expected. The trainer was walking around the room watching our moves.

'Good work,' he said to Flo.

We changed positions. I caught a glimpse of myself, all flushed and shiny. I put on the gloves.

'Punch harder, Mum,' Flo said.

Sweat had started to trickle between my breasts.

'Imagine I'm someone you really don't like and you want to knock me out.'

I brought Lori Kerwell's face to mind and I started to find a rhythm. It was cathartic and I was using muscles that had seen little action in a long time. The trainer clapped his hands again and made us form a line in front of him.

'Now for the group exercise,' he said.

Flo and I stood at the back of the line. The woman at the front put on gloves and the rest of us had the pads on. She had to move all the way down the line doing ten punches on each pad, then the next person would take her place. I hated the idea that everyone would be watching me.

'I don't want to do that, not in front of everyone,' I whispered to Flo.

'You *have* to,' she said.

We were moving up the line and Flo had reached the front. She punched down the line looking vigorous and in control. I was the last to go and it nearly finished me off. My arms and shoulders were shrieking their protest and my hair was plastered to my forehead. The trainer clapped his hands.

'Time for warm down,' he shouted.

I was elated to have got through it. We were both on an endorphin high and linked arms as we headed home.

'I loved it,' Flo said.

'You were good at it. I'm Mrs Beetroot Face. That's a class for you and Rosie, I think.'

The day had ended better than it had begun and I had my weekend with Douglas to look forward to.

CHAPTER TWENTY-THREE

Chalk Farm flat, Saturday

My arms and legs were sore from the class last night and I had a good long soak in the bath. I spent the rest of the morning fussing around Flo, overcompensating because I was going away. Douglas arrived and I brought him in.

'Flo, come and meet Douglas,' I called.

She came out of her room but stood on the threshold with her arms crossed as he tried to make conversation. He asked her about the fashion shoot. She wasn't rude but she wasn't the friendly, charming girl she can be sometimes. She was watching us like a hawk as I showed him around our home and it made me feel awkward.

'I guess we need to get on our way,' I said.

I had a last-minute tremor about leaving Flo. Maybe she was really nervous about the shoot tomorrow and here I was leaving her to deal with it on her own. I went to give her a hug.

'Janis will be here by four, sweetheart, and I'll call you when we reach the hotel. And Harriet will pick you up at quarter to nine on Sunday.'

'I know, Mum. You already told me that,' she said.

I have a habit of repeating myself when I'm anxious. She followed us out and Douglas put my bag in the boot of his dark grey Saab. Flo's expression was watchful as I kissed her on the cheek. We set off for Sussex and in spite of my guilt it felt good to be getting out of London.

'Tell me about your friend and his hotel.'

'Dan, he's a good bloke. He ran a bar in Shoreditch, which then became a second and then a third bar. Against everyone's expectations it turns out he's a brilliant businessman. He made a mint when he sold the bars. But this hotel is a major step up for him.'

'I can imagine. How did you meet?'

'He was married to Claire's best friend at school and she introduced us.'

My stomach contracted. Did this mean that Claire Cooper-Pitlochry was going to be at the opening? I found the idea of an encounter with her alarming.

'They split up a while back. It was a nasty divorce. Claire stayed friends with his ex and Dan and I, well, he's a good mate and we've got closer recently.'

Since they both broke up with their wives, I thought. I relaxed. Of course Douglas would never be so crass as to invite me to an event where his estranged wife would be present.

He played David Bowie tracks through his speakers and we made good time getting out of London. As we reached Arundel he turned on his satnav.

'The next bit is all twists and turns and it's easy to miss his turning,' he said.

He drove along a series of smaller roads which were framed by trees meeting overhead to make a tunnel of green dappled light. The hedgerows were a mass of wildflowers, and birds dipped and swooped in front of the car. Douglas drove slowly round a deep corner and we reached two gateposts. Stone lions sat atop each of the gateposts and as we turned between them there was a vista of mature trees lining a long drive. The hotel came into view, an elegant Georgian building with two other barn-like buildings standing behind it. Douglas parked and turned off the engine and we sat and looked out.

'It's a boutique hotel and he's got fifteen rooms. There are eight in the house and seven in that great barn,' he said.

The barn had been converted and had skylights in its roof.

'And the third building?'

'He uses that for staff accommodation.'

'And you've been here before?'

'Oh yes, when Dan was planning the refurbishment I spent two weeks here and we camped in the house. I painted some of the upper corridors.'

'Really?'

'Nothing too demanding. Dan's done a huge amount to get it to this point.'

Douglas carried his bag and mine and we entered the main house to find Dan standing there.

'Dougie! So glad you made it.'

He was a broad-shouldered stocky man with ginger hair and warm brown eyes.

'I wouldn't have missed it for the world.'

They did that punching each other on the shoulder thing which men do when they'd like to hug but feel it would be too much.

'This is Liz Lyon.'

'Welcome, Liz.'

We shook hands and he was looking at me with interest, taking the measure of Douglas's new woman.

'What a setting with those magnificent trees,' I said.

'Aren't they wonderful? There are some ancient trees in the mix. And it's a ten-minute walk to the beach from here. Come on, I'll show you to your room.'

He had allocated us a room in the main house on the first floor. It was pretty, with pale yellow walls and dark wood furniture.

'Get comfortable. There's tea and coffee in the main sitting room or something stronger if you prefer it. I'm needed in the kitchen.'

He left us and we stood and grinned at each other. Our room was dominated by the large and luxurious bed with a thick duvet covered by a white bedspread. Douglas hauled our bags onto the bed. I went into the bathroom which was a splendid affair with a free-standing bath on claw legs and a large shower with a rainforest fitting.

'Great bathroom, come look,' I said.

He joined me in there.

'That bath is big enough for the two us,' he said.

He put his arms around me and we embraced.

'You can scrub my back,' he said.

'It will be my pleasure but I'm going to unpack now because I've got a dress for tonight and it needs to hang.'

Douglas pulled off his shoes and arranged two pillows behind his back and sat on the bed watching me as I hung up my dress and chattered nervously. I carried my wash things into the bathroom. I locked the door and used the toilet, flushing it as I peed so he couldn't hear. I knew I was being faintly ridiculous. This whole weekend was about getting intimate. He took two minutes to unpack. I called Flo but she didn't pick up and it went to answer machine. I said we'd arrived safely and she could WhatsApp me as the phone signal was patchy but the Wi-Fi was good.

'I'm not ready to mingle with the other guests. Shall we go for a walk and I'll show you the beach?' he said.

We headed for the wood beyond the converted barn. There was a gully running down the side of an overgrown path and you could hear water gurgling over stones. It got darker as we went in deeper. There was some leaf fall and that earthy, musky smell you get in woods. Mushroom smell, my mum calls it. We heard movement in the canopy of trees above us and small rustlings at our feet but we didn't encounter anyone as we followed the twists and turns of the path. We emerged and the horizon appeared in front of us; bright and open after the dark spaces of the wood. The beach was divided by wooden breakwaters stretching in orderly sequence to our right and our left. A gull sat on the post of the breakwater closest to us, surveying the scene. It was a pebble beach and I was glad I'd changed into my walking boots.

We crunched over the pebbles, hand in hand, a light wind in our face. In the distance I saw a woman throwing a ball for her border collie and the dog splashing into the waves to retrieve it. After about fifteen minutes of the pebbles we reached a small bay and there was a patch of sand. We sat down and I breathed in deeply.

'This is wonderful. Flo and I don't get out of London enough.'

'Stew and I like to get away at weekends if we can.'

He picked up a shell and examined its pink interior and handed it to me.

'That's a pretty one,' I said.

We watched the waves coming in and I was lulled by their hypnotic rhythm and didn't feel the need to say anything.

'I find the sound of the sea comforting, probably from all those holidays in Sheringham. I remember an argument I had with my mum once. We were trying to describe what the sea sounds like and I said it roared but she said it growled,' he said.

'It's more of a loud whisper today,' I said.

'It's a gentler coastline here than on the east coast, a lot less exposed.'

'And no sandy cliffs to climb either.'

He smiled at that and put his arm around me. He started to talk about Stewart, how he spent more time with him now, more time than he used to, and he was glad about that.

'He's taken the break-up hard, you see. I guess being an only child you feel responsible for your parents. So he keeps trying to set up meetings between Claire and me and they always end up with recriminations and drive us even further apart.'

'Flo is possessive about me too. That's why she was prickly with you.'

'She was OK. I understood where it was coming from. They don't want to share us, do they?'

'I guess she still hopes that Ben and I could get back together, though she must know that isn't going to happen,' I said.

'He's in Dubai, right?'

'Since last December.'

The woman with the collie passed us. He was a fine-looking dog and was running along by the sea's edge, his tail in the air and his posture joyful.

'That's a happy dog,' Douglas said to the woman.

'Oh yes, he just loves to paddle,' she said.

As we walked back to the hotel Douglas told me how he had always wanted a dog, a proper dog a labrador or a collie, but Claire had refused point blank saying dogs brought in mud and destroyed furniture.

*

It was the sort of hotel that comes into its own in the autumn and winter; deep sofas, logs piled in a basket by the fireplace and thick emerald green curtains, not yet drawn. I took my boots off at the door and we sank down on one of the sofas and Douglas fetched us each a brandy.

'To warm us up before we get ready for dinner,' he said.

I snuggled up to him and we watched the light through the windows change as the sun started to sink slowly behind the trees. I was held in a cocoon of contentment.

Thirty guests had been invited to the opening and they were a mixture of Dan's friends and food and travel writers. As we were getting changed, Douglas said Dan had invited a few money men along too.

'He needs to raise some extra cash and hopes this weekend will wow them.'

He zipped me into my little black dress.

'Suits you,' he said.

I kissed him on the cheek but he pulled me to him and kissed me on the lips.

'Ready?' he said.

I put in my crystal drop earrings and we walked down the staircase hand in hand. We had been asked to assemble in the main sitting room at seven-thirty and everything was done to make us feel cherished. We were offered an aperitif of champagne or Tio Pepe. Most of the people there recognised Douglas and were taking covert looks at me to establish who his date might be. There was one guest there who I wished had not spotted me: Austin Lane. He used to work at StoryWorld, on the money side. I hardly knew him as I'd been in a junior role at the time, but I knew that he and Julius were still in touch. He noted that I was with Douglas Pitlochry and gave me a small nod across the room. I wondered if he was going to approach us but Dan came just then.

'Please take your time but we'd like to know your choice for the main course before you sit down. Can you mark your card and put your name on the top.'

He circled the room handing each of us a handwritten menu and a small gold pencil. He stood next to us as we read through the menu. There were four dishes on offer: fish, meat, poultry and a vegetarian choice called a pithivier which I had never heard of.

'What is pithivier?'

'It's a traditional French pastry in the shape of a dome and we've filled ours with roasted butternut squash, blue cheese and walnuts,' Dan said.

'I'm going to try that.'

'Good choice.'

I circled the dish with my pencil and printed my name at the top. Douglas chose the roast pheasant and Dan took our cards.

'Now, do you think I should put in a croquet course? There's plenty of room for one, or is that twee?' he said.

'No, it's a nice idea,' Douglas said.

'I agree. It will get people out and admiring your grounds,' I said.

We were both slightly drunk when we said goodnight to Dan and congratulated him on the marvellous food and wine.

We found our way up the stairs and Douglas had difficulty getting the key to our room to work and I started to giggle which was uncool of me. Douglas pulled the bedspread off and we fell onto the bed and undressed each other. He laddered my tights as he pulled them off. At last we were naked and able to feel each other's bodies. It started as an awkward fumble and became more and more intense and satisfying. I had worried momentarily about his back but it wasn't a problem. Afterwards, we lay under the duvet with my head on his chest and the smell of sex between us and it felt so good. I hadn't had sex for a year and realised I had shut down the part of myself that wanted it. We rolled over and cuddled and fell asleep.

On Sunday morning Douglas got up and went into the bathroom. I heard him turn the taps on.

'I'm running us a bath,' he called out.

'Lots of bubbles, please.'

On the bedside table there was headed stationery and post-cards featuring the hotel. I took a postcard, addressed it to Fenton and wrote on the back:

Fourth date. Magic! Liz xxx

I'd post it later.

The breakfast was as splendid as the dinner. There was a silver tureen of porridge with a choice of cream, honey, maple syrup and even whisky to add to it. Whisky at breakfast! The full English was all local produce or you could order had-dock cooked in milk, or kippers. Douglas chose the kippers.

He spread butter and marmalade thickly on his toast and took one bite of kipper and a bite of toast and marmalade.

'That's a strange mix,' I said.

'A discovery I made some years ago. You must try it; the sweetness of the marmalade is perfect with the salty kippers.'

Austin Lane walked in and he nodded at me but did not approach our table. Douglas saw me noticing him.

'You know him, don't you?'

'He used to work at StoryWorld when I was a lowly researcher,' I said.

'I've seen half a dozen folks I know. They've had the good manners to keep their distance. Now, Sunday newspapers by the fire or another walk?'

'I'm feeling awfully lazy,' I said.

We took the papers to our room and got back into bed.

The traffic was awful on our return to London. I'd started to feel tense and Douglas picked up on this and reassured me that he'd get me back to my flat by four p.m. as promised. Flo had WhatsApped me this morning when she was in the taxi with Harriet en route to the shoot, but I'd heard nothing since. There would have been no opportunity for her to contact me while the shoot was going on and I would hear all about it soon enough. We drew up outside my flat at ten to four and he switched off the engine.

'Thank you for getting me back on time.'

'The time flew by,' he said.

He leaned over and we kissed and nuzzled for a few minutes. I didn't want our weekend to end. He got out, retrieved my case and carried it to my door.

'I've had a wonderful time,' I said.

'Me too. I'm going to make myself scarce now because Florence needs your full attention.'

We hugged for a long moment and then he was gone.

It was nearly six and I had unpacked and still there was no sign of Flo. I looked in her bedroom. She must have been trying on lots of outfits before she left for the shoot because half her clothes were piled on her bed. My mobile pinged and it was a text from Harriet.

> In the cab and nearly at yours. Flo is upset.
> ☹ Hx

I texted straight back.

> Why upset? Lx

No answer came back and I went and stood on the pavement, scanning our road for an approaching taxi. I was trying to think what could have upset Flo. Finally I saw the taxi chugging up our road and I waved. Flo got out and as she said goodbye I heard Harriet say:

'You looked fantastic, the best of the three, *honestly*.'

Flo had her head down and she rushed past me and into the flat. Once inside she burst into tears.

'He made me look like a freak, like something out of *American Horror Story*!'

She flung herself into her room, pushed all the clothes off the bed and sobbed into her pillow. I sat and waited for the storm of emotion to subside. Finally, she sat up and rubbed at her face. I handed her a tissue. She was wearing a dark lipstick

I had never seen before, plum in colour. It was smeared and her lips were swollen from the crying.

'Mum you *have* to get him to edit me out. They can't put it out on TV.'

'I don't understand.'

Her eyes widened and she groaned.

'Oh my God, I told all my friends about it. They can't see it. They can't!'

'Calm down, sweetie, and tell me what's wrong.'

'I *hated* what he made me wear. I *hated* the make-up and the way they made my hair all wild and curly. The other two girls looked normal but I looked like a *freak*.'

More noisy tears followed this.

'But I heard Harriet say you looked fantastic,' I said.

'I looked *horrible* but I couldn't say anything because he works for you!'

She was becoming angry now.

'Why did you ever let me do it? Everyone's going to laugh at me when they see it. You *have* to stop it going out.'

She threw herself back on her pillow. I reminded myself that no matter how self-dramatising and silly teenagers can be, I must not make light of her concerns.

'Have you eaten anything, darling?'

Her only response was more noisy tears. Flo has a tendency to get emotional when her blood sugar is low. Maybe if I could get some food into her she would calm down.

'I'm going to make you some cheese on toast,' I said.

I got the grater out. What I really wanted to do was to call Fenton and tell her all about my heavenly weekend and relive it in the telling. I was like a silly lovesick teenager myself and it would not do for Flo to hear what a wonderful time I'd had.

CHAPTER TWENTY-FOUR

StoryWorld TV station, London Bridge

As soon as the morning meeting was over I asked Harriet if she would show me the rushes of the fashion shoot.

'Is Flo still upset?' she said as we went down to the edit suite.

'I'm afraid she is. I wanted to check what it is that's causing her so much anguish.'

'I don't understand it. She looked wonderful, honestly.'

The shoot had been done as a series of freeze-frame stills rather than as moving footage. We saw the three girls arriving in their own clothes in a long room which had a clothes rail along one side with the makeover outfits hanging on it. Then Harriet spooled through the series of shots, showing each girl in her makeover outfit.

'Guy had three themes, you see: Sport Luxe, Nineties Revival and Twisted Beauty.'

She brought up the images of Flo. She was dressed in a high-necked black Victoriana blouse with a velvet bolero on top and black trousers finished off with lace-up boots. Her hair had been teased into extravagant curls and her make-up was dramatic, a pale face and dark plum lips. I hardly recognised her. But the make-up was not extreme and it was definitely not in horror movie territory, as she had claimed. She looked otherworldly, a fragile beauty and older than her fifteen years.

'Doesn't she look wonderful?' Harriet said.

'Yes, she does, but she's convinced she looks like a freak. Can you show me the other girls?'

They both looked far more contemporary. The Sport Luxe girl was wearing black leggings, a print jumper and a red puffa jacket. Her hair was in a high ponytail and there was a splash of blue on her eyelids. The Nineties Revival girl was in a pink slip dress with a white T-shirt underneath, a choker necklace and a washed-out denim jacket. Flo had been shot inside the building sitting on a chair with a high back and the lighting was moody, one side of her face in shadow. The other two girls were standing on the roof terrace. They looked more like teenagers out having fun. Flo looked striking and she stood out, and fifteen-year-olds do not like to stand out. This must have been what was disturbing her.

'She's begged me to get her edited out of the story.'

'Oh, please don't. It won't work as an item with only two models and Guy adored the way Flo looked. He said she was the jewel in the crown.'

She was right that the item wouldn't work with only two makeovers. There wasn't enough contrast without Flo. And could I really be so unprofessional as to insist that Guy edited out my daughter, having agreed that she would do the shoot? What possible grounds could I give him? That she looked too striking? No, this had to go out and I had to persuade Flo that it was fine. Which was not going to be easy to do. I felt a vein start to throb in my temple.

'I'll talk to her tonight. Hopefully she'll have calmed down. Fifteen-year-old girls can be very up and down.'

'She's a real beauty but maybe that scares her,' Harriet said.

I found it interesting that Harriet had said that.

★

Mid-afternoon I got a second call from Ledley's agent Angela Hodge. She had called that morning and left a message with Ziggy. I had been putting off calling her back, expecting a hard time from her. There was no opening greeting and she was extremely clipped with me.

'We need a meeting at the earliest opportunity,' she said.

I find her abrasive and I didn't want to meet with her.

'Do we? What do you want to discuss?'

'Ledley's position on the show, of course; how you plan to develop his screen presence now he's the co-host.'

'We can meet in due course to discuss Ledley's terms and conditions but I'm afraid I'm swamped this week.'

'I'll be blunt, Liz, we feel you are showing favouritism.'

'I find your choice of words inappropriate,' I said coldly.

'And I find the way Ledley is being sidelined deeply disappointing,' she fired back.

'It's early days. I suggest you wait and see how the show settles down over the next month.'

'I cannot agree to that. I promised Ledley we would meet soon. I've got my diary open.' Her voice was glacial.

I agreed to a meeting next week but as I put the phone down I was cursing Angela Hodge and her persistence. I think I'm getting infected by the prevailing nastiness at the station. I'm not sure where nice, accommodating Liz has gone.

Chalk Farm flat, 7.35 p.m.

Flo pounced on me as soon as I opened the flat door, not even giving me time to take my jacket off or put my bag down which irritated me.

'Did you see it?'

'I looked at the rushes and you look wonderful. I can't understand what the problem is.'

'You're just saying that. You know I look weird.'

I filled the kettle and put out two mugs and she looked at me suspiciously.

'You are going to cut me out of it, aren't you?'

'I need tea. Sit down and we're going to have a proper conversation about this.'

I made us tea and took the mugs to the table. I opened the biscuit tin and offered her a ginger nut. She shook her head.

'OK. I agree that you look different from the other girls but that's because Guy thought you could carry off that look. Harriet said he considers it the best look by far and he was so complimentary about you.'

She shook her head.

'They look normal. He made me look like something out of a horror movie!'

'That's not true.'

'Why can't he drop the bits with me in?'

'He wants to show three different looks and he needs the contrast. I can't insist that he edits you out.'

'Of course you can. You're his boss. You pay him. You can tell him what to do.' Her voice was rising.

'It doesn't work like that. It will ruin the item if we leave you out and—'

'I can't believe you're putting the programme above me.' She pushed up from the table and started to shout: 'No, I can believe it, actually, because you *always* put your job above me!'

'You wanted to do the shoot, Flo. I didn't want to mix work and family but you pressed and pressed me. You have to learn that actions have consequences and anyway, I think you look lovely.'

But she had gone, had hurled herself into her room and slammed the door so hard that it reverberated for a full minute. Mr Crooks had been heading to join her. He stared at the closed door then started to lick his front paw and clean his face.

There was a letter on the table from the small claims court. I ripped it open and Ron Osborne has made a counter claim against me. I read his statement with mounting fury. It was full of lies. He claimed that I booked him in for four days' work and then changed my mind about the dates at the last moment. This resulted in him losing four days' work at a cost of eight hundred pounds to himself. He was therefore prepared to pay me back two hundred pounds of my deposit but not a penny more.

'You liar!' I shouted it out loud and Mr Crooks gave me a quizzical look. I dug out my mobile and my fingers were trembling as I spooled back through my texts to him. There had been some discussion about dates but no change initiated by me. How I wished now that I had put everything into writing more formally.

'You lying bastard,' I said.

He wanted to fight and he was going to get a fight. I would reject his counter claim and see him at the small claims court. I opened my fridge. I was out of cheese and eggs and there was only a piece of soggy frittata and a bowl of green beans left over from Friday.

I was in the bathroom when Douglas rang our landline.

Flo picked up and I could hear that she was being far from friendly to him. I hurried out and grabbed the phone from her. He kept his call short. He must have picked up that Flo and I were at loggerheads. We arranged to meet in Covent Garden on Thursday. He said he fancied going to Joe Allen for dinner and would tell me why later. I wanted to say something warm and tender after our lovely weekend but Flo watched me the whole time I was talking to him, her arms crossed and her eyes narrowed.

'Don't do that,' I said crossly when I'd hung up.

'Do what?'

'Listen in on my private conversations.'

'You care more about him than you do about me,' she said.

'You know that's not true.'

'If you cared about me you wouldn't let that shoot go out!'

When Flo gets an idea in her head she won't let it go. There is no way I can invite Douglas back to the flat on Thursday.

Later, I heard her talking to Ben on Skype. She wasn't making any attempt to lower her voice. I shouldn't have listened in. I'd told her not to listen to my private conversations. But I was rooted to the spot outside her door. I seem to be doing this recently and it makes me feel bleak. Where were the cosy mother and daughter chats we used to have? Her complaints at my heartlessness over the fashion shoot were long and detailed. I wondered if Ben was putting up any resistance. I had to remember what friends had told me; that teenage girls pull away from their mums but come back eventually. Then Flo started in on my relationship with Douglas and it was clear how much she resented me seeing him.

'Mum doesn't care how I feel any more,' she said.

I had become the Wicked Witch of the West.

CHAPTER TWENTY-FIVE

StoryWorld TV station, London Bridge

Martine and I were sitting on the sofa in Julius's office. I'd been called in at short notice. She had her pad open to take notes and he was pacing up and down his large office looking irritable.

'We've heard from WayToGo; from their head of comms. He's been very specific about what they want in the pilot,' Julius said.

'I bet he has,' I said.

'Each week we are to feature one of their twelve key destinations. They're all in Europe. They want moving footage as well as stills. And, here's the killer bit, a competition at the end so they can collect emails and mobile numbers.'

I hated doing Phone-in competitions. There had been some scandals about the ones where viewers called in to answer a simple question and paid a premium rate to do so. The regulator had stepped in and on-air competitions were now hedged around with all kinds of regulations and required legal wording. We hadn't run one for ages.

'Competitions are a major pain,' I said.

'They are a major pain and are tacky, to boot, but the sponsor has spoken and it's a requirement. The prize will be two WayToGo tickets to the featured destination.'

'Who does Ledley speak to?'

'That's up to us, but not to viewers. We're going to have to use footage from viewers so you need to find a tame expert who doesn't expect a big fee. A woman would work better with Ledley. Lori wants to have something to show them in three weeks.'

'That's really pushing it! We've got to get the footage in,' I said.

'That's the time frame and it's non-negotiable, that's the phrase she used.'

I saw Martine stiffen at that. She gave me a tiny nudge with her elbow. She wasn't used to having Julius dictated to in this way. Nor was I. She snapped her pad shut and we got up to leave.

'A quick word about something else, Liz.'

I sat down again. The thought of making the pilot was depressing me. What could I do so that it didn't look cheap and dreary?

'I saw Austin Lane last night. Said he saw you at a hotel opening with Douglas Pitlochry?'

It was inevitable that word would get out but I resented Julius raising it.

'Yes, a pleasant event. I would recommend the hotel, it's a great location,' I said, trying to sound blasé.

'I'm sure it was but you need to be careful around *him*,' he said.

'For heaven's sake!'

'Don't be offended. Well, you will be offended, but I wouldn't trust him as far as I could throw him.'

I stood up.

'Stop it, please. I don't ask you about Amber. Don't ask me about him or we're going to fall out.'

'He's an operator, Liz. Always has been. He has feelers out

everywhere and would love to get one up on StoryWorld. You should ask yourself what his motives are.'

'I'm not listening to any more of this. It's frankly insulting and what I do in my free time is my business.'

I left his office but his words had lodged with me and, like an annoying song that won't leave your head, I felt unsettled for the rest of the day.

I'd got into the habit of having a coffee with Henry and it was an oasis of calm and sanity in my day. We both felt the show was a car crash at the moment and it felt good to talk about it freely. We vented about how badly Fizzy was behaving and how much Ledley had changed for the worse. Timing discipline on the show is a thing of the past. This morning it was Ledley who ignored the timings on his slot with Betty. Henry and the director had to give him his countdown three times.

We stood outside with our coffees and he smoked. Recently he had moved over to roll-ups. They were less toxic than ready-mades, he said. He knew he should stop and this was stage one of his mission.

I told him Ziggy was about to lose her bedsit; that she was frightened and that it was affecting the whole team.

'Simon and Harriet are looking on rental sites every day but no joy yet,' I said.

'Poor kid.'

He blew smoke out and crinkled his eyes as the smoke curled up.

'I might be able to help,' he said.

'Really?'

'My sister Annie had a granny flat built for Mum at the back of her house. Flat is too grand a term for it. It's a bed-sitting room with a separate galley kitchen and a shower.'

'That's exactly what she's looking for.'

'Annie hasn't had the heart to do anything about it since Mum died. It's taken her nine months to give Mum's stuff to the charity shop.'

'Where is it?'

'In Lewisham, a bit out but you can get here. I could have a word with her.'

'Oh, Henry, would you? You'd be doing us such a favour.'

'I'll call her tonight.'

In my lunch hour I was eating a sandwich at my desk when Harriet tapped on my door. She hovered on the threshold looking awkward.

'Sorry to interrupt your lunch,' she said.

'Is something up?'

She finally stepped into my room and closed the door.

'It's kind of difficult...'

Last year, when Harriet had that awful problem with Julius, she clammed up on me. It was weeks later that I found out what had happened and I could feel my anxiety rising now.

'A problem shared,' I said.

She came further into the room.

'It's just that, well, Flo called me and she asked me to give her Guy Browne's phone number.'

'She did what?'

I stood up immediately and Harriet flinched at the expression on my face.

'She said she had to tell him how unhappy she was about the shoot and if only he understood...' Her voice trailed away.

'Did you give her his number?'

'No, I didn't, and she was nearly crying and I felt awful.'

I was furious with Flo. She had never done anything like this before, crossed a boundary at my work.

'Flo is *so* out of order. I'm really sorry, Harriet.'

'*I'm* sorry I ever mentioned the fashion shoot to her. If I hadn't done that...' Harriet said.

'Never mix work and family. Well, we've both learned that, haven't we? Look I need to call Flo at once.'

'Of course. I hope she won't hate me over this.'

Harriet left my room looking miserable and I punched in Flo's mobile number. The fashion item is going out tomorrow and this was her last-ditch attempt to stop it. Her phone went to voicemail and I blurted out my anger.

'Don't you even think about calling Guy Browne! I am so angry about this, Flo. You're way out of order.'

She would be back in her class by now and our showdown would have to wait till I got home.

It was nearly five when Simon came into my office. He must have noticed how I'd been slumped at my laptop for an age, staring at the screen. I had been trying to think about the travel pilot and had not come up with a single good idea. Instead I had been rehearsing what I would say to Flo when I got home.

'What's up, Liz?'

'I've got to make a bloody travel pilot in three weeks. The budget is zilch, the idea is tired and I don't know where to start.'

'Three weeks?'

'Yes; as decreed by Lori Kerwell.'

I shoved Martine's typed notes at him.

'Take a look.'

He sat down and read the short document.

'The tricky thing will be getting hold of viewers' footage,' he said. He took off his glasses and polished them. 'I could run a campaign on our Facebook page. Ask viewers to send their videos in, digital files only. It might work,' he said. 'There'd need to be some kind of inducement, of course. What can we offer them? One of our delightful StoryWorld mugs?'

I grimaced at the mention of the mugs which a previous marketing person had ordered in their hundreds and which took up valuable space in our prop store.

'Have you ever used one of those bloody mugs? They chip so easily,' I said.

'Can we offer an on-air mention? Footage sent in by Harry Smith from Leeds. People love to hear their names on the telly.'

'Or see it. That might work better as a caption,' I said.

'Leave it with me.'

'Thank you, Simon.'

It was the best thing I've done in years, making Simon my deputy. I called Janis and said she could leave early as I needed to talk to Flo and was on my way back.

Chalk Farm flat, 7 p.m.

Flo had decided to confront me head on and the minute I got in she came out of her room and started to shout at me.

'I called Harriet because you don't get it. I can't bear it if those pics of me go out.'

'Don't you ever do anything like that again. You put Harriet in a really difficult position,' I said.

'I had to do something. You weren't listening.'

'You were going to ring one of my presenters? You crossed a line, Flo, and I won't have it.'

The landline had started to ring. I ignored it.

'It's my body and I don't want your bloody awful TV station using those pics of me. Dad said I have the right of refusal.'

The reference to Ben was like a red rag to me and I started to shout. The phone was still ringing.

'Oh, did he! Did you tell him you signed a permission form before the shoot started? You're behaving like a totally spoiled brat and the shoot is going out tomorrow morning so bloody get over it.'

I went over to the phone and snatched it up. It was one of those stupid recorded calls about payment protection. I slammed the phone down. Flo had gone into her room and I heard her pulling her chair to wedge against the door. She was barricading herself in. Our relationship had come to that. I paced up and down the sitting room thinking I would phone Ben and tell him to butt out. He had asked me to let her do the fashion shoot, for chrissakes, and now there was trouble he was backing her; anything so he could be the good-time dad and I could be in the wrong. I went into my bedroom and called his number. It rang and rang but he didn't pick up. Then I called Fenton at home. She didn't answer either; probably still at work. I took off my boots and I felt like crying. I heard the front door slam and I rushed out. Flo had left a note on the kitchen table.

I hate you.
I've gone to stay with Rosie.

I did what I always do when I'm feeling stressed and turned to comfort food. I made myself macaroni cheese with an extra helping of Cheddar. It was death by cheese. My flat has always been my haven from work but at the moment it's warfare at work and warfare at home.

CHAPTER TWENTY-SIX

StoryWorld TV station, London Bridge

The teenage fashion item went out this morning. I saw Guy Browne briefly before he went into the studio.

'Your daughter has such a great look about her. Maybe we could use her again sometime,' he said.

He thought this would please me but my toes were curling inside my shoes.

'Thank you.'

I smiled back at him knowing that it wasn't going to happen, ever. Fizzy's discussion with Guy overran, but only by a minute. We've started to feel grateful if it's less than a two-minute overrun. The director thought the item was well done and we've had a good response from our viewers, several saying who was the lovely young woman in the black blouse and how cool she looked. I'd like to show these comments to Flo but she isn't talking to me!

I told Henry about it over our coffees.

'What really bugs me is the role Ben played in this. He called me from Dubai saying you must let Flo do the shoot. I had reservations from the start. Then he tells Flo she has the right of refusal. I mean, that's irresponsible, isn't it? He should have backed me.'

'Did he back you when you were together?'

'Sometimes he did. But he always had this tendency to be the good-time dad. He used to bring little presents home for

Flo several times a week. I know I sound curmudgeonly but honestly, Henry, it was too much.'

'She'll be home tonight, won't she?'

'I hope so.'

But I was going out and Flo would be asleep by the time I got in. There would be no chance of a reconciliation tonight.

'You could do without this,' Henry said. 'Anyway, Annie is happy for Ziggy to come look at the flat. Tell Ziggy to give her a call.' He pulled a piece of paper out of his back pocket with his sister's number and address written on it.

'That's great. Thanks so much. I'll tell her straight away.'

I wasn't meeting Douglas till eight and had planned to work till seven but all afternoon a feeling of restlessness and antici-pation had been growing in me. I decided to get the Tube to Waterloo and walk to Covent Garden from there. My team had left for the night when I met Julius at the top of the stairs. We walked down together.

'Saul is taking Fizzy out to dinner tonight. He said she needed to feel more cherished by the station,' he said.

'I'm pleased to hear that. Where's he taking her?'

'The Dorchester; bit of a traditionalist, is our Saul. She's been misbehaving but with Fizzy blandishments work better than rebukes.'

'That's true, and anyway, she had cause to feel aggrieved,' I said.

We had reached the exit and he stopped and looked at me. I wished I'd bitten my lip. It was foolish to make a point about Fizzy's grievance.

'Where are you off to?'

He must have noticed my date dress and my touched up make-up and earrings. I was not going to mention Douglas after our last conversation about him.

'A reunion with friends,' I said.

'Do you need a lift into town?'

Julius never gets the Tube. He drives in every day and parks his Mercedes in his designated spot on the forecourt.

'Thanks, but I'm going to walk. I need the exercise,' I said.

I watched him sweep out of the station as I headed towards London Bridge Tube. We were allies at the moment and I wanted it to stay that way. I got out at Waterloo and crossed by the giant IMAX cinema which sits like a great lit bowl on the approach to the bridge. It was a mild evening and halfway across the bridge I stopped for ten minutes. The rush of commuters was thinning and I watched the traffic on the river and felt myself unwind. When Fenton comes to London we come here sometimes because she loves the way so many landmark buildings rise on either side of the bridge. She prefers the view downriver with the brutal bulk of the National Theatre and the Oxo Tower and St Paul's on the other bank, refusing to be overshadowed by later high-rise additions. Fenton looks at the view with fresh eyes and has made me appreciate it. One time she talked me into taking the river bus from Charing Cross to Greenwich and her enthusiasm was infectious.

I continued up to the Strand and turned towards the piazza at Covent Garden. A man on stilts wearing candy-striped trousers and a tall hat was entertaining a clutch of sight-seers with a strangely graceful bending dance. The music was provided by his partner, also in motley, who played a mournful tune on an accordion. I was still early so I joined the ring of spectators until his dance ended with an elaborate bow. We clapped our appreciation. He loomed in front of us, whipped off his hat and presented it to us. Close up he looked older than I expected and his make-up was that of a sad clown. It was the kind of face that would have scared Flo when she was a little girl. I dropped some coins into his hat.

As I walked up to Covent Garden Tube my longing to see Douglas was growing in me. The last time was our delicious weekend. It was five to eight and he was already there. He hugged me.

'I wanted us to go to Joe Allen because my boss took me there when I got my first big break. We sat at the bar and drank far too many martinis. I've had a soft spot for the place ever since.'

You enter Joe Allen by a staircase leading down to a large, well-lit basement, the walls covered with posters of theatre productions. The bar runs the length of the right-hand wall. We perched on barstools and he ordered and paid for two martinis. I rarely drink them. The barmen at Joe Allen are artists and use the bar as their stage and the bottles as their props, pouring the spirits from on high into the mixers. We watched ours mix the martinis and decant the clear liquid into two glasses. We clinked.

'Cheers.'

You get a mighty strong hit from that small glass with its single green olive.

'How's your week been?' Douglas said.

'Awful, actually. Flo hated how she looked in that fashion shoot and we've had a bad old time over it. I'll never mix work and home again.'

He smiled sympathetically. He was sitting facing the

entrance and his expression changed as he spotted someone he recognised over my shoulder.

'Ledley just came in with two women,' he said, and I was surprised that he sounded put-out.

I looked over my shoulder. The maître d' was showing them to a corner table in the second room.

'Who are his two admirers?'

'The woman in the orange suit is Lori Kerwell, our head of sales and marketing. And the other woman is Angela Hodge, his agent.'

He stood up.

'I think we should eat somewhere else.'

'Really?'

He took my hand, apologised to the maître d' that something urgent had cropped up, and steered me up the stairs and out into the street. I was surprised that he was so eager to leave, even though seeing Ledley with Lori had taken the shine off the place for me.

'We couldn't have talked freely with them in earshot,' he said.

We wandered around for a while, walking away from Covent Garden and towards the garish lights of Chinatown with eager proprietors urging us to enter their establishments. But Douglas paid them little attention. I could tell he was annoyed that our plan had been thwarted and I was asking myself why he had made us leave Joe Allen. Was it because he didn't want to be seen with me? The idea made me miserable. He hailed a cab.

'Let's head back to Camden. Plenty of good gastropubs there.'

We ended up at the Lord Stanley off Camden Road and finally we were sitting opposite each other with our food ordered and a bottle of red between us. Something was bothering him and we skirted around a few topics. I updated him on Ron Osborne and my claim but he wasn't really listening.

'Look, I didn't want to start the evening with this but there's something about Ledley I need to share with you,' he said.

'Go on, I'm on tenterhooks.'

I had said it flippantly but he looked serious. He swilled the wine in his glass, drank it and glanced around the bar then back at me.

'Ledley approached a journo at my station. Told him he knows the identity of Fizzy's lover; Zachary's father.'

I was frozen with horror. He didn't take his eyes of my face as he said: 'Bob.'

Now I looked down at the table. I was shocked at Ledley's betrayal; to have gone to our rival station. I could think of nothing to say, had no idea how to deny it. The silence built between us.

'I told the journo we don't deal with tittle-tattle,' he said finally.

That was why he had hurried me out of Joe Allen. But was Douglas trying to get me to confirm it?

'This is so hateful,' I said.

'I think he might try to find another outlet, someone who is prepared to use the info. Fizzy is news, as you know.'

'It's pure speculation on Ledley's part,' I said. I felt that Douglas was digging for information and it disturbed me.

'They might make a friendly duo on screen but this sure ain't comradely of him!' Douglas said.

'He's changed so much, and not for the better.'

'Maybe you need to warn Fizzy,' he said just as the barman arrived with our plates of steak frites.

He placed them on our table. We engaged in a stilted conversation about whether mustard or béarnaise sauce was better with them. We didn't seem able to get back to the easy mood of the start of the evening. I chewed on my steak and swallowed with difficulty. We had been lovers that once and it had been lovely and I wanted to be able to open up to him and tell him what was going on at work and how miserable it was making me. But I could not do it. My loyalty to StoryWorld ran too deep and what I was thinking about was how I was going to confront Ledley with his treachery.

We left the pub before closing time.

'I'm going to have to get back to my very angry daughter,' I said.

We walked down to Camden Road but didn't link hands and he flagged a taxi for me.

'Sorry to have cast that shadow over our evening,' he said.

I kissed him on the cheek.

'I know you had to tell me.'

He opened the cab door for me.

'Good luck with Florence,' he said.

CHAPTER TWENTY-SEVEN

StoryWorld TV station, London Bridge

We had gone to an ad break when Henry's voice came over my earpiece.

'I need an urgent word about our next guest,' he said.

I had booked in ageing rocker Paul Angel who was doing his final tour all around the UK. It was actually his second final tour but tickets were selling and he was a name. I told the director there might be a problem and hurried out.

'He smells of drink. I think he's drunk. Do we let him go on?' Henry said.

'Where is he now?'

'In make-up. Ellen alerted me and it seems he's been up all night.'

Henry waited outside the make-up room and I went in. Paul Angel was sitting back in the chair as if the lights around the mirror were too bright.

His dyed black hair was backcombed, his cheeks were sunken and his eyes were bloodshot. He sipped on a mug of coffee.

'Paul, good to meet you. I'm Liz Lyon,' I said.

''S'all my pleasure,' he said.

He stood up and handed his mug to Ellen, winked at her.

'Thanks, love. Where do I go now?'

I needed more time to assess how he was going to perform on the sofa.

'I want to check the dates of your tour. Can you run through them with me?'

'Me roadie does all that. He's the man to ask,' he said.

He wasn't quite slurring and I decided we would risk it.

'This way please,' I said.

Henry led him to the studio to be miked up as I ran back to the gallery.

'A guest who's borderline drunk,' I told the director.

I got on the earpiece to Fizzy.

'Fizz, Paul Angel's been up all night, and he's a bit the worse for wear.'

She nodded and I watched as Henry placed him on the sofa next to her. Ledley was in the kitchen in preparation for his next item so there would be no help from that quarter if Paul Angel went weird on her. We came out of the ad break and Fizzy did the introductory link into camera.

'If, like me, you're a fan of rock and roll, my next guest needs no introduction. This morning we're joined by the legendary Paul Angel. Welcome to StoryWorld, Paul.'

'Good to meet ya, Fizzy.'

He was sitting with his legs spread wide and one arm looped over the top of the sofa grinning at her. His black shirt was unbuttoned to his breastbone. Strangely, he looked slightly better on camera than he had under the lights of the make-up mirror.

'Fizzy, that's a funny kind of a name,' he said.

'Oh, I know. My real name, which I've always *hated*, is Felicity. I mean honestly, Felicity.'

'Felicity,' he said, looking confused.

'We're going to keep this short,' the director said to the crew.

'You can see why I wanted to change it. Now, your many fans are thrilled about this tour, Paul. How's it going so far?'

'Going OK, ta.' He leaned forward and looked into the camera nearest to him. 'Hello, fans,' he said, grinning.

'We're playing his track in thirty seconds,' the director said.

'I believe you're taking in twenty venues, Paul?'

'Yeah.'

'And you were in Newcastle last night?'

'Good town,' he said and he pinched the bridge of his nose.

'So there's plenty of opportunity for your fans to see you live. Let's watch now what is certainly *my* favourite Paul Angel track.'

The director let the track run for a minute and a half. Paul Angel was nodding his head along to it and Fizzy was telling him that when it ended she was going to ask him what his favourite track of all time was.

'That was fabulous. We had the whole studio tapping along,' she said. 'Do you have a favourite track, Paul?'

It was the right question to ask because he talked for over a minute about how his first number one had come about. It was a story he had told many times.

'And wrap it,' the director said.

'If you go onto our Facebook site you can see all the dates and venues of Paul Angel's Final Tour. Don't miss it. And thank you so much for coming in today, Paul,' Fizzy said.

The director mixed to the cameras trained on Ledley in the kitchen as Henry guided a dazed-looking Paul Angel out of the studio. We had got away with it, just.

As soon as the morning meeting was over I went down to Ledley's dressing room and tapped on the door. I had been thinking about little else and knew he had to be confronted straight away. At the meeting Julius had thanked Fizzy for coping so well with a drunk guest. I had looked over at Ledley and thought, You swine. I shut the door behind me. He was on the phone and waved me in with great bonhomie but it felt false.

'Lovely to see you but I'm rushing off to a PR event with Lori, literally in the next fifteen minutes. Can it wait?' he said.

'No, I'm afraid it can't.'

He had picked up on my voice and threw his mobile onto the sofa.

'Is there a problem?'

'Yes, there is. I heard something disturbing last night, something about you which I find hard to believe.'

He rocked back on his heels and then stood very still. We stared at each other for a long moment.

'I was told you approached a journalist at a rival station and offered them information about Fizzy's private life.'

'Says who?' his voice was sharp.

I was pretty sure he hadn't seen me with Douglas last night. We had left sharpish and they had been in the other room.

'An impeccable source from that station. How could you do that?'

'Don't you dare get all high-handed with me, Liz.'

He was angry but he hadn't denied it.

'A rival station? Where's your loyalty?'

'Don't you talk to me about loyalty. You never stick up for me.'

'That's rubbish. You wouldn't have a TV spot without me.'

'Which no doubt you'll never let me forget!'

I was getting sidetracked.

'You talked to the opposition. You crossed a line. This gets out and it hurts the show.'

'The show!' He was contemptuous. 'That's all that matters to you. Bob's wife needs to know she's being cheated on.'

'And of course that's all that matters to you.'

'Meaning?'

'Fizzy. You don't care that you'll ruin Bob's marriage and what that'll do to his wife and daughters. You just want to get back at Fizzy.'

'So I'm supposed to let her undermine me day after day? *She's* hurting the show.'

'What's happened to you? This stinks, Ledley.'

'Don't play the guilt card. The woman's a tramp.' He spat the words out.

I wasn't going to shame him out of his determination to expose Fizzy. I would have to frighten him.

'Drop it now and I won't say anything to Julius. But if you carry on and approach anyone else I'm telling you now that you'll be in breach of your contract. Leaking to a rival TV station is gross misconduct.'

He smirked.

'And?'

'We can sack you for it.'

His face shut down. He pulled on his jacket and pocketed his mobile.

'It's your word against mine and everyone knows know you're on Team Fizzy.'

'You forget I have an impeccable source,' I said.

There was a light tap and before I could say anything else Lori had opened the door.

'Taxi's waiting. Oh, hello, Liz. Are you finished?'

'She was just leaving,' Ledley said.

I passed Lori, giving her the merest nod. Getting angry

makes me feel ill and I had a fight on my hands. Ledley was going to brazen this out. Was I prepared to involve Douglas to make my case? I did not want to do that at all. I could imagine how Julius would react if I told him that Douglas was the source of my intelligence.

The door to Fizzy's room was open and as I went by she called me in. She was standing by a bouquet of red roses on her table.

'These arrived from Saul, and in this lovely vase.'

My row with Ledley was scouring my head. The roses were dark red and flawless and arranged in a crystal vase. I bent over them and they had a delicate scent. I had expected a richer, darker scent, given their colour.

'You deserve these after this morning,' I said.

'Read his message.'

She pulled the card from its holder and handed it to me. It said: *A wonderful evening. We must do it again soon. Saul*

She took the card back and put it into her bag with a small satisfied smile.

'He's always fancied me. I have to tell you about my dinner with him last night. Sit down,' she said.

I sat on her chaise longue.

'He took me to the Dorchester. The food was fabulous and they know him there. We got one of the best tables.'

'What's he like off-site? I find him difficult to talk to,' I said.

'Quite a sweetie. Kind of shy and finds it easier to talk about sport. Cricket especially. He went to Australia once to watch the Ashes tour.'

I couldn't imagine Fizzy enjoying talking about cricket. She sat down at her mirror and started to brush her hair.

'He likes to travel. And it's five star all the way.'

'Did you find out anything more about his family life?'

'Not to begin with but he opened up later. I'd heard his divorce was bitter so I didn't probe too much. His two boys are grown up and I think he may be lonely, you know.'

'But you enjoyed it.'

'I did. He was charming and attentive. He's kind of old-school gallant and he insisted on driving me home and opening the door for me. Rather nice to be treated like that.'

Saul had to be in his fifties and he sounded conventional, even a bit dull. He was not Fizzy's usual type who tended to be men who represented a challenge to her. She had told me once how much she enjoyed making a resistant man fall for her charms.

'And will you see him again?'

She smiled at me from the mirror.

'I might just do that.'

I had agreed that Ziggy and Simon could leave work early as they had arranged to meet with Henry's sister Annie to look at the granny flat in Lewisham. Ziggy was packing her rucksack. She was wearing one of the tops Harriet had given her and looked better turned out than usual. Every few months Harriet brought in a bag of clothes she wasn't going to wear any more and Ziggy had been the recipient of some well-cut shirts and cashmere jumpers. She was thinner than Harriet so they tended to balloon on her thin frame. Ziggy was the least vain person I knew. I never saw her look in a mirror or put on make-up. Harriet would take her to the dressing rooms downstairs and insist she try on the things she had brought in.

Ziggy would accept a few and the rest would go to our local charity shop. Harriet told me she wished Ziggy would take more; that she felt to take more than two or three things was excessive.

'We're off then.'

'I hope it goes well,' I said.

I sat down with Molly and Harriet. Harriet keeps her desk pristine. Her research notes are filed away and her pens are corralled in a pretty container decorated with seahorses. Molly's desk was covered in papers and pens and books. She's a voracious reader and is always suggesting that we book in writers for the show. Her laptop had post-it notes stuck around its edges like a frill.

'What do you think of her for the pilot?' Molly said, swinging her laptop around to me.

I had asked Molly to find us a travel expert. Images of a rather severe-looking woman filled her screen.

'She does a lot of radio, doesn't she? I've heard her,' I said.

She was an experienced broadcaster who did consumer investigations.

'She's good at holding travel companies to account over late take-offs or lost luggage, but that could be a problem.'

'Why is that a problem?' Molly said.

'With WayToGo as sponsors? With their track record?'

WayToGo had poor ratings on customer service. We had to make the travel slot pro-business and upbeat. They would want an uncritical expert, who was preferably pert and pretty.

'She's a pro but she's not right for us,' I said.

'We won't get anyone better-known, not for the fee we're offering.'

The travel pilot was proving a chore. Simon had been

posting appeals for footage on Facebook but we weren't getting a lot of response from our viewers.

'Can we find an up-and-coming travel writer? Someone who is hungry to make their mark,' I said.

'There are loads of travel bloggers on Twitter,' Harriet offered.

'Time is short,' Molly said.

She sighed with frustration and Harriet rolled her eyes. Those two are an argument waiting to happen. I was glad it was the weekend, though I wondered what awaited me at home.

Chalk Farm flat, Friday evening

Flo had invited Rosie to stay over and Janis had fed them by the time I got in. The girls were in her room all evening and I probably exchanged ten words with Flo. The stand-off continues.

CHAPTER TWENTY-EIGHT

Chalk Farm flat, Saturday, 2 a.m.

I heard a weird shriek from the sitting room and leapt out of bed, my heart galloping. I had been deeply asleep and got up so quickly that I felt dizzy and had to hold on to the door frame. That strange unearthly shriek again. I fumbled for the light switch. Mr Crooks was crouching by our TV stand in a state of high excitement, every limb ready to pounce. I caught a glimpse of movement among the plugs and wires as Mr Crooks leapt. But the frog out-jumped him and landed under the table by the sofa. I grabbed Mr Crooks and shut him in my bedroom. He yowled his protest and scratched at my door. I dug out a plastic measuring jug and a small plate and approached the table. It was a fully grown frog and it didn't look injured but its body was all a-tremor. As I lowered the jug he caught my movement and leapt away towards a pile of magazines near the French doors.

'Stupid thing! I'm trying to save you.'

I moved forward slowly, got down on my knees and made myself be still. The frog was very still too now, playing dead. This time I got the jug in place and as it jumped up to escape I lowered the jug fast and trapped it. Gently, I pushed the plate under the mouth of the jug.

'Gotcha.'

I opened my French doors and there was the brightest moon shining into our garden. There was a clicking noise by my shed which slightly unnerved me. I went over and discovered it was the bamboo stick I'd used to stake my tomato plant. It had worked loose and was hitting the wall. I stood and looked round my little plot. It is walled all round and there was nowhere I could put the frog so that Mr Crooks wouldn't get him again. It would be better to leave him out front. Holding the plate tightly over the jug, I pushed my feet into a pair of Flo's slippers which she'd left by the door. I opened the front door and walked along to the third garden before depositing Mr Frog in a nice dewy clump of grass.

Saturday, 11 a.m.

Douglas had told me he was going to an away match with his son Stewart. I've taken to checking Norwich City Football Club fixtures and results, which I know is stalkerish of me but there you go. It was a bright blowy autumn day with clouds scudding across the sky. I'd already cleared the backlog of washing, deadheaded the flowers, restaked my tomato plant and swept our garden. I was itching to get out and do something nice with Flo, to heal our horrible breach. Maybe I could suggest we go out with Rosie.

Teenagers seem able to sleep the sleep of the dead till lunchtime. I took in mugs of tea for them and they sat up.

'Ta.'

Flo's face was puffy from sleep and her hair mussed up.

'Thank you,' Rosie said.

'Did either of you hear me last night?'

'No, nothing,' Rosie said.

'Mr Crooks brought in a full-grown frog. It made the most awful shriek, almost human-sounding.'

'Did he kill him?' It was Rosie again. Flo was sipping her tea and looking at me over the top of her mug.

'No, I managed to get it out in one piece.'

'He's Hunter Cat,' Flo said proudly to Rosie.

'I was thinking let's do something today. We could go to Regent's Park and hire a boat again. And you'd be so welcome to come, Rosie.'

'Thanks, but I've got to go. Mum has plans,' she said.

'Flo?'

'A rowing boat, not one of those silly pedalo things,' Flo said.

'You're on.'

Boating Lake, Regent's Park

I rowed us away from the boathouse, the water dripping off the oars. We watched a mallard dip, his rear sticking up as he tugged at something below the water.

'What do ducks eat?'

'All kinds of things; snails, worms, even small fish and fish eggs,' Flo said.

'I thought they lived on weeds and algae,' I said.

'They eat that too. They have to forage all the time to get enough.'

Flo knows a lot about birds and animals. It's a major area of interest with her and I think in time she may study zoology.

'Do you want a turn on the oars?'

We swapped places and she rowed us round the lake. I felt a fragile peace growing between us. She went near the edge where a tree leaned its branches into the water and the leaves made their own little current. She rested the oars and we sat looking at the eddies in the water. There was a distant rumble from the traffic like a low bass accompaniment. A pair of swans glided past our boat.

'Is it serious with that man?' she said.

It was a sudden change of topic but we needed to talk about Douglas.

'We've been on a few dates. It's early days.'

'But you had sex with him?'

'Yes, I did. I like him a lot.'

'Are you going to have a baby with him?'

'Oh, darling, whatever made you think that?'

'When he calls you your face goes all moony,' she said.

She pulled a silly face and I laughed.

'No babies planned at present.'

'Good! There's this girl at school and she went to fourth base and she may have got herself pregnant but she refuses to do a test.'

'Poor kid, she's probably frightened.'

'You should hear the things the boys are calling her,' Flo said.

This must be the girl I had heard Flo talking about with a friend.

'I hate that. There are such double standards, aren't there? I mean, when I was your age a girl who had a few partners was called a slut or a slag but if a boy had several partners he was a bit of a lad and was sowing his oats.'

'It's rank. But she's been an idiot, Mum. She should have known they would do that.'

'She may have been mad about the boy. I bet she's feeling very alone now. I think you should give her some support,' I said.

Later, I treated her to ice cream. She wanted three flavours and sprinkles on top and I think she has forgiven me for the fashion shoot.

Sunday, 9 p.m.

I was already in my pyjamas and on the sofa when Simon called me.

'The granny flat was perfect. Ziggy loved it and we're going to move her in next week,' he said.

'That's the best news.'

'Annie's really nice. And have you seen the all-staff email from Saul Relph?'

'No. I try to avoid work emails on Sunday.'

'Sorry to bring it up then,' he said.

'What does it say?'

'We've all got to go to a presentation by Lori Kerwell. Results of some big survey she's done.'

We said goodnight and I opened the email from Saul Relph which he'd sent that morning. We had all been instructed, presenters as well as journalistic staff, to attend a presentation in the atrium at twelve noon on Tuesday on the findings of a survey Lori Kerwell had conducted into the lifestyle and viewing habits of our audience. He believed that all editorial staff, including the news reporters, would benefit from knowing more about our audience. The last time we had got an all-staff email from Saul Relph it was to warn us about budget cuts and redundancies. This looked harmless in comparison but it hauled me back a few hours too soon into thinking about work.

CHAPTER TWENTY-NINE

StoryWorld TV station, London Bridge

There was such a good atmosphere among the team this morning. It was relief all round that Ziggy has found a new home. She looked the best I've seen her in weeks and I heard Simon and Harriet offering to help her move in. I love it when the team pulls together like this.

In my lunch hour I walked to London Bridge to a bakery that do a nice line in mini-cakes. I bought a box of little glazed fruit tarts and mini éclairs for the team. My next stop was an upmarket off-licence called Quaff. I was pleased that they stocked Bushmills Black Bush and bought a bottle.

Back at the station I put the cake box on my desk and went downstairs. The floor managers have a designated space off the main studio. It's a draughty nook because the giant studio door is usually kept open. Two battered tables have been placed end to end which the floor managers share. Henry was sitting at one end poring over a rota. I put the bottle bag down.

'*You* are our man of the month,' I said.

He pulled out the bottle.

'How did you know I like Irish whiskey best? Did I tell you?'

I nodded.

'My favourite brand, too. Thank you, Liz. You didn't have to.'

'Oh yes I did. I can't tell you what a relief it is that Ziggy's found a place, a place she loves.'

'Annie is happy about it too,' he said. He stood up. 'Is everything else OK?'

He was looking at me, really looking at me.

'Flo is speaking to me again.'

'Glad to hear it.'

'And Ziggy is sorted and that's down to you,' I said.

'You're still looking troubled.'

I wondered for a moment if I could share Ledley's treachery with Henry. I trusted Henry and knew he wouldn't gossip. He was a discreet man, an honourable man, and it would be a relief to share it. But my mother had always impressed upon me that gossip was toxic and that if you knew something unpleasant you should keep it to yourself unless the telling of it was essential.

'It's this place. The on-screen conflict is wearing me down and viewers are starting to notice that the chemistry is wrong.'

'Knock their heads together,' he said.

I laughed.

'Wish I could.'

'Well, I shall open this tonight and toast you,' he said.

Late afternoon I had my scheduled meeting with Angela Hodge, Ledley's agent. We had agreed to meet at her office near Trafalgar Square. I was not looking forward to it and was preparing myself for a tongue-lashing about my 'favouritism' towards Fizzy. If she came on hard I would have to restrain my temper. My role was to reassure her that we were looking after Ledley's screen presence and I had to be careful not to reveal my true feelings about him.

The offices were in a Victorian red-brick building on

Shaftesbury Avenue. Hers was on the fourth floor. I waited for the ancient lift which had one of those old grille doors and could fit four people in at a squeeze. I clanked the door shut and it ascended slowly. I checked my face in the lift's speckled mirror. There were lots of small offices off a long corridor. I hadn't rung in advance to confirm our meeting and when I was shown in Angela Hodge was sitting behind her desk and she looked rough. Her hair was lank and her face almost grey. It was as if she had forgotten that we were meeting. Her room had been carved out of a larger room. It had a high ceiling but was otherwise tight on space and there was a musty smell. Five minutes in she excused herself and said she would get us some water. She was gone for nearly ten minutes.

When she returned with a bottle and two glasses she looked slightly less grey. I was going to ask her if she was feeling ill but there was something so forbidding in her expression as she poured me water that I didn't. She sat back in her chair and took a sip.

'What can you tell me about your plans for Ledley?'

'We loved Ledley's interview with Bethany Burton. He was relaxed as he cooked and chatted. So I'm developing a series with him doing his interviews from the kitchen, cooking a favourite dish for his guests.'

I thought she might object. After all, Ledley had started out as our chef but now he was making the transition to being an anchor on the sofa. In a way this was returning him to his former role. But she didn't object.

'Noted. Look, I'm up against it today. You can email me the guests, OK.'

She stood up and saw me to her door. She wanted me out of there and I felt at a loss as I went down the four flights of stairs. I emerged on Shaftesbury Avenue opposite a theatre which was running a revival of a Noël Coward comedy. It had been the most peculiar meeting, or rather non-meeting.

There was time to go back to the office but I decided to walk home and get back early for a change. When I reached Heal's I couldn't resist crossing the road to look at the gorgeous furniture on display which was well out of my league. There was a sitting room set up with an elegant brass and glass drinks trolley as a feature. A drinks trolley was something I associated with my grandparents' generation when they would serve up whisky sours and Singapore slings. Were drinks trolleys coming back into fashion? And then it came to me that maybe Angela Hodge had a drink problem. The only explanation I could find for how she'd been was that she was massively hungover. Had she been sick while I sat and waited for her? She'd been gone a while. I recalled her grey face with a stab of pity. She worked in a high-stress business and had to spend her time soothing egos and pushing through deals. You can't get away from socialising and drinking in our industry. Maybe the pressure was getting to her. I had known more than a few casualties to alcohol over the years. Was Angela Hodge a high-functioning alcoholic?

Chalk Farm flat, 5.45 p.m.

Flo was sitting at the kitchen table and Janis was putting two pizzas into the oven.

'Shall I put one in for you?' she said.

'I'll eat later, thanks.'

There was a letter from Luton County Court on the table and I ripped it open. The date of my hearing is in November at eleven in the morning.

The kitchen was filling with the smell of dough and cheese and herbs and I wished I'd said I'd have a pizza with them.

'I've got a date at last but I'll have to take a day's leave to attend,' I said.

'The man's a menace,' Janis said.

'I'm not looking forward to seeing his nasty tanned face again.'

'Will you have to swear on a Bible, Mum?'

'Yes, I think so.'

'"I promise to tell the truth, the whole truth and nothing but the truth".' Flo intoned the words in a strangled theatrical voice and Janis and I laughed.

I sat with them while they ate their pizzas and told Janis she could go early.

Later, Flo joined me on the sofa to watch a rerun of *Inspector George Gently*. This is one of my guilty pleasures and Flo teases me about liking it. It is set in the 1960s and she always comments on the fashion. Tonight, a young female character was wearing a Mary Quant shift dress with white tights and bar shoes.

'I like those white tights,' Flo said.

'That was the Mod look,' I said.

I always admire the way the actor Martin Shaw, who plays the inspector, is able to convey disgust with a withering look. I'd love to be able to do that. My mobile buzzed and it was Douglas. Talking to him would break the cosy mood Flo and I had going so I let it run to voicemail. I would call back as soon as the drama was over.

I went into my bedroom and called Douglas and told him I had the court date at last.

'I'm sure you'll nail the bastard. But why Luton?'

'It's near where he lives.'

'So *you'll* have to travel.'

'I know. That annoyed me too.'

He said that Norwich City had lost. I knew that already because I'd checked the score. But he'd had a good time with Stewart and he sounded upbeat. We arranged to meet on Thursday, which has become our night.

It was after eleven and I was turning in. Flo was in her bedroom and I wanted to kiss her goodnight after our lovely bonding session on the sofa. I tapped on her door. This is now a requirement. If I ever barge in without knocking she gives me merry hell. The room was dark except for the light of her phone and she looked upset. When she saw me she put the phone on the floor, face down. Her eyes were full of tears.

'Darling, whatever's wrong?'

She sniffed and shook her head.

'Leave me alone.'

I came nearer.

'Darling, tell me, please.'

'It's all your fault!'

'What are you talking about?'

'Ethan. He liked me.'

She flung herself back on her pillow.

'But now he's dating someone else.'

'How do you know?'

'I just saw it on Instagram.'

I thought of sitting on her bed but there was a dangerous light in her eyes.

'I'm sorry it hasn't worked out, sweetheart.'

'I *know* he liked me. But then he saw me looking like a freak! That's when he went off me.'

'You know that's not true. I doubt any teenage boys watch our show, ever,' I said.

She looked at me with such contempt then.

'A girl who hates me posted it up on Facebook. The whole item. *Everyone* at school has seen it.'

'But you looked lovely. I bet that girl was jealous.'

'You don't get it, do you?' She was shouting now. 'I looked bloody weird and he went off me.'

'And it's always my bloody fault, isn't it?' I shouted back, leaving her room.

I'd left the garden lights on and as I went to turn them off I stubbed my big toe and hopped around the room in agony. No one can press my buttons like Flo.

CHAPTER THIRTY

StoryWorld TV station, London Bridge

'I'm not going. She can go and boil her head,' Fizzy said as we walked down the stairs together and saw the rows of seats that had been laid out in the atrium. The meeting room upstairs wasn't large enough to accommodate all the staff who were expected to attend Lori Kerwell's presentation. A podium had been set up with a screen behind it.

'Come in for a minute,' Fizzy said.

I followed her into her dressing room.

'It's my second date with Saul tonight. He suggested the opera but I told him I have to be in bed by ten. Truth is, I find opera terribly tedious,' she said.

'So what are you doing?'

'A cosy dinner for two at his club cooked by their top chef; much nicer.'

She picked up a perfume bottle and squirted behind her ears and onto her wrists. She was in a good mood. As far as I knew she was still meeting with Bob at Loida's flat; taking Zachary along so that Bob could have some kind of relationship with his son. Fizzy had the chutzpah to juggle two men in her life.

'Are you still seeing Douglas Pitlochry?'

'I am, when he can get away from his bulletins and family commitments,' I said.

'I hope you're being careful around him. This is a leaky ship and Julius has his suspicions about Douglas Pitlochry.'

I could not leave this unchallenged.

'You've discussed it?'

'Yes. I know Julius can be a bit of a control freak about stuff but he told me that Douglas Pitlochry is an operator. He stabbed his predecessor in the back to get the anchor role at News Nine.'

'I never heard that. Are you sure that's right?' I said.

'Julius has his sources and he said that under the charm he's ruthless and not to be trusted.'

I shook my head in disbelief.

'Are you serious about him, Liz?'

This was uncomfortable territory for me.

'It's early days. He's good company when we do get together. Look, I'd better go and listen to Lori. Three-line whip and all that.'

She grinned mischievously.

'They can whip away. I'm going home.'

I headed to the atrium feeling troubled by what Fizzy had said. I did not see Douglas as a backstabber and I wouldn't believe that. But the idea of them talking about me behind my back and that Julius saw my connection with Douglas as a possible source of leaks was unsettling. I stood and watched reluctant news journalists trickle down the stairs and choose seats at the end of the rows. They would consider this a chore and an irrelevance since news was news and why should you change it because of who the audience were? I didn't want to attend any more than they did but I thought they were arrogant to think that. Bob had clearly instructed them to be there and he had seated himself in the front row next to Ledley. The first of my presenters to arrive was Betty.

'This should be interesting,' she said.

Simon found her a seat and sat next to her. Guy had sent his apologies. Gerry arrived late looking flustered but cheery. He has lost weight which is usually a good sign with him, a sign he is feeling happier. I gave him my seat and went and stood at the back of the gathering. Julius was standing there watching the atrium fill. I found a spare chair and carried it to the back, asked him if he wanted one. He said no and he stayed standing next to me.

'She said half an hour. It better not be any longer.' He spoke in a low voice so only I could hear him.

I had expected Julius to introduce Lori, but she was not a woman who needed any introduction. She was striding down the stairs dressed in her usual boxy suit, orange with an acid yellow blouse underneath, and her poodle hair was pinned up. As she took her place at the podium it struck me again how she was a person who did not suffer from self-doubt. She was in her element with her PowerPoint ready and a captive audience in front of her. She put on her glasses and started to speak.

'I need your attention for thirty minutes and by the end of that you will know a great deal more about the people who watch StoryWorld.'

She clicked up her first slide, a graph showing the salary bands of our viewers. The next one analysed where they lived. She might have a captive audience but they weren't a sympathetic one. Journalists do not like being told what to think by salespeople. The slides came in quick succession, outlining the leisure activities of our viewers and what soaps they watched. I saw some of the news journalists fidgeting at this. Why did they need to know if our viewers watched *Coronation Street* or *Emmerdale*? She had produced a comprehensive piece of work and I did learn something. Her last slide ended at exactly thirty minutes from the first one. She must have rehearsed and timed it.

'I won't keep you longer. I know how busy you all are. If you have any questions please email them to me. Copies of my survey are available,' she said.

The screen behind her went blank and Ledley and Bob started to clap. Betty and Gerry joined in, as did a handful of others. Julius hurried away, taking the back exit through the studio as if he did not want to talk to anyone. I watched Ledley go up to Lori and congratulate her.

'You nailed it, clever lady,' he said.

They left the atrium together, heading for his dressing room. Everyone was filing out as I joined Gerry.

'You're looking great,' I said, sitting down next to him.

'Thanks, darling. I've taken up dancing. It's such a fun way to lose weight and the pounds are melting off me.'

'What sort of dancing?'

'Zumba once a week and on Saturday I went to my first ever ceilidh. There's a caller and a live band and you get to dance with all sorts. I loved it. You must come with me next time. So what did you make of that?' He nodded towards the empty podium.

'I guess it's useful information for us all.'

He raised his eyebrows.

'Well, it's the first time I've ever been told to attend a presentation here. Lori has asked to meet with me. Is that OK?'

'Of course, that's fine.'

Lori should have cleared her meeting with Gerry through me but we had got beyond such courtesies.

'But I'm asking my agent to come along. That woman has missionary zeal and if I'm honest I find her scary,' he said.

I kissed him on the cheek.

'Let me know how it goes.'

I went upstairs wondering how Lori intended to monetise his astrology slot. No doubt she had some plan for viewers to pay for phone-in predictions from Gerry. I heard Harriet telling Ziggy about the presentation because Zig had had to stay behind to monitor our calls.

'I mean, the most ghastly people,' she was saying, her pretty little nose wrinkling in distaste.

'For heaven's sake! They're our audience. Stop being such a snob,' Molly said.

I went into my office and spent longer than usual reading viewers' comments about the show. They are definitely starting to notice that something is amiss. The chemistry between Fizzy and Ledley is all fake bonhomie and banter. Some viewers are seeing through it. And we've had a bit of a Twitter backlash, too, with viewers saying bring back Fizzy in a solo role.

Simon and Harriet were going to help Ziggy move into her new place that evening. I heard Ziggy insisting that they didn't need a van; that a taxi would be enough for her stuff.

'But what about your bed?' Harriet asked.

'I'm leaving my mattress behind. It's a horrible old thing anyway and Annie has put a proper bed in for me.'

'And your kitchen stuff?'

'It's all in a box.'

The three of them set off and I sat down with Molly. She had a packet of pistachios open on her desk and poured me a handful.

'I found out something about Lori Kerwell,' she said.

'Really?'

'I get this health magazine. Did you know she was fund-raiser of the year for Cancer Research?'

'No, indeed.'

'Yes, she raised thousands of pounds.'

'That's impressive. Actually, I can imagine her being a formidable fundraiser.'

I threw the pistachio shells into the bin.

'Have some more,' Molly said.

She poured me another handful and we opened and munched the nuts.

'And it's something to be proud of, isn't it? But when I mentioned it to her today it was like she was angry with me for knowing about it, which is odd.'

'That is odd,' I said.

'I told her about the article. She cut me off literally mid-sentence.'

The bag was empty. Molly pushed the shells into a little pile.

'But then I thought that maybe someone close to her had died of cancer and it was too painful for her to talk about.'

Last year Molly had made a short film with a young woman who was dying of cancer. It had been a powerful piece of film-making and had affected her deeply.

'Good on her for doing something so positive,' I said.

I recalled Fenton telling me that maybe Lori's hard exterior was an armour she put on to protect herself. Perhaps I needed to think better of her. I had been out of sorts all day. The row with Flo last night had darkened my mood.

Chalk Farm flat, evening

Flo was not speaking to me. She was still brooding on Ethan and she rebuffed my attempt to make up with her. She was in her bedroom and I went to mine. I spent the evening watching a drama series on catch-up on my laptop, three episodes back to back. It was a dark drama and involving. I heard Flo go into the kitchen and make herself a drink; heard the kettle boil and her open the fridge. I stayed put. I didn't even go into the sitting room to watch Douglas's bulletin. I took ages to get to sleep as the drama I'd been watching had got into my head. One particularly disturbing scene kept playing behind my eyelids.

CHAPTER THIRTY-ONE

StoryWorld TV station, London Bridge

Flo had left for school still in high dudgeon. It has been going on for days now. I'd told her I'd be back late and all she said was 'Whatever', which I think is the teenage equivalent of 'I almost care.' I was seeing Douglas at seven-thirty and my anticipation at that was buoying me up.

Mid-morning, I got a call from Angela Hodge, Ledley's agent.

'Liz, have you heard the news about *Magic on Ice*?'

'Sorry, Angela, I'm not sure what you're talking about.'

She sounded impatient.

'The ice show you got Ledley involved with? He was one of the judges of an ice-sculpture contest.'

It came back to me. Lori had got Ledley a gig on a panel of judges. The ice-sculpture contest, which had been filmed, was to launch a dancing on ice show in Birmingham.

'Yes, I remember now. Actually, it was Lori Kerwell who got him that gig,' I said.

'Well, she should check out the companies she works with!' Angela snapped. 'The Serious Fraud Office has only gone and shut the event down. The organiser is wanted for money laundering and he's scarpered with the proceeds. No customers will get their money back and Ledley won't be paid.'

'That's not good,' I said.

'Not good! Far worse is that news companies are using a clip from the ice-sculpture contest to run the story. Everyone can see Ledley in the clip and this harms his reputation. I'm not happy,' she said.

This was the old Angela Hodge, back on form. But as I recalled, she had been keen enough to let Ledley do this event. Maybe she was mortified that she had agreed to it. Maybe she had agreed to it on one of her bad days. I was still convinced that she had a drink problem.

'As I said, I did not set up the event. I will let Lori Kerwell know about this at once.'

'Tell her that in future I expect her to properly check out any companies she wants Ledley to work with. We expect due diligence from StoryWorld.'

Angela had clicked her phone off.

'Rude woman,' I said, but she had a reason to be cross. This was embarrassing for the station as well as for Ledley; one of our co-hosts associated with a money-laundering operation. That was what came of working with cheapskate companies. A small, mean part of me felt pleased that Lori's work was at fault. I walked down to her office. She was out and the door was locked. I called her on her mobile and it went to answer machine. I left a quick message relaying what Angela Hodge had just told me. As I went past Julius's office I decided he needed to know too.

'Go on in,' Martine said.

Julius had been furious. What had particularly enraged him was that the clip showing Ledley was doing the rounds on the news networks. He hates it when StoryWorld becomes the story. I was scheduled to leave the station at noon. Simon and I had been invited to a presentation in Westminster on changes to broadcasting law and I didn't plan on missing it.

Simon and I decided to walk to the conference centre along the riverside. There was an autumnal nip in the air and we walked briskly. We passed a mother with twins in a double buggy. She was kneeling down trying to comfort one of the toddlers who was yelling his head off and banging his legs against the buggy in a total body fury. He would not be comforted. The other twin looked at him with interest and sucked on his dummy.

'I remember those temper tantrums. I'm glad I don't have to deal with them any more, though teenage tantrums can be a challenge too,' I said as the sound of the toddler's cries receded.

A young couple rollerbladed past us at speed. They were wearing knee pads and racing each other, swerving in and out to avoid the obstacles in their path.

'Ziggy had so little to move in to her new place. I unpacked her kitchen box. There were a couple of mugs, three plates and a frying pan. When I think of what I've got, well, it cut me up actually,' he said.

'She's been looking happy since she moved in,' I said.

'She *is* happy to have that little flat. And it is nice. I've learned a lot from Ziggy about being grateful.'

We arrived at the conference centre and were given our name badges and printouts of the presentations to come. We queued for the coffee and pastry that was on offer and I spotted a lot of TV people I'd met over the years. There were high tables to rest your cups on and Simon and I headed for one. The woman who covers economics on Douglas's bulletin approached our table. I recognised her from watching his show. She's clever and her presentation style is acerbic. I've seen her lance a few politicians with tricky questions in her filmed reports. She didn't say hello and she was scanning the room to see if there was anyone she knew. When she looked back I saw her read my badge and a look of recognition flashed on her face. But I had never met her. Simon broke the ice.

'Hello, we're from StoryWorld.'

'Greetings from News Nine,' she said.

She gave me a penetrating but not a friendly look. It occurred to me that she knew I was dating Douglas.

'Is it true what I read that there's all-out sofa wars at your station?' she said.

She had to be referring to the Lou Gibson piece. I was chewing on my pain au raisin. I swallowed and tried to sound light-hearted.

'Have you had any dealings with Lou Gibson? She should be a novelist. She invented a lot of that.'

I noticed she was drinking her coffee black and had no pastry.

'I would certainly fight it if News Nine suddenly said I had to share my slot with a newcomer,' she said crisply.

'Ledley's not exactly a newcomer,' I said.

'I thought he was your chef?'

Her manner was so supercilious and I was trying to think how to answer her when Roomana, who used to be in my team, arrived at our table with a shriek of joy and embraced Simon and me. We were called into the main room and Simon, Roomana and I sat together.

'She was a cold fish, wasn't she?' Simon said to me.

'Arctic,' I said.

'And she was digging,' he said.

I was thinking about her as the first speaker started his presentation. It was only when she read my name that she knew who I was and she had been far from friendly. Did the News Nine team know about Douglas and me? I didn't like the idea that he had talked about our relationship. But maybe they had heard about it indirectly, as Julius and Fizzy had.

I was back at the station by five. I had a session booked in with Molly to look at three screen tests she had organised with travel bloggers as possible candidates for our travel pilot. I found her in the edit suite lining the tests up. We watched three young women do the same script. The first one was awful. The other two were competent but neither of them leapt off the screen.

'That's a bit disappointing. I was hoping for someone with that extra something. Do you have a preference between the last two?' I said.

'The last one edges it for me,' Molly said.

'Let's go with her then. Thanks for doing this; I know it's been a terrible rush.'

I went upstairs to get ready for my date. I changed into a green velvet blouse and laid out my make-up by my mirror. As I applied mascara I was thinking about whether I should ask Douglas about his frosty colleague. He rarely talked about his work with me, though he asked me about StoryWorld, particularly about Fizzy. A small worm of suspicion uncurled. I put concealer under my eyes and was using my brush to add blusher when Lori came into my office without knocking. She shut the door behind her, I swung round to face her and she launched straight in.

'I do not appreciate you running to Julius and winding him up like this,' she said sharply.

'Are you talking about the *Magic on Ice* fiasco?'

'There was no need to involve Julius.'

'Oh, but there was. This is an issue about the reputation of the station. He needed to know,' I said.

'I bet you laid it on with a trowel.'

'I find that rich coming from you when you went running to Saul the moment I disagreed with your fashion ideas.'

'You've been against me from day one,' she said.

'I've tried to resist your cheap and nasty ideas. And working with cheapskate companies gets us into difficulties, as per *Magic on Ice*.'

'You've been working against me and working against Ledley.'

'That's not true but go ahead and think that if you want to. You're the one who screwed up on *Magic on Ice*. Thanks for linking the station with a money launderer.'

She looked like she wanted to slap me or better still stab me with her hideous statement brooch. I glared back just as hard and she turned on her heel and exited my office. I sat down. My heart was pumping hard and I was breathless. For once I hadn't held back. It felt good to have given her the two barrels and sod the consequences. My phone rang. It was Douglas and he sounded stressed.

'I'm so sorry, Liz. Tonight is off.'

'What's happened?'

'My mother-in-law has had a stroke, a bad one. She's hanging between life and death.'

'That's awful.'

'I'm driving down to Cornwall in the next hour, picking Stew up on the way.'

'I'm so sorry.'

'I'm sorry to miss tonight.'

'Don't worry about that. I hope the news is better when you get there.'

'I'll be in touch,' he said.

I sat at my desk and felt immensely deflated. I couldn't stop myself from resenting that his mother-in-law was sick and that he had been called away; which then made me feel that I was a bad person. I sighed deeply.

'Get a grip,' I said aloud. 'It's a cancelled date.'

Chalk Farm flat, 7.15 p.m.

As I unlocked the door to our flat I could hear Flo chatting happily to Janis in the kitchen. I took off my jacket and joined them.

'I thought you were out with him tonight?' Flo said in an unfriendly voice.

'A last-minute change of plan. One of his family is very ill.'

Flo got up and went to her bedroom. She shut her door with a click and Janis and I exchanged knowing looks. I wondered if Flo had told her about Ethan. I followed Janis out onto the pavement.

'It's a shame your date was called off,' she said.

'Yes, and I'm in her bad books. Oh joy.'

'It's her age and her hormones. She loves you loads, you know,' Janis said.

I could not face another night of Flo and me sitting in our separate rooms with an atmosphere in the flat. I tapped on her door.

'Shall we cook a cake? We haven't made one for ages.'

She was probably as miserable as I was about our stand-off.

'OK.'

We went through the cupboard together. I laid out flour, butter and baking powder and got the milk from the fridge.

'I think we've got everything for a Victoria sponge,' I said.

She opened the egg box.

'We've only got three eggs.'

'It's enough.'

'And can we just have jam? I've gone off buttercream.'

She beat the ingredients into a batter while I lined the sandwich tins with baking paper. She divided the mixture between the tins and smoothed the surface with the back of a wooden spoon.

'That's nicely done,' I said.

The oven was ready and she put the two tins in carefully. We sat at the table while the kitchen filled with that most comforting of smells, a baking cake. I tried not to think about my missed date with Douglas. The priority was to mend fences with Flo.

'Granny's birthday next week and I'm thinking I should get her something useful to take to Kenya,' I said.

'I wish she wasn't going.'

'Me too, but I am proud of her. She likes to help people,' I said.

'Granny would be Abnegation,' Flo said.

I must have looked blank.

'In *Divergent*. I told you. Everyone belongs to a category and Abnegation are the people who help others. They always put their own needs last.'

She was reading *Divergent*, in fact she was completely

enthralled by it and had mentioned it before. Society was arranged by character class and she had explained the categories at length to me. She had said I was a mixture of Erudite and Candour. Erudite were into knowledge and power and Candour were the truth-tellers.

'I wouldn't want to be Abnegation. They have to wear grey all the time,' she said.

This made me think of a story my mum used to tell me about her childhood and I told it to Flo again. Money had always been short. My granny would buy cheap meat cuts and make a basic stew at least once a week that would last for two days. My mum hated this stew and dreaded those nights when it was all that was on offer. One evening she had arrived home from a bad day at school, had smelled the stew cooking and had burst into tears. Granny had said, if you were in the Russian Revolution you would be grateful for a bowl of my stew. It had been known as Russian Revolution Stew ever afterwards.

Later, as the cakes were cooling on the rack, Flo reached for the jams.

'Mum, do you want apricot or raspberry?'

'You choose. I like them both.'

'I'm going for apricot this time.'

I watched her spread the jam thickly on the sponge.

'I can't wait to taste it,' I said.

We ate the cake with mugs of tea and agreed it was a good one. When Flo and I cook together it unites us.

CHAPTER THIRTY-TWO

LATE OCTOBER
Chalk Farm flat, afternoon

I've been in bed for two days with my worst bout of flu in years. My legs ache so much, my throat is raw and my head is heavy and throbbing. No word now from Douglas for nearly a month.

I couldn't get warm and was shivering under the duvet. I pulled on my dressing gown before going into the kitchen to make yet another Lemsip. I put on the kettle. There was no point in going to see my doctor. With flu you have to endure the symptoms while the virus works its way through your body. Douglas had called me a couple of days after his dash to the hospital, said that he and Stewart were staying in a hotel in Truro while Natalie Cooper's condition hung in the balance. I poured boiling water onto the powder and added a large spoonful of honey, watching it melt into the mix. I'm trying to keep track of how many of these I've drunk. I had texted him a few days later saying I was thinking of him and hoped that things were improving. He hadn't texted back. He would be spending a lot of time with his wife Claire. She would be frightened about her mum and crises bring people together.

I refilled the kettle and fetched the hot water bottle from my tangled sheets. It's Flo's Peter Rabbit hot water bottle and the fur on his stomach is flat. Stewart wants his parents to get back together, of course he does; it's only natural. The kettle boiled again and I filled Peter Rabbit. I shuffled back into my room and tried to straighten the bed. But he could have called. He could have kept me updated. Even a text to show I was important to him. I always knew he was too glamorous for me. We met at that award ceremony and I was only on that table because Julius was away. I was wearing the dress of transformation and, looking back, the whole thing has a feeling of unreality about it. I sat against my pillows and cried. Another failed relationship. Why does it hurt so much?

I've seen the articles on how your emotional state affects your health and that misery makes you ill. Perhaps it does. For the last two weeks I hadn't been sleeping well. I was brooding about no word from Douglas and October is also a difficult month for me because my darling dad died suddenly in October. Every night I'd long for sleep but would wake up, usually around five, still bone-tired. I tried to make myself go back to sleep so that I would have enough energy to face the demands of the day. Sometimes I managed to drift off. When I woke again I would feel this heaviness pressing on my chest, like a weight I couldn't throw off. I'd drag myself up and make myself go through my morning routines. There was a certain salvation in habit and in having to get Flo up and having to go to work. But I could not remember feeling so bleak for a very long time. And now this wretched flu has felled me.

I can't imagine feeling good about myself again. I know I'm failing at work. I've got nowhere with the Young Fashion Designer competition. We filmed the travel pilot and it was lacklustre. But who cares, what does it matter? I rolled onto my side, hugging Peter Rabbit.

It was nearly dark when the phone rang. It was Fenton, calling from work.

'How are you, love?'

'Still one great big ache.'

I know she is worried about me. When Douglas stopped calling she'd told me there were parallels to the troubles she'd had with Bill and his ex-wife. When they were starting out on their relationship Bill's ex made a move to get back with him and it had been fraught. She reminded me how she had been on the rack for months but it had come good in the end. We didn't talk about Douglas today. I was glad she didn't ask me if he had rung.

'You're not to go back until you're completely well. I know you. You always go back too early,' she said fondly.

I had told Janis not to come to the flat. I heard Flo unlocking the front door and she came straight to my room.

'Poor Mum. You look awful.'

'Darling, can you heat me a tin of tomato soup?' I croaked.

She warmed the soup and brought it to me in a mug.

'Thanks, sweets. There's some ravioli in the fridge and a jar of sauce you can put with it.'

'It's OK, Mum. I'll cook something.'

I sipped at the soup. She sat on my bed and plucked at the duvet.

'How was your day?'

'I hate boys,' she said.

'What happened?'

'You remember the girl I told you about who had sex with a boy who's a total dick.'

'Yes, I remember.'

'I heard him calling her all kinds of horrible names so that *everyone* could hear. I went over and told him he was disgusting. And Rosie said he should grow up and then he and his mates were jeering at us and calling us frigid skanks and other things.'

I felt a starburst of pride explode in my chest.

'That was brilliant that you did that, just brilliant.'

CHAPTER THIRTY-THREE

NOVEMBER
StoryWorld TV station, London Bridge

I'm peaky but I'm standing. My team were glad to have me back and made me feel wanted. Ziggy got me a coffee and a Twix from the Hub and Harriet brought me a bunch of pale pink camellias at lunchtime. She arranged them in a vase and placed them on my desk. I cupped one bloom in my hand, the petals unfurled in a perfect spiral from the centre.

'These are so lovely. Thank you.'

'You've lost weight,' she said.

I had lost nearly half a stone and wasn't taking my usual pleasure in food.

'It's a silver lining, but I wouldn't recommend the flu diet,' I said.

My emails had accumulated to an alarming number. Many were out of date and I spooled through and did a mass delete. Around twelve-thirty Martine rang, sounding apologetic.

'Sorry for the shortness of notice but Julius said can you come down to his office? And Lori's in there with him.'

I went down and as I got to Martine's desk she said: 'Keep your cool and don't let her get to you.'

'Thanks for the warning.'

But I was detached rather than anxious as I went in to his office. Lori was sitting on the sofa with her back straight and Julius was standing by the window. You couldn't see anything outside, a thick fog hung over the river and I could hear the mournful note of some kind of foghorn tolling its warning. Julius looked tired.

'Sorry we have to throw this at you on your first day back,' he said.

'Throw what?' I said.

'I'm afraid we've just heard that WayToGo has rejected the pilot.'

'I'm sorry to hear that,' I said.

'They want another pilot,' Lori said.

Julius looked irritated that she had spoken out of turn. I addressed my remarks to him.

'What didn't they like?'

'They thought there was no chemistry between Ledley and the expert.'

'And they thought the footage was below par,' Lori interjected.

She was getting well and truly above herself. It was for Julius to comment on the editorial content, not her. I continued to look at him as his left eyelid twitched and I found that I didn't really care.

'We'll rethink the expert. That's why you do a pilot. To test it out,' I said.

'How soon?' she said.

Now he strode to his desk and sat down on his ancient leather Baedekar.

'That's enough, Lori! Liz and I will discuss timings and let you know.'

'She needs to know the three words,' Lori snapped back.

Lori had become so confident about her position at the station. The way she talked over Julius showed that. No one else did that. Ever. He looked murderous as he picked up a piece of paper.

'WayToGo has given us these words to describe the kind of item they want: "family-friendly", "budget-conscious" and "zany".'

I have always hated the word 'zany'. When someone describes themselves with that word I know to give them a wide berth.

'Noted,' I said.

I have no idea how we can make the second pilot any better than the first. I have no reserves of energy and it feels as if my creativity has dried up. Spiritual exhaustion; that was what I was feeling as I left his office.

I left it till nearly four before I got Simon and Molly in to my room.

'I'm afraid it's back to the drawing board on the travel item. WayToGo rejected our pilot. They didn't like the expert or the footage.'

'Bugger!' Simon said.

'Another pilot?' Molly looked mortified.

'Don't beat yourselves up. I've been in the Slough of Despond about this project from day one.'

I had been but somehow we needed to make a second pilot work better. I told them the three words which WayToGo had specified as their brief. Molly snorted in disgust.

'That's such crap, it doesn't really tell us anything.'

We sat in glum silence for a few minutes.

'I guess "family-friendly" is the key word,' I said.

We pondered some more.

'And we still need a competition?' It was Simon.

'Yes.'

'So what if we ask viewers to send in holiday pics of their children, say ten-year-olds and under. And the cutest pic wins the prize.'

'That's so cheesy,' Molly said.

'Yes, but I think cheesy is good. I think WayToGo will like cheesy and flashing up a pic of little Johnny is going to be popular,' I said.

'It shall be done,' Simon said.

'We need to find another expert. And she needs to be "zany", of course,' I added.

They smiled at that.

'I know what we can call it: Postcards from our Viewers,' Molly said. 'We'll make a virtue of the fact that we're getting our footage from them.'

'That's really good. Thank the stars you two are still firing creatively,' I said.

Chalk Farm School

It was parents' evening at Flo's school and I went there straight from work. Flo was hanging out in the hall with two girls I didn't recognise. She hurried over to me and I held back from kissing her as her body language was saying don't hug me, don't make a fuss. The assembly hall had been set up with tables in rows and three chairs for parents and pupils to sit opposite the teacher. I picked up the sheet which explained who was sitting where and Flo said we should do the head of science first. We had to queue and the couple in front of us were getting irritated at how long the seated parents were taking with the teacher.

'They should realise she's got a lot of people to get through,' the father said loudly enough for several of us to hear.

'Selfish,' the mother replied.

Their daughter seemed embarrassed at this. She was a wan-looking girl who chewed on her nails anxiously. These evenings bring out a competitive spirit in some parents and I vowed not to embarrass Flo.

The head of science, Mrs Ingmere, was wearing a black and white Norwegian-style jumper and hoop earrings. She could not have looked more different from the science teachers at my school. She was warm about Flo.

'Your biology project was first-rate,' she said.

She consulted a sheet of marks and test results.

'We do need some more attention to the chemistry and physics side of things. You'll need good grades in those as well but I'm delighted Florence wants to pursue zoology long term.'

Next we waited for Mr Williams, who is her form teacher, and Flo is usually positive about him. I saw Rosie and her parents getting up from his table and waved at them. Rosie whispered something to Flo. Finally, we were settled in front of him. We shook hands but then he addressed his remarks directly to Flo, which I thought was a good thing to do. She did not like her teachers talking to me about her as if she wasn't there.

'I don't want to overstate it but it's been a bit of a bumpy half-term, hasn't it?' he said.

'I got an A star in biology,' she said.

He looked at his chart of figures.

'You did, and well done on that. Your grades in other subjects are slipping. You're a clever girl, Florence. I've noticed that you're getting drawn into a group who think that being clever is uncool.'

This was news to me. We'd had a bad time last year when she had got close to a toxic older girl called Paige who got Flo into trouble. But that friendship was well and truly over.

'It's not uncool to do well in your subjects. It's a passport to all kinds of opportunities,' he said.

'You mean uni,' she said.

'Yes, I do. You're capable of top grades. I'd like to see more focus for the rest of the term.'

I didn't say anything other than to thank Mr Williams. We went to the room where they were selling teas and snacks and I asked Flo if she wanted anything.

'No. I think we should go now.'

'But we haven't done languages and I'm getting myself a tea,' I said.

She crossed her arms.

'What's the point?'

I insisted we see two more teachers before we left and a similar picture emerged. Flo had always scored highly but was currently showing less interest in her work and her grades were down.

As we came out of the school it was raining lightly. I had an umbrella in my bag.

'You want to share this with me?'

She shook her head and drew out a navy woollen hat with a fur pom-pom on top from her rucksack. I'd bought it for her last Christmas. She pulled it down low on her head and we trudged home without talking. Her hands were deep in her pockets and her shoulders were slumped. The evening had been a wake-up call for me. I was wondering how I could help her get back her mojo. My motivation was in the cellar.

'I wish you and Dad were still together,' she said finally.

'Oh, darling, what's brought this on?'

'Seeing all my friends with their mums and dads there tonight.'

'Not everyone, sweetheart,' I said

We were not the only ones. There had been other lone parents in the hall, others who had only needed two of the chairs, so why did I feel that I had failed her? We passed a place that did fried chicken and fat chips served in little buckets. Flo and her friends loved the place though I found the food greasy. I wondered if she'd ask to go in. I would have said yes, anything to lift the low mood between us. But she walked by without a glance. She was the one who brought up the fall in her grades so it must have been bothering her.

'Mr Williams thinks grades are all that matters. It's only so he can impress the head.'

'Is that fair? He's got a lot of time for you and wants you to fulfil your potential, which you've got in spades.'

'Maybe I don't want to have a great career. It's not the most important thing. You and Mr Williams seem to think it is.'

'But one day you're going to have to get a job.'

'So?'

'Believe me, it's better to get one that stretches you. Not for the money but for the satisfaction,' I said.

'Having a great career doesn't make people happy. It doesn't make you happy.'

We had reached home and I was rummaging for the key. She had hit home with her last remark.

'I may not be happy at the moment but having my job let me buy this flat and pays for our holidays, so don't knock it.'

CHAPTER THIRTY-FOUR

StoryWorld TV station, London Bridge

I was in the gallery and Gerry was discussing those zodiac signs which were drawn to power. I have limped through this week on half-power and was grateful to have reached Friday. I felt low about the parents' evening last night. I needed to spend more time with Flo and encourage her to get back on track. Maybe I needed to talk to Ben about it. Ask him what we could do to help her. Tonight I'd buy pizza and pretzels and cream cheese dip which we love. We planned to watch another series. Maybe I could get her to open up about what was going on at school.

Gerry had turned to talk directly into camera.

'Now Aries, the first sign of the zodiac, is of course a born leader. You thrive on competition and command the respect and attention of others. You are confident, which is good, but you can be headstrong, so watch that.'

He turned to Fizzy.

'As a Leo you're also a natural leader, Fizzy. You know what you want and you're good at convincing people to do your bidding. In fact, it's not unknown for you to persuade others to do the tasks you'd rather avoid.'

He said this archly, in mock reprimand, and Fizzy giggled while I thought what a lot of nonsense it was; although Fizzy did get Loida to do a lot of the tasks she found boring. It may be nonsense but Gerry rates consistently highly with our viewers and he is a dear.

At the morning meeting Bob was in trouble. He had run a story about a birth that had taken place in a toilet at a company that was known for exploiting its workers. The story claimed that the woman had been scared to miss her shift and had struggled in to work. One of his journalists had found the story on the web and they had run with it without making the proper checks. She hadn't actually given birth on the toilet floor. This was particularly bad timing because only this week MPs had called for media outlets to be more alert to the 'contagion' of fake news stories on the web. Julius had been called to a seminar of the subject by the regulator.

'How did it slip through?' Julius was clipped.

'We should have doorstepped but we don't have the resources. We have to get some of our stories from the web and it's like the Wild West out there, bloody hard to sift the true from the false,' Bob said.

'Don't let it happen again. If you have doubts, don't run it. This damages our credibility.'

Bob scowled. I made a point of not looking at him. He would think I was pleased that he was being carpeted.

'We're going to have to run a retraction,' Julius said.

Bob nodded. I glanced over at Fizzy and she was positively glowing, a woman without a care in the world. This seemed odd if she still cared about Bob. As for Ledley, we had hardly exchanged a dozen words since our bust-up and I hoped he had heeded my warning. Outside the morning meeting we actively avoided each other. These days I sent Simon down to talk through the briefing notes and scripts with him.

I went downstairs to meet Henry for our coffee and we took our cups outside. This has become my favourite part of the day. He rolled me a smoke and lit it for me.

'You need fattening up,' he said.

I was the thinnest I'd been in years and when I lay down I could feel my hipbones again, which I liked.

'On Monday I'm going to buy you a bun.'

'Thank you, kind sir,' I said.

'It will be my pleasure,' he said.

'Even though I spend the whole time moaning about my lot? Now today's problem is Flo and her poor grades at school. Her form teacher told me last night that she's got in with a crowd who think it's uncool to be clever.'

Henry laughed.

'I was in with that crowd when I was at school and it drove my mum and dad to distraction.'

'And did you flunk at school?'

'Oh yes. I had to resit my exams. My anger at that drove me to work harder and I passed well the second time,' he said with a rueful smile.

'So you're saying you came good in the end?'

'I guess I'm saying don't stress about it too much or make it a federal issue. That didn't work with me,' he said.

We smoked and watched the activity on the river. There were fewer river buses at this time and more working boats churning up the water. On the bridge above we could see buses and cars inching along. The date for my case against Ron Osborne was fast approaching. I had told Henry the whole saga already.

'Wouldn't it be nice to get on a boat and just sail away?' I said.

'It would.'

'I'm due in court next week and I'm feeling stupidly nervous.'

'You're bound to be. It's a fight.'

'I'm wondering whether to throw the towel in. It will be his word against mine.'

'But you're telling the truth and he's lying.'

'I bet he's a good liar. I'm not sure I've got the fight left in me.'

'That doesn't sound like you, Liz.'

Everyone thought I was still strong capable Liz, not the beaten creature I had become. I could feel tears pressing up and I swallowed hard.

'Where's the court?'

'In Luton. We're scheduled for eleven next Thursday.' My words came out slightly squeaky.

'I could come with you,' he said.

'That's so kind of you, but I've got to take the day off work.'

'I can take the day off too. I can drive you there.'

'I was going to go by train.'

'Let me drive you. That's what friends are for.'

The thought of having Henry drive me there and be in court with me was immensely comforting. I threw my butt into the bucket of sand by the studio door.

'Yes, please,' I said.

I was back in my office when Fizzy appeared at my threshold.

'Come in. You look nice.'

She shut the door but didn't sit down. She had changed out of her studio clothes into jeans and a pink jumper with a huge cowl neck and she looked excited.

'I'm about to set off for a weekend in France, with Saul,' she said.

'Goodness.'

'Our first weekend away and without my darling Zac. Loida's holding the fort, bless her.'

She was walking round my room as she talked. She stopped at the mirror by my door and looked at her reflection.

'I mean he's taking me to this *amazing* hotel in Le Touquet and it's not the kind of place you'd bring a baby.'

'I hope you have a great time.'

'And Bob just gave me third degree because he wants to see Zac this weekend and I said he couldn't. He'd wind Loida round his little finger and I'm not having that. He's got a bloody nerve. I'm doing him a favour, and since when did he get to dictate the terms?'

'He may be feeling raw after what happened this morning,' I said.

'What was that all about? I mean, saying it was like the Wild West. Does he see himself as some kind of cowboy? Ridiculous.'

Bob's charms had clearly diminished in Fizzy's eyes.

Chalk Farm flat, Friday night

A quattro formaggi and an American hot pizza had been consumed. We'd watched two episodes of the second series of *The Missing*, which was Flo's choice for our night's viewing. We had a really good discussion about it. For me it was the French detective Julien Baptiste who made the show work.

'What a wonderful man he is. He cares so much,' I said.

Flo is clever at predicting the direction of the plot. She was suspicious about one of the characters and pointed out with great precision a number of inconsistencies in that character's story.

'I hadn't thought of that,' I said.

'You wait and see, Mum, I'm sure I'm right.'

I hugged her to me.

'Clever clogs. I am proud of you, you know.'

She shrugged.

'I'm not clever,' she said.

'Oh, but you are. You're just having a dip. We all have dips from time to time.'

Chalk Farm flat, Saturday morning

My cafetière of coffee had been made and I was warming milk when I heard our mail box clatter. I stirred the milk in so my drink was the colour of caramel and took a first sip. It was perfect. There were three flyers and a letter on the doormat. My address was handwritten in a hand I didn't recognise. I opened it and actually gasped when I saw the letter was from Douglas. I leaned back against our front door and read it through twice while my heart did a strange dance.

> Liz, dear Liz,
>
> You are the loveliest woman I've met in years and I'm sorry I've been so distant these last few weeks.
>
> All I can say is that there have been serious family commitments which I had to attend to. We thought Natalie Cooper was going to die. Thankfully she is now recuperating at home.
>
> There has been a lot of other private stuff going on too and I let it take me over.
>
> I know I've been an idiot. Will you see me again? Please say yes.
>
> Douglas

I didn't know what I felt about his letter. Hearing nothing from him for weeks had brought me so low. I read it a third time. No matter what private stuff was going on he could have kept in touch. It had been weeks and even a text would have made me feel I mattered to him. I had been getting used to the idea that I wouldn't see him any more. My self-esteem was in the cellar and I wasn't sure I could risk getting involved with him again. I would think about it tomorrow. No, I would think about it after the court case.

CHAPTER THIRTY-FIVE

StoryWorld TV station, London Bridge

Monday, and this week we're running the heroic-women series which we first discussed at the end of the summer. It has taken Molly this long to find and film five stories and each one of them is compelling. The first one was about the wife of the Saudi blogger and her campaign to stop her husband receiving any more lashes from the state. She had fled with her children from Saudi Arabia and she said more lashes would kill her husband. It was a powerful film. It's a funny thing with our audience that they like the froth and the frippery but when we do run a hard-hitting series it scores highly with them. We've had a lot of positive tweets and emails this morning and it cheered me up. This was a series we could be proud of.

When I got back from my coffee with Henry there was an email from Julius asking me to meet with him at five p.m. on a serious matter. That was all it said and it put the wind up me. Martine usually sets up his meetings and might have some idea what it was about so I went down to her desk.

'I really don't,' she said. 'It's odd that he wrote to you like that.'

'I thought that was odd too.'

'He seemed to be down this morning and he's with the regulators all day so I can't reach him. My best guess is that it's a budget thing. Could be more cuts coming your way, perhaps.'

'Oh joy,' I said.

She looked sympathetic.

I went back to my office and pulled my budget sheets up with a sense of great weariness stealing over me. There was no fat left. We had been cut to the bone last autumn. Only once did I let myself think about the letter from Douglas. It was at the back of my mind all day and I still didn't know what to do about it. He had unfinished business with his wife, that was the private stuff he referred to in his letter. He said he had let it take him over. And it probably would again; it was still early days in his break-up. My landline rang and it was Fizzy calling from home.

'We couldn't talk this morning but I wanted to tell you about Le Touquet. It was the most gorgeous hotel, real old-world glamour with black and white pictures everywhere of the famous people who've stayed there. Saul booked us a suite with a sea view.'

This was a big weekend for Saul and it seemed he'd wanted to impress her. He was dating a woman fifteen years younger than him who in terms of looks was well out of his league.

'The service was sensational and the swimming pool was a dream.'

'Lucky you.'

'And at dinner on Saturday he gave me diamond earrings, Liz, real diamonds.'

'Diamonds are a girl's best friend.' I said it ironically but Fizzy laughed in delight, not picking up on my tone.

'You betcha. It's lovely to be cherished.'

'How do you feel about him?'

'I'm not going to marry him, but it's nice to have a man around. It's tough being a lone parent.'

'Tell me about it,' I said.

Fizzy, as ever, was doing the smart thing rather than the right thing.

I was outside Julius's office at five p.m. sharp. I tapped on the door and Julius asked me to sit down. I had brought a folder with my budgets and I rested this on his desk. He glanced at my folder and then at a document he had in front of him.

'This is going to be a difficult conversation, Liz, one I hoped I would never have to have.'

In my depressed state I hardly had the energy to be alarmed.

'Is it my budget?'

'Your budget? No, nothing to do with your budget,' he said quickly.

I felt relieved but he was looking serious, almost pained.

'Saul has asked me to give you a formal warning.'

That felt like a punch in the stomach.

'What! What have I done?'

'A case has been made against you that you've been trying to sabotage the new presentation arrangements.'

'Says who?'

'You were opposed to the Fizzy and Ledley double act from the beginning. You're still committed to Fizzy having the solo role.'

I shook my head in disbelief and said it again: 'Says who?' Although I knew the answer.

'In addition, it's claimed that the travel pilot failed because you do not want Ledley to succeed as the co-host.'

'It's Lori, isn't it?' I said.

'Lori believes you're deliberately sabotaging the sponsorship deal with WayToGo. And the ratings are slipping.'

I could feel something stirring inside me, a small ember of resistance.

'The ratings are slipping so let's blame me,' I said.

He put his hand on the document on his desk.

'Lori has made a case to Saul that you are actively working against the new format.'

'She would. She's been against me from the start. And let's remember it was her big idea to mess with the format, a woman with no programming ability at all.'

'She's not the only colleague who thinks you've been working against the station,' he said.

The ember inside me was flickering into life and I could feel the heat of long-suppressed anger in my body.

'Let me guess, Bob is in on the act.'

Julius tapped the document again.

'Yes, he's backed up what Lori said.'

'So the two of them concocted a case against me?'

Saul would have been swayed that an editorial person like Bob had joined the head of marketing on this. This was no simple programming versus sales split.

'I don't want to discipline you, Liz. You're a good producer. I'd much rather you resigned and we can give you a pay-off for long service and you can leave here with your reputation intact,' he said.

The embers had now burst into roaring flames and I leapt to my feet. I leaned across his desk.

'Oh no; that's not going to happen. Resign after all these years when I've done *nothing wrong*?'

I pointed at the document on his desk.

'I can't believe you've been taken in by them. Bob and Lori are both gunning for me and I'll tell you why. Lori made a huge error in insisting on the double act and she has to get rid of me because I saw that coming. It's her fault we're losing ratings. She hasn't got a clue about programming. Bob wants me out of here because I know something that will blow his marriage apart.'

Julius had sat back in his seat and was watching me intently.

'What do you mean?'

'He's Zachary's father and I'm the only person in the station that knows it.'

I didn't count Ledley. He didn't *know* for sure. That took Julius by surprise. That wiped the lordly expression off his face.

'You're saying Bob and Fizzy...'

'Yes, Bob and Fizzy. They had an affair and she got pregnant. He tried to persuade her to have an abortion. He hates me because he thinks I persuaded her to go through with it. And he's terrified Pat will find out. He's been threatening me for months. This is his latest ploy.'

I could see that Julius was trying to absorb what for him was a bombshell. He had had no idea. He had thought that Geoff was Zachary's father, as did nearly everyone at StoryWorld.

'And I've never said a word to anyone, and you know why? To protect Fizzy.'

'Sit down,' he said.

'Not until I've had my say. You've let Lori get away with far too much. You should kick her out of the morning meeting, for a start. She's a saleswoman and has no place being there. You've allowed her to grow in influence and to poison

Saul's mind against me. You've let her take power away from you too.'

I had hit home there. He knew how close Lori had got to Saul and that it had weakened his position at the station.

'Now you can do one of two things, Julius. You can choose to take my side and fight for me. You can put that document in the shredder and I hope that's what you will do. Together you and I could turn the programme around. Or you can choose to discipline me and I will fight it every step of the way and use everything I've got.'

I turned to leave his room.

'Don't you walk out of this meeting! I decide when it ends,' he said.

'I'm leaving you to consider those two options. There's nothing more to say. Goodnight.'

I left his office with my head held high. I didn't want to go back to my office and see the team so I called Ziggy and asked her to bring my coat and bag down to reception. She hurried down to me with my things and I asked her to lock my office.

'Is everything OK?'

She looked worried.

'I need to get home,' I said.

I left the building. I was desperate for some air and space. I walked by the river, heading towards Westminster, fast to begin with, fuelled by my fury, but gradually I slowed down and my heart settled. I was not ready to go home; I needed time to process what had happened. Julius wanted me to resign.

The small lights strung along the bank were lit and there was a faint smell of smoke on the air. StoryWorld had been such a huge part of my life for so many years that it was part of my identity. The injustice of it burned strongly, that my years of work and dedication seemed to count for nothing. At the same time that bastard Saul Relph was consummating his relationship with Fizzy, he was deciding to discipline me. I felt utter contempt for him. A lone jogger passed me. He had a light attached to his head like a miner's lamp. I recalled Flo saying the other night that my career had not made me happy. The last three months had certainly not been happy. In fact, since Lori Kerwell had arrived there had been one nasty shock after another. What if I did resign? Was this the time to make the break, to take the money and to work fewer hours so I could spend more time with Flo? Too often I had let the problems at StoryWorld be my priority, not her.

The London Eye came into view. I pass it so often but have never been on it. On an impulse I joined the queue. I was shocked when they said it cost twenty-five quid for a thirty-minute circuit, but I'd waited in line so I bought a ticket. I hadn't had to wait that long as a November night was not the optimum time for viewing. I wasn't there to see the London landmarks which I knew so well. What I wanted to experience was the sensation of being lifted into the sky and seeing the ground fall away.

We entered our capsule. There were no children present, it was mainly young couples and one elderly pair who sat on the bench in the centre and held hands. I stood and looked out. As we rose in a slow and stately manner what wowed me most was the white metal framework of the wheel, the struts and the giant shaft, the sheer feat of engineering that had allowed this structure to go up and to turn so smoothly. We could see into other capsules, faces pressed against the glass, people pointing at buildings. As we rose higher I gazed at the sequence of floodlit bridges that spanned the river and the boats passing beneath them becoming smaller, becoming toy size. I walked round the capsule to get a three hundred and sixty degree view. There was the Shard and Charing Cross station and I could make out Buckingham Palace surrounded by trees. Closer, and dominating one view, was Big Ben, glowing in the dark. We had reached the top of the circle and we hung there. The city lay spread out beneath me, a panorama of slowly moving tracks of light. Red lights burned on Titan cranes. This was my world and I knew I had to fight. I would find the strength to take on Saul and Julius because even if I lost it would force them to increase any financial offer they made me.

We started down the other side. The old couple on the bench got to their feet and I made room for them next to me. The boats on the river and the buses on the bridges and the people on the South Bank became larger, became normal size. We had reached the exit platform.

'Such a treat, wasn't it?' the old lady said to me.

'It was. Gives you perspective,' I said.

CHAPTER THIRTY-SIX

StoryWorld TV station, London Bridge

I was in the gallery and a small part of me was watching Ledley as he cooked for his guest and the greater part of me was thinking how I would manage the morning meeting, seeing Lori and Bob, my attackers, across the table. Ledley's guest was a Romanian weather presenter. She had acquired a cult following because of her mispronunciation of words when she did her weather reports. She was a gift to the impersonators with her gaffes and she took how people laughed at her with good grace. You couldn't help liking her. Ledley was making her smoked bacon with cabbage rolls on the side. It didn't sound appealing and it didn't look very nice either, but apparently it was her favourite dish. I wouldn't let Lori and Bob know they had got to me. I would appear calm no matter how much my stomach was clenching. I would say little and watch how things played out.

The cameras had moved back on to Fizzy. A text pinged on to my mobile from Simon.

> Need to show you something before morning
> meeting.

It was rare for him to text me while the show was on air so something was up. The credits rolled and I hurried upstairs. He was waiting for me and followed me into my office.

'Look at this.'

He handed me his phone and I read a short spiteful piece published in a weekly satirical magazine. It referred to Fizzy as *the fragrant Miss Wentworth*, and went on to say that *as speculation continues as to who the married father of her six-month-old son Zachary can be, we are told on good authority that the baby is a StoryWorld in-house production. Miss Wentworth, a favourite with the viewers, has been the face of StoryWorld for nine years. She hails from Burnley, as does StoryWorld's seasoned news editor Mr Bob Taylor.*

An *in-house production*; I remembered that Ledley had used that exact phrase to me when he first voiced his suspicions. And that reference to Burnley and to Bob, putting him right in the frame. It was hideous.

'It was just posted on their Twitter account. It's small circulation but you know how fast word gets out,' Simon said, his eyes round behind his glasses. 'She's with Saul Relph now, isn't she?'

So the team knew about Saul and Fizzy's relationship. You can't keep a secret in a TV station although God knows I've tried to keep Fizzy's secret for months.

'It's horrible. The person who leaked this wants to do maximum damage to Fizzy. I've got to go. Thanks for alerting me.'

We were sitting round the meeting table waiting for Julius. Fizzy and the director sat on either side of me and Ledley was next to Lori and Bob. I had been worrying about how I would deal with this meeting but the latest drama had pushed my concerns to the back of my mind. I looked at Bob. He couldn't have seen the story yet. He looked as he always did, slightly bored and scowly. He scratched at his jaw and suppressed a yawn. He had supported Lori in the plot against me and I was glad that trouble was heading his way. But I felt for Fizzy. She was going to have to deal with the fallout, which was always going to come at some point. She was looking pleased with herself so it hadn't crossed her radar either. I would have to tell her straight after the meeting and reveal that Ledley was the leaker. How would Saul Relph react to the news that Bob had fathered Zachary? As for Ledley, he was pulling at his cuffs as Julius came in and I watched him during the meeting as he said smoothly how much he'd enjoyed talking to Elena, the Romanian weather presenter, she was good fun. He had thrown a little pebble into the media pool but it was a hand grenade. There would be destruction in its wake. I suddenly remembered Pat, Bob's wife, and his two girls. They were all innocent parties but would be terribly hurt by today's revelation. What a Judas he was.

Fizzy's reaction, when I told her in the privacy of her dressing room, surprised me. I had expected her to explode at Ledley's treachery but she seemed alarmed rather than angry.

'Saul's going to hate this so much.'

She sat on her chaise longue and wound her hair round her fingers in ever tighter spirals. She looked up at me.

'Apart from Martine you're the only woman friend I've got. Tell me what I should say to Saul?'

That admission touched me. I sat on the chaise next to her.

'No point denying it, is there? You have to tell him the truth.'

'But you know men and their bloody pride. He'll hate that I slept with Bob. He assumed it was Geoff and could deal with that because he doesn't know Geoff.'

She was right. Saul Relph would hate that the affair had happened on his patch, his territory. Her mobile rang.

'Oh shit, it's Saul!' she said.

Her phone vibrated insistently on her dressing table and we stared at it. Finally it stopped.

'Fizz, do you want to be with him?'

There was a significant pause.

'I don't want him to reject me over this,' she said in a small voice.

I detested the man now but she had asked for help.

'Then build him up. Tell him what a difference being with him has made to you. That you felt alone before and stupidly took comfort with Bob but that it didn't mean anything to you.'

'That's good, that's very good. But what if he asks if I'm still seeing Bob? He'd loathe that.'

She had stopped twisting her hair and was looking at me for the answer. There is a childlike quality to Fizzy sometimes.

'You could say you felt it was the honourable thing to do, to let Bob see his son.'

'Yes, his only son. I was being honourable. You're brilliant, Liz. And I'll say that it's Loida who takes Zac to her flat where they meet. He can't object to that.'

It was a lie, of course, about Loida being the go-between, but Fizzy looked calmer. She stood up.

'You better go now. I'm going to ring him back.'

'Have courage,' I said.

She blew me a kiss and picked up her phone.

By noon the station was buzzing with the story. I saw Harriet talking to a couple of the news reporters who had wandered

over to our side of the building. They conferred over their
paper cups of coffee about where the story had come from.
Bob had locked himself in his office and had lowered his
blinds. Julius was nowhere to be seen. I stayed in my room
too and got Ziggy to screen my calls. No way was I going to
risk speaking to the likes of Lou Gibson again. Ziggy brought
in a list of names of journalists wanting to talk to me and sure
enough her name was there.

'There are cameramen outside,' she said.

I had already told the team to talk to no one. There would be
more paparazzi camped around Fizzy's house and I wondered
how she would manage to get in later without being snapped.
I did not return any of the calls. My usual impulse would have
been to call the journalists back and try to make things look
better for the station but I was damned if I'd do that after
the way Saul and Julius had treated me. Let them deal with the
media firestorm. I pulled out the letter from Douglas and read
it one more time. But I couldn't engage with it. Bubbles of
dread that I might be losing my job kept surfacing, making
me feel slightly sick and dizzy.

At lunchtime I bought a roll from the Hub and was passing
reception when I saw Pat Taylor, Bob's wife, giving her name
to the security man! I was rooted to the spot as I watched her
fill in the form all visitors have to sign. Pat looked unbelievably
tense. He handed her a pass on a lanyard. She grabbed it from
him and turned away.

'You need to wear it,' he said. 'We've got extra security today.'

She pulled it over her head in a fury and then she saw me.
I walked towards her.

'Is she one of yours?' she said.

'Sorry?'

'Lou fucking Gibson. Is she one of your journos?'

'No, no. She works for a news site.'

'She turned up at my work. Shoved this in my face.'

Pat was holding the magazine and her hands were trembling.

'She wanted to know how I felt. How I felt!'

'She's a piece of work,' I said.

But she had pushed past me and was heading towards the dressing rooms with great determination. She knew her way around the station, had been here several times and was a woman on a mission. Nothing was going to stop her from finding Fizzy. I followed her and dived into make-up. I used the phone on the wall and punched in Simon's extension. He picked up on the second ring.

'Get Bob down to Fizzy's dressing room *now*. Tell him Pat's here.'

Pat was outside Fizzy's door. She pulled the door open and flung herself in. I ran up in time to see Fizzy turning towards her and Pat slapping her face with great force.

'You cheap little marriage wrecker.'

Fizzy had stumbled backwards and was holding her face.

'You can have him, he's all yours,' Pat hissed at her.

Fizzy had put out her hand on the wall to steady herself. Pat turned and shoved past me. Bob had arrived at the end of the corridor to the dressing rooms. He was white-faced as he came towards us, his hands held out in an attempt to stop her.

'Don't you *dare* touch me,' Pat said.

He pulled back his arms and stood aside as she swept past him.

'Pat. Please.'

She was charging back towards reception. Bob followed her and so did I.

'Pat, we need to talk. Please.'

She didn't even turn to look at him.

'Don't think about coming to the house. You stay right away from us.'

She pulled the visitor's pass off and tossed it to the ground. She had reached the exit. There were paparazzi on the forecourt and when Bob saw them he stopped. He didn't want to be photographed chasing his wife out of the station. Pat disappeared from view. Bob leaned against the wall and looked as if all the stuffing had gone from him. The security man picked up the pass from the floor and looked over at me with his eyebrows raised. Bob was rubbing his face with both hands. Then he saw me and his eyes blazed with hatred.

'Bet you're loving this, you bitch.'

'It didn't come from me. You can blame your pal Ledley for this. He's the leaker,' I said.

He was shaking his head in disbelief but then he stood still. He was taking it in. I started to walk back towards Fizzy's dressing room when Bob rushed past me and started hammering on Ledley's door. It was locked. He banged his fists against the door in a fury. Fizzy came out of her room.

'Your wife assaulted me,' she said.

Her cheek was red.

'Fuck off,' he said.

Ellen had heard all the noise and kerfuffle and came out of make-up.

'What's going on?'

'Where's that fucker Ledley? Is he in there?' Bob roared.

Ellen looked at him as if he was a dangerous dog that needed to be placated.

'He's not here. I saw him go upstairs.'

Bob turned and raced towards the stairs as Fizzy fell into Ellen's arms.

'Am I going to have a black eye?' she wailed.

I followed Bob. He had taken the left-hand stairs up to the features side. Lori's office was on the other side of Julius's from mine. Like mine it was a glass box and I could see Ledley was in there with Lori. Bob sprinted to the door and burst in, leaving the door swinging wide.

'You treacherous little shit,' he screamed at Ledley, heading towards him with his fists clenched.

Ledley leapt up from the sofa and backed away from Bob. 'What the hell?' Lori said.

She stepped between Bob and Ledley.

'He's the fucking leaker,' Bob yelled.

That was news to Lori and as it registered with her she looked out of her office and saw me standing there. Ledley had now moved behind Lori's desk, was cowering there. Lori put both hands on Bob's chest and pushed him down on her sofa.

'Get a grip,' she said.

She slammed her door in my face. But I stood there anyway and watched the three of them hurling abuse at each other. Simon had joined me and we both stood fascinated by the tableau unfolding behind the glass. We couldn't hear what they were saying but it looked like each one of them was blaming the other with a lot of arms being thrown into the air. Lori was screeching at Ledley now and he was shouting back, his face a picture of outrage. No doubt he was justifying his action. Bob was on the sofa with his head in his hands.

'Oh dear,' I said. 'Team Kerwell seems to be coming apart at the seams.'

Simon burst out laughing and I joined in. Lori swung round and saw Simon and me laughing at them. Her face was contorted as we turned and walked away.

Ellen was waiting for me and followed me into my office.

'Fizzy's gone. She was in a terrible state. Said she was booking herself into a hotel. What's going to happen tomorrow?'

'I have no idea,' I said.

Martine had appeared on the threshold and came in, shutting my door.

'Please tell me what's going on,' she said.

I recounted the events of the last mad half-hour and Martine was aghast.

'What a mess. So bad for the station. And Julius is out. Can you get everyone to calm down, Liz?'

That was my role, to be the company woman and to steady the ship. But I wasn't going to do it this time. Though I didn't say as much to Martine and Ellen.

'You need to brief Julius asap,' I said.

'Will Fizzy present the show tomorrow?'

'All bets are off,' I said.

After they had gone I realised that I no longer had to keep Fizzy's secret. There was a relief in that, almost a lightness.

Simon came in around five and sat on my sofa.

'You wouldn't believe the wild rumours that are circulating out there,' he said.

'Enlighten me.'

'Pat Taylor slapped Fizzy. Bob punched Ledley. Fizzy has a black eye and Ledley will be presenting the show solo tomorrow,' Simon said.

'Bob certainly wanted to punch Ledley but Lori denied him that pleasure. I've always thought that Bob was a man who wants to punch a lot of people, including me,' I said.

'Seriously though, is Fizzy OK?'

'The thing about Fizzy is that she's the ultimate survivor and has a core of steel. There's no way she'll let Ledley go solo tomorrow,' I said.

The person Simon should have been worrying about was me. Would I still have a job in a week? Today's fiasco didn't change the fact that Julius had asked me to resign.

I locked my door at six and Molly was still working but the others had left.

'I don't suppose much got done today,' I said.

StoryWorld had become an even more dysfunctional place than usual. Yet I'd seen Molly at her desk all day working on her heroic-women series and putting the finishing touches to the third story which was going out tomorrow.

'So many more important things to worry about,' she said.

Molly hates the world of celebrity and gossip and some people find her high-handed, even haughty. I'm glad to have her in my team. Downstairs I saw there were now two extra security men in reception. I put up the hood on my parka and hurried past the lone paparazzo who was lurking in the forecourt.

CHAPTER THIRTY-SEVEN

StoryWorld TV station, London Bridge

I went down to Fizzy's dressing room before the show. She had called me last night and said she would present the show today. She was almost feverish this morning. Ellen had had to apply extra concealer to her face and her eyes were unnaturally bright. She told me she hadn't dared leave her hotel room and had hardly slept. Loida was holed up at her house with Zac.

'The hotel let me use the staff exit so at least I got away without being spotted this morning. I don't know how long I'm going to have to stay there.'

'How did Saul take it?'

'He was *so weird* about it being Bob. He was deeply offended and didn't say it but I could tell he thought I'd stooped by sleeping with a mere news editor. Things with him are on a knife edge. Men and their bloody egos!'

'You know he's into status in a big way,' I said.

She pulled a face. Saul Relph was the kind of man who treated junior members of staff as if they didn't count.

'He said the station could do without the scandal. Does my face look bruised?'

'No, you look fine.'

She glanced at her reflection.

'But your line about what a difference he'd made to my life played well and I was the contrite woman, of course. I cried, actually.'

I had only seen Fizzy cry once and it was last year when she decided to have a termination. She had sobbed on my shoulder that having the baby would ruin her career. We had gone to the clinic together, a sad and tense journey, and then she'd had a last-minute change of heart.

'He was nicer then, said I wasn't to fret,' she said.

'You told him that Ledley is the leaker?'

'Of course. He said they need proof before he and Julius can take action. But that prick better watch his back, he's on borrowed time. I can hardly bear to sit next to him on the sofa!'

Yesterday she had been stunned by Pat's attack but she seemed to have no guilt at the wreckage she had caused. I could imagine the unhappy scene that was going on at Bob's house, if Pat had actually let him past the front door. I recalled meeting Pat and her daughters in Selfridges. She'd told me their older girl was off to university. How awful for them to learn from the press that their dad had cheated on their mum and that they had a baby half-brother.

'Time to get to the studio,' I said.

'I saw the anthropologist in make-up. He's hot for an academic, isn't he?' she said.

'Fizzy!'

Molly had booked in an anthropologist whose book on polygamy was proving a surprise big seller. I slipped into the gallery as the title credits were rolling. Fizzy read her opening link faster than usual. The director switched off the shared mic and leaned in to me.

'Is she OK?'

'She's all over the place,' I said.

There was a manic quality to her reactions as she talked

to the handsome anthropologist. He was telling her that a large number of countries allowed a male to have more than one spouse.

'I bet it doesn't happen the other way round,' Fizzy said.

'It's much rarer, but there is a group of people in southern India who practise fraternal polyandry. That is when the woman marries *all* the brothers in a family.'

'Goodness, how truly bizarre.'

'The brothers rotate the nights they sleep with her.'

'It makes my head spin to think about it,' she said.

'It's a way of making sure that the farmland in such a remote area is concentrated in one family,' he said, matter-of-factly, while I could imagine our many female viewers reeling at the idea.

The next item was Ledley talking to Betty on the sofa. I had watched Betty's face as she got miked up and caught her looking at Fizzy with thinly disguised distaste. Betty was deeply conventional. She didn't do social media but by now everyone at the station knew that Zachary had been fathered by Bob Taylor.

The end credits rolled and the best thing about the show had been Molly's story. I went upstairs to the morning meeting. Ledley, Lori and the director were already there. Julius marched in and sat at the top of the table.

'Where are the others?' he said.

No one said anything. Martine came in and I heard her tell Julius that Fizzy had a bad headache and had left the station for the day.

'I bet she has,' he said tartly. 'And Bob?'

'I haven't seen him this morning,' Martine said.

Nobody had seen Bob and there had been no word from

him. We all knew the reason for his no-show and I wondered if he was going to survive the scandal. Would he be coming back to StoryWorld?

'Well, get his deputy in now,' Julius said irritably.

We waited while Martine walked over to the newsroom.

'I hear yesterday was like something out of a Wild West bar brawl,' Julius said. 'I was disgusted to hear about it. You're supposed to be ambassadors for StoryWorld and to set an example.'

Martine returned with Bob's number two who sat down and looked like a rabbit caught in headlights.

'OK, we'll start and I'll draw a line under what happened yesterday but if there is a repeat of it there will be serious repercussions,' Julius said.

Martine sat down next to Julius and opened her pad.

'Martine is joining us as I'd like today's meeting to be minuted,' he said.

That was unusual. The morning meeting was rarely minuted and it gave me an uneasy feeling that something else was up. Julius asked the director for his technical report and he spoke briefly.

'Anything to add, Liz?' Julius was looking at me.

'A good mix of features today and I thought Molly's piece was particularly strong,' I said.

'I agree. It was first-rate work,' Julius said.

He didn't ask Ledley or Lori for their views. He pulled his papers together and straightened them. He waited for a minute before speaking again so that he had everyone's full attention.

'Before we leave I want to put on record my appreciation to Liz Lyon for her work. Liz should be commended for fighting to maintain editorial standards at StoryWorld. She knows that if we compromise on quality we lose ratings. We are not, I repeat *not*, going to become bargain-basement television.'

He was looking at Lori as he said the last sentence and she actually rocked back in her seat, her face frozen. Ledley was looking at Lori aghast, and Martine was noting Julius's comments down with a small smile. I was amazed, gloriously, deliriously amazed at his words.

'I appreciate that,' I stammered.

'Very well deserved, Liz,' the director said.

'In addition, from now on this will be a purely editorial meeting, with immediate effect,' Julius said.

He was banning Lori from coming to the morning meeting. I cheered inside.

'With *immediate* effect.' He repeated the phrase, looking at Lori.

There was a moment of stunned silence. Then Lori sat up even straighter than usual.

'Saul will be informed of this,' she said icily.

'I've already explained to Saul that this is an editorial meeting and you are a salesperson. You're not needed here.'

'I need to know what's going on,' she hissed.

'You need to focus on selling ads and leave Liz and me to do our jobs. Please leave now,' he said.

He went to the door and pulled it open. Lori pushed her chair back, stood up and hugged her lever arch file to her chest. She didn't sweep out. She had her chin down over her file as she turned towards her office. Martine and I exchanged glances and I tried so hard not to grin. Ledley didn't know what to do or what to say or where to look. His champion had just been publicly kneecapped and I guessed he was suddenly feeling very alone. Julius left, with Martine in close attendance, shortly afterwards, and I floated out of that room.

Julius had decided to back me and to take on Lori. Her document was in the shredder and his praise for my work was on the record. He had stood up to Saul on this. I guessed that he had backed me because I had made him see that once I was out of the way Lori would have him in her sights. There was no end to her ambition.

Before I left for the day I drafted a memo to Julius making the case for Ziggy to have a permanent role in my team as a digital technician. She had passed her editing course with distinction. I detailed how it would save us money as we wouldn't need to hire in freelance editors. I'd got some power back and I reckoned that today was the day I could get what I wanted.

Chalk Farm flat, evening

When I got in I tapped on Flo's door. She was sitting cross-legged on her bed and Mr Crooks was sprawled across her lap. I sat down and tickled him under his chin and rubbed his cheekbones.

'That's his all-time favourite thing,' she said.

He closed his eyes in ecstasy, opening and closing his paws to show his pleasure and purring loudly.

'I've got the court case tomorrow so I'll be here when you get home from school.'

'Great. I'm dying to watch more of *The Missing* tonight,' she said.

'Let's do it.'

She lifted the sleepy Mr Crooks from her lap and laid him on her bed. He opened one eye and stretched out languorously on the duvet.

'Hunter Cat is Duvet Cat tonight,' I said.

We cosied on the sofa and she sat sideways, resting her bare feet on my lap, wriggling her toes now and then to prompt me to stroke her feet. I tucked a blanket round us as we watched episode four of *The Missing*. Flo's insight into the character from the other night proved to be right. We started on episode five. My mobile rang and Douglas's name flashed up and I was startled to see it.

'I'd better take this.'

Flo paused the drama.

'Don't be long,' she murmured as I took the phone into my bedroom, and only then did I click the answer button.

'Hello, Douglas.'

'Hello, Liz.'

I was thrown by his calling me. I had planned to call him in my own time, when I felt ready. And I didn't feel ready, not tonight, not after the last few days I'd had. I searched for something to say to bridge the weeks we hadn't spoken to each other. All I could come up with was a polite: 'I was glad to hear that your mum-in-law recovered.'

'Thanks. It was a close-run thing. So you got my letter.'

'Yes, I did. On Saturday.'

'Look, I know this is a bad time but, well, I guess I wanted to know your answer,' he said.

The words I picked up on were 'bad time'.

'How do you know it's a bad time?' I said.

'Oh, I meant all the shenanigans at your station. I hear that Fizzy has had some of her fragrance slapped out of her.'

He was trying to be light-hearted, to make a joke of it, but it jarred badly with me.

'It is a bit of a bad time,' I said.

There was an awkward silence from his end.

'And I'm sorry but I don't want to talk about it,' I said.

'I'm sorry, for the bad timing and for my big foot,' he said.

'It's OK, it's just that I'm kind of right in the middle of something with Flo and—'

'Of course, of course. Shall we talk tomorrow?'

'I'm at the small claims court tomorrow,' I said.

I was shutting down the conversation and he got the message.

'I see. Good luck with that.'

'Thank you.'

'I'll wish you good night then.'

'Good night, Douglas.'

I clicked the phone off. Why had I pushed him away? He had made a throwaway remark. But it showed that he knew what was going on at my work and it had played to all my doubts about him. There would always be awkward moments between us; boundary issues. He was News Nine and I was StoryWorld. If I had a relationship I wanted it to be with someone I could trust, someone I could open up to and share my work problems. And my worries about Flo. It was sad but I knew I could never truly relax with Douglas. I would probably feel thoroughly miserable in the morning for what I'd done but for now I wanted to rejoin Flo on the sofa.

'No more calls please, Mum,' she said.

'You're right.'

I turned off my mobile and she pressed play.

CHAPTER THIRTY-EIGHT

Chalk Farm flat, morning

I was up at seven and felt more chipper than I expected. Taking Ron Osborne on no longer seemed such an ordeal. I didn't feel devastated about Douglas either; I felt OK. I kicked off the duvet and peered out. The sky was overcast and gloomy and rain was on its way. I'd thought about what I should wear and dressed in my black dress with its white scalloped collar because it was smart but also looked demure. Flo joined me in the kitchen.

'How are you getting there, Mum?'

'I've got a lift.'

She was buttering toast and she stopped for a moment.

'With him?'

I knew she meant Douglas.

'No, it's someone from work, Henry – you've met him though you might not remember him.'

'I do; the one that fancies you.'

'Henry? Don't be silly.'

'He does. When you were wearing that bead dress he couldn't stop looking at you.'

He had liked that wonderful 1920s dress. So had I. It had made me feel glamorous on that night.

'We're mates, good mates,' I said.

What I liked about Henry was that I never felt self-conscious with him and we could talk freely. She carried on buttering her toast.

'And he's nicer than Douglas,' she said.

'You don't know him; you don't know either of them.'

That sounded a bit hard. Was she teasing me?

'Jam or Marmite, darling?'

She took the jam from me.

'Will you get some crunchy peanut butter next week? It's my new fave thing.'

I added it to the shopping list I keep in the kitchen. The bell rang and Flo got there before me.

'Morning, Flo.'

'Hello, Henry.'

I came up behind her to see Henry dressed in a smart navy coat.

'Good coat. Makes you look like an Italian football manager,' I said.

He laughed at that.

'I'm taking that as a compliment. What a great room,' he said, looking around. He walked to the French doors, as everyone does when they come in, and looked out at our little garden.

'Italian football manager? Sounds like you fancy him too,' Flo said softly to me and I gave her a playful punch.

I joined Henry by our French doors. It had started to rain and fat drops were hitting the ground.

'These are the doors that are warped, the ones Ron Osborne was supposed to replace.'

He ran his hand down the wood.

'They're a nice feature. I can recommend a good carpenter, after you win,' he said.

'Wish I had your confidence.'

Flo was doing a last check on her rucksack and had pulled on her woolly hat.

'I'm off, Mum.'

'Would you like a lift to school?' Henry said.

'Well, I go with Rosie.'

'We can pick her up too. It's chucking it down.'

'OK, ta.'

We ran to his car which was an old Volvo with well-worn seats. Flo got in the back and called Rosie.

'We're coming by car to get you in five,' she said.

The rain was hammering on the roof of his car and Rosie was waiting under the portico of her house as we drew up. She sprinted to the car and jumped in, breathless and giggling.

'What a storm!'

Henry drove to the gates of their school and parked.

'Thanks for the lift.'

'No, wait, girls. You'll get soaked. I've got a big umbrella in the boot.'

He got out and opened the boot. Flo leaned forward and said: 'He *so* does fancy you.'

'Behave!' I said, but I was smiling.

Henry returned with a huge golfing umbrella in the blue and white stripes of StoryWorld's logo.

'Out you get.'

'Good luck, Mum. Text me as soon as you know.'

He is so tall he stood between them and held the umbrella so that Flo and Rosie could both shelter beneath it. There was a lightning flash which lit up the school sign, followed three seconds later by a rolling crack of thunder. Students were running through the gates, some holding school bags over their heads as the rain pelted down. Lightning flashed again as Henry got back and flung the umbrella into the back of the car. He got out of his coat.

'Thank you for doing that. That was apocalyptic,' I said.

He keyed in the postcode of the county court and we set off for Luton. His windscreen wipers were working flat out and we didn't talk much as he drove us out of London. I looked at his profile as he focused on the road.

The storm had spent itself and the rain became less heavy. I had my folder with all the papers on my lap, my statement and Ron Osborne's counter claim.

'I suppose we'll have to swear on a Bible,' I said.

'I guess so.'

I kept looking at my statement.

'Would it help if you read me his statement and then yours?' Henry said.

'I think it might.'

I read them both out loud and it did help. My statement was clear and all I had to do was stick to the truth and not allow myself to get sidetracked or riled by Ron Osborne's lies.

'Anyone hearing that will know you're telling the truth,' Henry said.

His presence calmed me. I put my folder down as he fiddled with the radio and found BBC 6 Music. 'I Heard It Through the Grapevine' came on.

'Oh I love this,' I said.

'Me too.'

We sang along to it and he knew all the words.

'Annie's got very fond of Ziggy. She's been joining them for Sunday lunch,' he said.

'I'm happy to know that.'

'Annie's got a heart as big as a house. She said Ziggy brings out the mum in her.'

'And I'm going to get her a permanent job at StoryWorld. But keep that under wraps until I get the piece of paper from Julius. I can't wait to tell her.'

'She's lucky to be in your team.'

The rain had stopped. We approached Luton and drove past the same shops you find on every high street. We passed the county court, an ugly impersonal building, and Henry parked in the next road.

'Plenty of time for a coffee,' he said.

We walked to the next block, avoiding the puddles on the pavement, and found a café with its windows steamed up. He pushed the door open and I could smell bacon and toast.

'I'm sticking to tea,' I said.

'Can I treat you to an iced bun?'

'Oh, go on then.'

It was a spiced iced bun, full of fruit. The icing was generous and the dough soft and it melted in my mouth. Henry had got himself a cheese and pickle roll.

'I'm eating all the time since I gave up the fags,' he said.

'You needn't worry. As my mum would say, there's more fat on a chip.'

I swigged my tea.

'I'm not looking forward to seeing that Ron Osborne again.'

'He's a shyster and you'll make mincemeat of him.'

I used the Ladies before we left and checked my appearance. I combed my hair and thought about putting on lipstick before deciding not to. So often I handle things on my own and I'm used to it, but it had felt good to be driven to court and to know that Henry would be sitting in there with me.

We came out onto a busy road and waited at the lights.

'Thank you for being here,' I said.

He put his hand on the base of my back as we walked across the road.

Dear Reader,

Thank you so much for reading *Behind Her Back* and I hope you enjoyed it.

I wanted to tell you a bit about what inspired me to create the character of Liz Lyon, her daughter Flo and the StoryWorld TV station. Like Liz I was a lone parent and a TV producer working on the live show *Good Morning Britain* and later in charge of feature programmes at WestCountry Television in Devon.

I struggled to be a lone mum and a TV producer. I remember how hard it was to keep all the balls up in the air. I felt horribly conflicted about competing pressures and sometimes felt that I wasn't doing either role properly. Feelings of guilt would lurk and pounce on me at two in the morning! Television is an exciting place to work but it is not a family-friendly industry and I left when my daughter Amelia was nine-years-old. I wanted to explore this world and these pressures in *Behind Her Back* and the earlier Liz Lyon novel *Woman of the Hour*.

I have seen many novels about women's family and emotional lives but much less fiction about women's lives at work. Yet so many issues and moral dilemmas are thrown up by this aspect of our lives. There are power struggles, personality clashes, gossip and intrigue as well as lovely moments of camaraderie, praise and the satisfaction of a job well done.

What happens at work offers such a rich seam to mine and I'm intrigued why there isn't more fiction about it. I would love to know what you think about the book and about writing about women's working lives. Let's start the conversation on my Facebook page: https://www.facebook.com/janelythellbooks/ or you can email me at: janelythell@gmail.com and I will write back to you within the week.

My warm wishes,
Jane Lythell

ACKNOWLEDGEMENTS

My warmest thanks to my agent Gaia Banks, the best champion anyone could ask for.

I worked with two brilliant editors on this book, Laura Palmer and Victoria Pepe. Thank you both for your insights, your suggestions and for helping me to make the book better. Thanks also to the wonderful team at Head of Zeus with a special mention to Madeleine O'Shea and Nia Beynon.

A bouquet to Amelia Trevette, my daughter, who put me right on all the fashion aspects in the novel. And thanks to Jan Thompson who gave me an excellent idea for a character trait in Harriet.

I think the book cover, designed by Anna Green, is terrific, and sincere thanks to Liz Hatherell for the meticulous copy edit and to Jon Appleton for the proofreading.

When I was working on the last chapters of *Behind Her Back* I went on retreat with my best writing buddy Kerry Fisher who gave me loads of encouragement – thank you Kerry.

I want to salute the book bloggers who are passionate about reading and do so much to promote our books. I am also very grateful to readers who find the time to write reviews. Your reviews mean a great deal to me. Thank you all.

Finally, thank you so much Barry Purchese for your loving support and your masterly feedback.